Selected as an
OPRAH'S BOOK CLUB 2.0 RIVETING READ
and an INDIE NEXT PICK

"The Edge of the Earth enticed me—the details of time and place are vivid, yet the dilemmas of Trudy's new marriage certainly transcend this beautiful novel's dreamlike setting. Schwarz is a masterful storyteller: perfect pacing, secrets and suspense, and characters who aren't what they seem kept me entranced as the pages turned."

—LAURA MORIARTY,
New York Times bestselling author of *The Chaperone*

"The Edge of the Earth invites us into the lives of a young married couple in the late nineteenth century drawn to a lighthouse above the forbidding cliffs of Point Lucia, California—an isolated spot filled with marine life that few have seen before and, perhaps, a mermaid. But there are human secrets too—and as you learn what they are, you will almost hear the crashing waves. A gripping story."

—KATE ALCOTT,
New York Times bestselling author of *The Dressmaker*

"Christina Schwarz's gift of detail makes the characters leap off the page and her expert handling of suspense allows for a cliffhanger ending that you won't see coming. I loved this book!"

—SARAH JIO,
New York Times bestselling author of *Blackberry Winter*

Praise for the #1 *New York Times* bestseller *Drowning Ruth* and Christina Schwarz's other captivating novels

"Powerful . . . suspenseful . . . richly textured."

—*The New York Times*

"Schwarz's multilayered storytelling makes this novel spellbinding."

—*People*

"The book's pacing races. . . . When you read the last page, you will want to start over, to see the clues you missed and appreciate Schwarz's delicate weaving of family histories that leave legacies of guilt and revenge."

—*USA Today*

"A brilliantly understated psychological thriller. . . . Schwarz's prose is spare but bewitching."

—*Publishers Weekly* (starred review)

"An absorbing tale. . . . Readers will be entirely under Schwarz's spell."

—*Salon*

"Schwarz pays meticulous attention to her characters."

—*The Washington Post Book World*

"The immediately impressive thing about *Drowning Ruth* is not the author's talent, though that is apparent within the first few pages, but the ambitious narrative scheme she's devised to tell her tale."

—*San Francisco Chronicle*

ALSO BY CHRISTINA SCHWARZ

Drowning Ruth

All Is Vanity

So Long at the Fair

The
EDGE
of the
EARTH

A Novel

C H R I S T I N A   S C H W A R Z

WASHINGTON SQUARE PRESS
New York   London   Toronto   Sydney   New Delhi

WASHINGTON SQUARE PRESS
A Division of Simon & Schuster, Inc.
1230 Avenue of the Americas
New York, NY 10020

First Washington Square Press trade paperback edition April 2014

WASHINGTON SQUARE PRESS and colophon are registered trademarks of Simon & Schuster, Inc.

For information about special discounts for bulk purchases, please contact Simon & Schuster Special Sales at 1-866-506-1949 or business@simonandschuster.com.

The Simon & Schuster Speakers Bureau can bring authors to your live event. For more information or to book an event, contact the Simon & Schuster Speakers Bureau at 1-866-248-3049 or visit our website at www.simonspeakers.com.

Designed by Dana Sloan

Manufactured in the United States of America

10 9 8 7 6 5 4 3 2 1

The Library of Congress has cataloged the hardcover edition as follows:

Schwarz, Christina.
    The edge of the earth : a novel / Christina Schwarz. — First Atria Books hardcover edition.
        pages cm
    1. Young women—Fiction. 2. Self-actualization (Psychology) in women—Fiction. 3. Lighthouse keepers—Fiction. I. Title.
    PS3569.C56783E34 2013
    813'.54—dc23   2013000480

ISBN 978-1-4516-8367-7
ISBN 978-1-4516-8370-7 (pbk)
ISBN 978-1-4516-8372-1 (ebook)

For Ben and Nicky

and in memory of
Margaret Meyer,
who walked on her own feet,

and Scout

Jane
1977

I'M NOT GOING to let on I was born here. People always ask what it was like to grow up in a lighthouse, and then they're disappointed by the answer. I'm not much of a storyteller. Anyway, growing up in a lighthouse isn't all that remarkable when you don't know anything different, and I didn't know anything different until I left Point Lucia at nineteen.

Which was in 1912. And I haven't been back since. Not that I wouldn't have been glad to visit, but it was a lot of trouble back then, back before Route 1 came through. I allowed the usual preoccupations—studying and teaching, marriage and children—to chivvy me on, away from the place of my childhood.

I wish that my grandson Danny and I could be climbing the morro alone now, without this straggling handful of tourists who, in their very charmlessness, remind me that Mrs. Swann is no longer at the top.

I remember the day she came to us from the sea. The mountains behind us were too tall and squeezed together to let anyone through, but the ocean before and below us was like a carpet and ships slid past on it every day, some with big white sails stretching out in the wind, some puffing steam like a whale's spout.

My father was chief keeper, but Point Lucia was important enough to need three, and red-faced Mr. Finnegan went to Cuba to kill the

1

Butcher, so we were getting someone new. We children hoped he would bring along more of our kind.

My brothers were first to see the tender, and then we all shouted, "*The Madrone! The Madrone!*" and ran to the edge of the morro.

"Stand back, Jane!" My sister took my hand, but I knew better than to fall off a mountain, so I snatched my fingers away and stood where, straight below, the milky foam spilled around the black rocks.

The wind was blowing hard enough to lean on, and sometimes when the waves were that big, the tender would anchor and wait for better weather, so we were prepared for disappointment. Soon enough, though, the longboat full of barrels was dropped into the ocean. It was always a nervous thing, watching a longboat come in. Plenty of times it would swamp, and we would have to do without flour or sugar or library books or Christmas oranges.

We couldn't be certain until they'd rowed in a ways that the creature with a hat tied around her head was a lady. Childishly expecting Mrs. Swann to be a large white bird with the neck of an eel, like the letter "S" in my alphabet book, I was a bit let down. My father came with the spyglass and held it for each of us in turn. The woman's face was covered with a cloth.

"She must be very ugly," one of my brothers whispered.

Gertrude Swann. Danny—I suppose I should call him Dan now, but grandmothers are forgiven these lapses—had come across her name in a book assigned for one of his courses down in San Diego. Did I know, he asked when he phoned, that an early marine biologist had lived and worked at Point Lucia? A woman who studied the tide pools.

Of course I knew. I'd introduced her to her first anemone. Or at least one of my brothers or my sister had. Danny was impressed that my world might, after all, have a snippet of relevance to his. Infuriating, obviously, but I take what I can get. Riding high on our moment of connection, I told him I'd read that the lighthouse was open to visitors; maybe the two of us should go and see it.

I meant only, I think, to talk and plan with Danny; I didn't believe such an outing would actually come to pass. But up to San Jose he came, driving his little Japanese box with its back window stuck halfway down, his shaggy blond head nearly touching the roof. I treated him to crepes at Rosemary and Tim and grilled him about college life and so on, and this morning we got up early and here we are, in a place unsullied by the current cultural detritus.

"Actually, there were a few other female lighthouse keepers in those days." The volunteer guide is responding to a question from a wide-shouldered woman in an olive-green anorak who has clearly done some, if not much, homework. The guide tells about Charlotte Layton, who stayed on as keeper at Point Pinos after her husband was shot by a bandit, and fashionable Emily Fish, who kept racehorses and painted china. "And often," the docent goes on, "wives served informally as keepers. The lighthouse service encouraged men to bring their families, because the women and children would work as assistants—unpaid, of course." Even now, in 1977, the ladies in our group nod and pull their mouths into bitter little smiles, acknowledging the obvious truth.

The docent stops walking. She's a retiree in knit trousers, her hair an unnatural shade of apricot beneath the rubberized hood of the raincoat on which the drizzle is beading. "Are you doing okay?" she asks me in the high tone reserved for children, pets, and the elderly, although it's really she who needs to catch her breath, what with all the talking.

It's a steep, very long climb to the top of the morro on which the lighthouse and its attendant buildings stand, along a narrow road that girdles the rock and was cut long after my time here. The volunteer, Linda or Lydia—I couldn't quite make it out—tried to discourage me at the bottom. Not wanting a heart attack on her hands, no doubt. It's true that I'm wizened as an apple doll—no point trying to deny my age, now that I've confessed actual dates—but, still, I'm a walker. I can go miles if I pace myself. Besides, I used to scramble up this mountain on all fours; I could do it again, if need be.

The drizzle has stopped. I look west over the ocean, an old habit, and am rewarded with a pale sheen in the sky. In an hour or so, before we start down again, I know it will be clear.

Our little group is breaking apart. Two sullen teenagers and their parents, intent on getting the climb over with, have taken the lead. Behind them, a little boy drifts, drawn by the sight of the waves tirelessly hurling themselves against the black rocks far below, and his young mother yanks him back, though he's nowhere near falling. We children spent a lot of time lying on our stomachs looking over the edge or standing with our toes jutting into the air. I don't believe we were foolhardy. We knew what was possible and what was unreasonably dangerous. I suppose that at any time the ground might have slid out from under us, but in fact, there was very little erosion. A morro is, after all, made of the hard stuff that remains after the softer rock falls away.

A thin-haired man and his brassy wife are arguing over who left the camera in the car. Now the anorak woman is asking more questions about the lady lighthouse keeper here at Point Lucia. The lady lighthouse keeper! As if she were a talking horse!

"She was from Minnesota," Linda—or Lydia—answers.

"Wisconsin," I whisper to Danny.

The child begs to be carried. The docent calls ahead to the teenagers, her voice shrill with anxiety. "Please stay together, everyone!" Thin Hair and Brassy are avoiding each other's eyes.

Danny spots a pod of dolphins surprisingly close to the shore, which gives us all a lift, pulls us forward another thirty yards. Someone asks how far out the light can be seen.

To keep our minds off the work of the climb, the docent tells us about shipwrecks: some boats foundered because the captain was drunk; some were smashed in storms or ran aground in fog; but most went down simply because people made mistakes and steered directly into what they should have avoided. All manner of goods were lost—beer and barley, paint and salt, lumber and butter and chrome—although in most cases, the crew survived. She tells one especially sad story that I remember hearing from my mother about a lighthouse keeper whose skiff overturned after he'd collected pay for himself and his men from the tender. He drowned because the gold in his pockets weighed him down. That's why my father was never paid in cash.

Finally, we reach the light. We're not yet at the top. The light had to be placed about a third of the way down, or it would have been smothered too often in the fog that settles around the summit. It's impossible, now that the sky has cleared, to imagine the kind of dense fog that's inevitable here, fog that hovers so close it blurs your vision and makes you lose perspective. Even I can hardly recall that kind of fog when the sun is shining.

The light tower itself isn't the tall, graceful cylinder one might expect in a place of such grandeur but, rather, a squat, four-cornered, medieval castle–like structure of heavy gray stone. It's even shorter than I remember. Otherwise, from the outside, it's remained essentially unchanged in seventy-odd years (while I have suffered the usual ravages). Inside the base, where the boiler once roared and hissed, it's quiet as a crypt. And vacant.

When I was a girl, that space was a sort of clubhouse, a game of solitaire and some piece of greasy machinery to be tinkered with on the table; the all-important keeper's log and a cup of yellow pencils on a shelf, along with a book or two, including one called *Flags of Many Lands* from which we liked to choose our favorites; the big black toolbox, full of useful devices we were not allowed to borrow, in its special spot at the foot of the stairs, beside the basket of mending with which the women passed the time. All of that has been cleared away. Then it smelled of pipe tobacco, kerosene, oil, and woodsmoke; now it smells only of stone.

Linda summons us to the winding staircase at the back, and we march up single file. I find myself gripping the metal banister as I did when I was five, afraid to put my faith in my feet. At the top, we pack into the small platform that extends between the light and the windows, the lamproom. We're expected to marvel at the lens—an enormous scalloped jewel—and Thin Hair obliges. The men generally are gung ho about the mechanical details. But I'm impatient. I resent that we can't move about as we please. The light, marvel of nineteenth-century scientific achievement and my family's bread and butter, was serious business and therefore not the scene of my childhood. It's not what I've come here to see.

There are bullet holes in nearly all of the windows.

"Vandals," Linda explains.

I imagine them trudging up here, going so far out of their way to casually destroy whatever strikes their fancy. There's modern life for you. It's true that in my day, we had our share of broken windows, though at least there was nothing casual about that destruction.

What is this? We've been shunted onto the catwalk outside to observe the view, but it's the exterior wall that grabs my attention. It's covered in a mosaic of stones, and abalone, mussel, and periwinkle shells. Here is the dried husk of a sea star. And here a bit of a sea urchin's shell. Here is the carapace of a crab. I touch the pieces, imagining her deft fingers pushing them into the soft cement, for I need no docent to tell me who's constructed this mermaid's castle.

Finally, we're trailing along the path on which I walked and ran every day for sixteen years. The surface is different—asphalt instead of rocky dirt—but the vistas are so much the same that I might be a girl again, my pinafore whipping in the wind. We shuffle through the workshop with its drill press and saws and whetstone—all manner of tools neatly organized—and pass the small barn where my family kept a cow and a few chickens, presumably empty now, and come at last to the big stone triplex where the keepers lived. As of three years ago, when electricity finally came to this remote outpost, no one need live in this building again.

"Most of Gertrude Swann's collections were scattered when she died," Linda says, wiggling her key in the lock, "but we've found a few of her things and a copy of the catalog she compiled."

We step inside, and I experience that disorienting feeling inevitable when you revisit after a long absence a place that was once as familiar as your skin. The few furnishings—a modern sofa in the parlor, a kitchen obviously outfitted in the fifties—are all wrong, but the big windows and wide window ledges are the same, and the narrow floorboards haven't been carpeted. Artfully arranged on a table in the parlor are some dried urchin shells—she did much of her work with urchins—and a few pretty curio slides she made with a bubble of glass and fancy paper. "Amusements," she called them, a little sheepishly, for they were not of scientific value. One contains a tiny starfish, another a curl of delicate seaweed.

"Eeew! There's hair in these!" one of the teenagers says.

It's my hair, my old, true color, and that of my brothers and sister. She cut the strands for keepsakes as, one by one, we moved away from Point Lucia. I was the youngest, the last to go.

A copy of her catalog is opened to a page devoted to kelp. "Among the rippling kelp lived a family of otters," I can hear her saying, for she was my first teacher and a storyteller, and I was an eager listener.

"She was pretty strange and secretive," Linda says. "She insisted on living alone after the original keeper and his wife retired, even though the station was meant to be operated by three keepers. The machinery was less labor-intensive by that time."

"I read that a kind of Loch Ness monster killed her husband." It's Anorak again.

I can see Danny, young scientist that he is, turning away to hide a smile at such a fantasy. Several others, however, who no doubt were beginning to think about the Bloody Marys they would order at Nepenthe or the comic books they'd left on the seat of the car, perk up.

"People think that it may have been a shark or an orca," Linda says. "Back then they didn't know what we do."

Such condescension toward the past is to be expected, but I know better.

After Mrs. Swann died, my siblings and I discovered that she'd willed things to us. Mary got the collections of slides and specimens—they're mine now; and Edward was to have her scientific instruments—he'd predeceased her, although she didn't know it—those are mine, too; Nicholas got the original hand-inked catalog; and I got a manuscript.

At the top of the first page, in the handwriting I knew as well as my own, she'd written a note:

> *My dearest Jane,*
> *I wrote this some time ago, and I'd like for you to have it. I hope it will interest you—you, of all the Crawley children, are the most intimately involved in this story. As I come to the end of my life, I suddenly find that I want someone to know how she lived.*

That last pronoun rankled, appearing as it did without an antecedent. But once I'd read, I believed I understood. I know what happened here. Or at least some version of it. As I say, she was a storyteller.

CHAPTER I

W E'D TRAVELED FOR days to reach California, and it takes only hours to steam from San Francisco to Point Lucia, but from the moment we heaved over the first of a thousand waves, I knew that this stretch would take me farthest from the home I'd so precipitously left behind. At first we pushed through a cold fog, guided only by the uneven clang of buoy bells. Standing on deck, I couldn't make out even the surface of the water. But in an hour or so, the sun began to filter through, revealing a picturesque coast of soft hills and low bluffs.

Dolphins (not fish, my husband said, but mammals just like us) arched in and out of the water beside us, shifting direction miraculously as one, as if attached by strings. Oskar seemed to be racing along with them, one minute sitting beside me and holding my hand, the next, hurrying to the rail, then off to have a word with the captain, then back to me to point out some feature of the landscape or to inform me of some remarkable attribute of the vessel or to hold before me an enormous, toothy fish one of the sailors had caught off the stern, its eye still alert and admonishing. At last I had to beg him to be less solicitous and allow me to weather the wretched waves in peace.

Along one stretch, I spotted a lighthouse and a pretty white cottage glowing together on a lush green lawn. I was able to hope for a minute that it might be ours.

"No, that'd be Pinos," a sailor said.

A woman kept that lighthouse, he told me, assisted by her Chinese manservant. The woman was from China, too, although she was white. The sailor claimed she kept racehorses, grew roses, spoke Italian, and played sonatas on the pianoforte.

"She doesn't sing opera?" I was thoroughly seasick by this time, and so, although I meant to be amusing, I must not have hit the proper tone, for the sailor only frowned, considering whether the white Chinese lady might lay claim to this refinement as well.

Some distance on, the landscape changed, the soft hills shouldered aside by steep and ragged mountains that didn't so much approach the sea as bang against it. Pieces of these mountains had broken off, littering the water with jagged black rocks and leaving wounds hundreds of feet high and gaping, impossible to heal.

"There's Lucia," the sailor said casually, politely ignoring the fact that I was bent over the rail.

I lifted my eyes for my first look at the lighthouse to which we'd been assigned, my new home. It stood three quarters of the way up the side of a small mountain—a morro, the sailor called it—a rough brown breast attached to the land by only a spit of sand. Point Lucia had no lawn, no white cottage, and no roses. Above the light, at the very top, stood a gray gabled hulk, built of the sort of blocks used for barracks and asylums and prisons. Around the main structure, a jumble of outbuildings was scattered. No trees grew on this mountain, and the stooped and stunted few that stood along the coast to either side reached inland with their branches, as though they would flee in that direction if they could.

I was loaded, along with our trunk and a number of wooden barrels and metal drums and the toothy fish, into a longboat and rushed through the surf until the ocean finally spat us onto the beach, where the sailors emptied the boat with remarkable speed. Some barrels—I could tell they were empty by the ease with which the sailors swung them—and a mail pouch, full, were waiting. Once the sailors had packed the boat with these, they pushed off into the surf again, leaving Oskar and me alone.

Oskar, who'd jumped into the waves to help steady us on the way in, was dripping.

"We look shipwrecked," I said.

"Not you."

It was true that no water had touched me. I felt wrecked nonetheless, standing there with my boots sinking into the sand. If appropriate dress exists for being stranded on a wild beach, my lavender gloves and dove-gray veil didn't approximate it. While Oskar tramped toward the morro, shouting hellos with his hands cupped around his mouth, I stood by helplessly, clutching our valise and breathing in the stink. Thick snake-like coils lay scattered over the beach, as if an army of Medusas had been slaughtered there. Swarms of black flies, the rotting smell made visible, buzzed around the tangled piles.

Suddenly, a boy flew out from behind the mountain, his bare feet throwing off sand as he ran. I saw him shake Oskar's hand vigorously and gesture in the direction from which he'd come.

When they came to me, the boy adjusted his cap by way of greeting. "I'm Edward," he said. "We didn't think the Service could get a lady to come." He grinned in such a winning way that I couldn't help but smile back.

He shouldered the fish and suggested that Oskar do the same with our trunk, explaining that the rest would be collected later. Then he led the way—a very long way, as it turned out—over the beach and around the back of the morro to a small open platform on wheels at the bottom of an impossibly steep track. We were to balance on this bit of wood as it climbed with painful, squeaking agony straight up the side of the rock.

I hadn't expected children at all, but three more stood solemnly at the top, a girl of about ten with smudged eyeglasses and tight, unflat-tering braids, who seemed to curl in on herself; another boy who was a slighter, younger version of the first; and a small girl whose ragged hair obscured her face. Their skin was dyed brown from the sun, and each successive child seemed to have soaked in more pigment, so that the eldest, the girl in braids, was the color of weak tea, and the youngest was dark as an acorn. A man with the beginnings of a stoop emerged from an outbuilding, wiping his hands on a cloth. And then, as we mounted the last creaking yards, a woman rushed up the path. She was tall, with long legs and neck, like a heron or stork. Her hair was brushed with white and pinned up in a messy nest, and she was wearing men's boots.

She smoothed her large, chapped hands over her soiled apron self-consciously, as Oskar handed me off the platform, and she rocked slightly while she stood, as if she couldn't bring herself to stay entirely still. "Good to meet you," she said with a sharp dip of her head. "Hope you can stick it."

The man with the dirty cloth shook our hands, nodding in a friendly way, as if we'd turned out to be just what he'd ordered. "Henry Crawley," he said, "chief keeper." He was a head shorter than his wife and seemed to have been bleached by the sun and wind; he was so fair as to be nearly colorless. His pale eyes watered in the bright light.

Over Mr. Crawley's shoulder, I saw the tender that had delivered us steaming unhesitatingly across the vast, restless plain of the ocean toward the northern horizon, and I felt an internal sinking so cold and overwhelming that I nearly cried out my dismay. But I held my chin high and didn't reach for Oskar's hand, for I was a grown girl who knew how to behave.

Another man was coming up the path. He was in no hurry to meet us but walked in a desultory way, his gait sinuous, his eyes turned mostly toward the ocean and the disappearing tender, as mine had been. The dark brown hair that showed below his bowler appeared to have been cut with a bowie knife.

"My brother, Archie Johnston," Mrs. Crawley said, and she sighed, as if she wished he weren't.

We greeted him, but he looked us up and down rudely before he responded. "I hear you've come from Wisconsin," he said at last.

"Oh, yes." I answered too eagerly, more than willing to overlook his poor manners for the comfort of some connection to my home. "Do you know it?"

"I know it's a long way to come just to be second assistant at a light-house."

Oskar laughed. "Do you suspect ulterior motives?"

Mr. Johnston stared at him. "I don't know what to think."

"Come now, Archie," Mr. Crawley said. "Don't make these good young people defend themselves. Most would jump at the chance for this post. Let's show Mr. Swann the light, get him acquainted with his work."

Archie Johnston was right to be suspicious, although the crimes for which we'd had to leave Milwaukee—shattering the fondest hopes of family and friends—were not the sort the law takes any notice of.

CHAPTER 2

M Y PARENTS HAD laid out a lovely future for me in Milwaukee with tender care, as if they were smoothing the white coverlet over my rose-wood bed. When I was graduated from the Milwaukee College for Females, I was to marry Ernst Dettweiler. Our wedding had been planned, mostly as a joke, while our mothers aired us as infants in Juneau Park. But why not? Ernst was a sweet, straightforward boy who met life's pleasures head-on and made clear that he believed I was among them. He was as dear to me as sunshine. As my mother said fondly, "You know what you're getting with Ernst."

We were to live on one of the newer streets west of downtown. Although a wedding date had not been set—indeed, Ernst had not yet formally proposed—my father and Uncle Dettweiler had looked at two or three possible houses, and my mother had selected the peonies she intended to transplant to my yard and the furnishings from her own house that would be mine. Of course, we young people were expected to have ideas of our own. Within certain boundaries, our parents were willing, even eager, to indulge us.

Despite all of this—or perhaps because of it?—I'd been vaguely but persistently discontent, as if a bit of straw had lodged itself in some un-reachable spot under my clothing. Back in early September, that glow-ing time that promises such riches for the academic months ahead, our college president had given a speech in Menomonee Hall, exhorting

us girls to be of service in the world. She'd drawn a loose but definite connection between a graceful translation of Ovid and a young
woman's ability to contribute to the uplifting of mankind. But the more
I'd thought about it, the less convinced I was of that connection, or
at least of my ability to make it in the ways others saw fit. President
McAdams had stressed the contribution of home management to the
good of society. She'd pointed to the teaching of home economics, the
practice of philanthropy, and the creation of literature as suitable fields
in which the college-educated woman might perform service. And there
was Florence Nightingale to provide an example of more elevated ambition. But I knew I was no Miss Nightingale.

Miss Dodson, my teacher of home nursing and biology, had held me
back after class one day. I'd assumed I was to be chastised for bandaging
my friend Lucy's head so carelessly, but Miss Dodson had pressed me to
consider teaching.

"I believe it's a good thing," she'd said, unscrewing the limbs from
the torso of her mannequin, "for a young woman to make her own way
for a year or two before she attaches herself to a man."

I admired Miss Dodson, with her bright brown eyes and uncompromising nose. She excited in her students—in me, at least—a sense
of wonder at the functions of living things even as she exposed their
secrets. She'd been afflicted with polio as a child and so walked with a
bit of a hitch that seemed to keep time for her as she paced the front
of the classroom, urging us to observe: "You must look, girls! Never assume; always examine!" While in everyday conversation she was rather
reserved and dry, she had been known to rhapsodize over such things
as "the clever lichen, which thrives where other plants would instantly
wither." We giggled, but only the most aloof among us could resist
being caught up in her enthusiasm for and devotion to her subject. At
her suggestion, I'd imagined myself presiding over my own classroom in
a crisp white waist and black skirt, confidently sketching a heart and its
attendant arteries with colored chalk on the blackboard.

"Why did you become a teacher?" I'd asked boldly.

Miss Dodson looked slightly startled. She was used, I think, to directing others, not to considering her own feelings.

"I suppose it's because I liked school. It gave me license to live in my mind." She gave a small, rueful laugh. "That was a far more interesting place than any other I seemed likely to have access to. Natural history obviously interests you," she went on, setting the conversation back on terms more comfortable to her.

I did like the way that science, like Latin, seemed to make sense of the world (whereas history and literature, to my mind, were apt to muddle it). When we studied the plant and animal kingdoms, Miss Dodson was always calling our attention to examples of symmetry and efficiency and cooperation. And I dearly loved classification, the neat way in which the most unusual species had features it shared with others and thus could be grouped into a genus, which in turn could be grouped into a family and so on, until the whole puzzle of life, theoretically, anyway, could be clearly mapped.

Perhaps I would never attach myself to a man, I'd pronounced boldly, relaying Miss Dodson's advice to Lucy.

"You mean like Miss Gregor?" Lucy's eyes were wide.

I laughed. "Really, you don't think much of me. Miss Gregor? What about Miss Dodson?"

"Oh, Miss Dodson. Yes, well, she's a special case, isn't she? She manages to put all of her passion into her work. Yes, I do admire that. But Trudy." She'd laid her hand earnestly on my arm. "Don't you think that she's a little sharp? She reminds me of one of those crabs that backs itself into a snail shell."

"And her eyes and forehead bulge so."

Lucy laughed. "But seriously, I don't want you to become like Miss Dodson, however much we admire her. That's not for you, is it? Don't forget that when you marry Ernst and I marry Charles, we're going to live next door and run in and out of the back door of each other's houses."

The thought of remaining in those schoolrooms or ones like them, passing on what I'd learned to other girls so they could pass it along in turn, made me as weary as all the rest. As a teacher, I feared, I would be making myself into a link in the very chain that was constricting me, holding me back from a future that seemed to shimmer just beyond my ability to perceive it.

What had I wanted? I'd been sure of only thing: I wanted something that I did not know. Well, I'd gotten it.

CHAPTER 3

"MARY'LL SHOW YOU around the place," Mrs. Crawley said, and for a moment she rested her rough hand tenderly on her elder daughter's shoulder. "Janie, would you like to go along?" The little girl was leaning her head against her mother's hip. She nodded, and Mrs. Crawley smoothed the child's hair behind two delicate ears that stuck straight out like the handles of a teacup, revealing inquisitive brown eyes. "You two," the woman said to her sons, "better fetch wood. We'll want a good bonfire tonight."

The boys went whooping off, and the look Mrs. Crawley sent after them was at once exasperated and fond. "I'll be providing the dinner tonight," she said, turning abruptly back to me. "Seeing as you haven't had time to set up your kitchen."

Set up my kitchen! What did that mean? In school, we'd been taught to brown flour and keep it handy in a jar for thickening and coloring. I knew how to make a white sauce and a fruit salad and how to clean a cake pan. My mother had shown me how to bake a coffee cake with the bacon grease she collected in a green ceramic jar and how to gently encourage custard to mingle with clouds of beaten egg whites. I remembered some of the lessons she'd given our girl: how to store glasses and cups in the pantry—upside down, so as not to collect dust; how to clean the ash from the stove without spilling it on the floor; when to change

19

the water in the reservoir. I feared that these random bits of knowledge wouldn't be enough.

Indeed, I felt much closer in station to Mary than to her mother, although I took pains to conceal it. My guide, who chewed at her thumbnail as we walked, was entering that awkward stage of a girl's life when she is no longer darling but not yet pretty, and it was difficult to know whether she would become so. She was unformed, her freckled face a plump, boneless disk, and she had a habit of adjusting her small glasses by pushing at them with one finger.

She took me first to the barn where several brown chickens strutted and poked about, entirely focused on the ground and uninterested in the fact that their patch of earth hung high over the ocean. A green-tailed rooster, suspicious, turned one black eye on us, rather in the way of Mr. Johnston.

The little girl, Jane, was more forward. "Ma says the hens wouldn't know a fox if it bit 'em," she said. "I've sure never seen a fox. Have you seen a fox?"

I informed her that I had.

"I've seen eagles," Jane went on. "They swoop down"—she made a huge gesture of wings with her arms—"and pluck the chicks right up." Here she reached forward, fingers outstretched like talons, and made a grabbing motion in the air. "It's gruesome."

"Ma says the eagles have to eat, too," Mary said, and Jane nodded at this piece of wisdom.

I was surprised to see a cow chewing its cud behind the barn.

"Ma says children must have milk." Jane squinted her eyes, sizing me up. "She said you'd churn us some butter. She said where you come from, everyone knows how to churn butter."

Apparently, Ma wasn't always right.

When we reached the workshop, Mary demonstrated the whetstone, hiking up her skirt so that she could work the pedals unencumbered.

Then, still sitting on its seat, she slid her glasses, which had slipped low on her nose, back into place. "Might I ask you a favor?"

I had to smile at her formality. "Of course."

"May I try your hat?"

I unpinned my hat and arranged it on the girl's head and folded the veil down for her.

"Oh!" She was disappointed. "You can see out perfectly well."

"Let me see," said Jane, so I had to settle the hat on her as well. "You're right, Mary," she said with similar dismay. "You can see out perfectly well."

Did they imagine that I'd been bumbling along blind?

As I'd observed from the tender, the lighthouse was set at a little distance from the rest of the buildings and somewhat lower on the rock. Its upper third reached the top of the morro, and the catwalk that encircled the light was accessible from the level where we stood by way of a little bridge. Oskar was up there when we emerged from the workshop, but he seemed to be looking at something far out at sea. In any case, he didn't notice the hand I raised.

"That one is ours," Mary said importantly, pointing at the southern-most entrance of the awful stone building where three apartments were clumped.

"We get the biggest," Jane announced, "because our father is the head."

The center house into which the girls led me was a sort of tunnel, a passageway pressed between the two other apartments; light could enter directly from the east at the back or the west at the front, but otherwise not at all. It was obvious from the smudges along the walls, the hard brown grease on the cooktop, and the skeins of dust against the baseboards that no one had prepared the place for us and that the previous tenant had been no housekeeper.

I was amused to see evidence of squatters. In the parlor, Mary quickly gathered up a doll, several squares of inky paper, a tin pot, and some other detritus she gave me no time to identify. In the kitchen, both girls were proprietary, demonstrating the running water in the sink and drawing my attention to the heavy china, patterned with a small navy lighthouse, in the plate rack; the iron pot and skillet in the cupboard; and the drawer of silver-plated utensils.

Upstairs were two little bedrooms. The front one was furnished with nothing but a bed.

"This one," Jane said, her palm pressed to the door of the back room, "is for your baby."

I laughed. "But I don't have a baby."

"Ma says you will," she insisted, "sooner or later. Mary and I are hoping for a girl, aren't we?" She turned to her sister.

Mary nodded. "In the meantime," she said boldly, giving me a sideways look as she opened the door, "we've been using this room for our collection."

The floor looked like a beach. It was littered with shells and pieces of driftwood, dried and flattened seaweed, and what appeared to be bones. Washed up here and there were small creatures at once gorgeous and monstrous. Some were bristly, some pebbly, some curly, some knobby. Almost everything was strange to me: white tubes, brown disks, and opalescent cups; shapes of orange and pink, blue and violet; branches and coils, spines and nubbins and surfaces that appeared glassy smooth. Confined in jars were more creatures, some sluglike, some waving tentacles. Presumably, they'd been plucked live from their homes (although most appeared to be dead, despite the attempt to provide them with an appropriately watery environment). I lifted one jar, half full of cloudy water, for a closer look and nearly dropped it again in horror. Inside, a blobbish thing floated and stank.

"I think this is dead," I managed.

"I suppose we ought to throw it away, then," Mary said regretfully.

"What can we do with all this?" I would speak to their mother.

"I don't know." Mary's tone was bright, as if the problem didn't concern her.

"You won't tell Ma, will you?" Jane said. "She don't like us keeping this stuff."

"No, she don't," said a deep voice from the doorway. I was so startled that I almost dropped the jar again, but it was only Mr. Johnston, who'd somehow crept up the stairs without our knowing. "Here," he said, his tone unexpectedly kind as he dipped one hand into his shirt pocket. "I picked this up the other day." He handed Jane a twisted tube of a shell, hollow as a drinking straw, while the two boys, who'd come up the stairs after him, crowded in.

"Thank you!" Jane handed the shell ceremoniously to one of the boys, who placed it with care, although seemingly randomly, among the other flotsam and jetsam on the floor.

Mr. Johnston hooked his thumb over his shoulder. "What's in the trunk? Rocks?"

"Did you really bring rocks?" the littler boy asked eagerly.

"It must be our books," I said. "I'm sorry it was difficult to move. We ought to have packed more novels and verse. The lighter stuff."

The children looked baffled, and Johnston, too, frowned at me for a moment before he raised his eyebrows. "Huh," he said, and smiled as if he'd discovered something he'd not anticipated that pleased him.

"Let's see!" All of the children piled down in a rush, so I felt obliged to follow. Archie Johnston came after us in a leisurely way, as if the place were more his than mine.

"Thank you, Mr. Johnston," I said.

I'd meant it as a dismissal, but he merely nodded. "Aren't you going to open it?"

I might have begged off, said that I'd misplaced the key or wished to wait for Oskar, but the children were so expectant, I hadn't the heart.

At least my night things were secure in our valise, I thought as I parted the two halves of the trunk, exposing my personal possessions to Archie Johnston.

The children's pleasure soon overwhelmed my discomfort. Opening my trunk before them had the quality of Sir Richard Burton's accounts of displaying matches and pocket watches to the Africans. My violin was stroked and plucked; my sketchpad admired, more, I fear, for its being nearly a whole volume of rich, blank pages available for marking than for the few stiff still lives, portraits, and landscapes I'd rendered. My pencils and pens were painstakingly tested. My feathered hat (only slightly crushed) and my paisley shawl were modeled; my rose geranium oil was sniffed. There was much scuffling and grabbing and shoving and poking, and when curiosity was sated, many items were grubby and disheveled. I supposed such behavior was typical of little boys, and the little girl was, after all, too young to know better, but I was surprised at Mary, who might be expected to fold a pair of stockings.

For me, the greatest treasure were the bedsheets between which my mother had slid the same sachets she used in her own linen cupboard. By the time we reached them, Johnston had become bored and wandered out, so I was able to open them wide without self-consciousness. I took them upstairs, turned the mattress to what I hoped was its freshest side, and slid the sheets over it. Then I lay facedown on the bed, breathing in the dear, lost scent of home. This was a mistake, however, for almost immediately, the rank odor of the mattress bullied its way through. I rose quickly and hurried back down the stairs.

"Is there anything to eat?" Jane asked. She was wearing my lavender gloves.

"I wish there were." Fully recovered from my ocean voyage, I was conscious of a keen hunger.

"Ma might give you some raisins," Edward said doubtfully.

Just then, as if he'd summoned her, Mrs. Crawley appeared at the open door. "Edward, you know we haven't got raisins." She turned to me and said, as if in explanation, "We never open the new barrels until after supper. Sort of a ceremony for the children. Not much other than beans and fish tonight."

With curiosity as frank as her offspring's, she studied the contents of my trunk, strewn about the parlor.

"Look at this linen," she clucked, holding up a scalloped-edged tablecloth. Her coarse fingers seemed likely to tear the dainty material. "I suppose you thought this was Pinos. Artist types visiting, painting vistas, writing poems, and whatnot. No need for fancy tablecloths here." She refolded it without bothering to match up the edges. "No one comes here." She appeared to take satisfaction in that alarming notion.

Were these people to be all of our community then? My mother's warm eyes, my father's enclosing arms, Lucy's bright laugh, and Miss Dodson's encouraging smile all came crowding suddenly into my mind, so that I had to make a little cough to mask the sob that threatened to escape me. I didn't see how this flinty and imperious woman could solace me for the loss of those I'd abandoned, and obviously, this lonely place would offer no one else. Oskar would have to be all to me here, and I to him.

"All right. Well," Mrs. Crawley continued briskly, dropping the linen back into my trunk, "the dinner is on. Get the men, why don't you?"

At first I thought this command was intended for me, but the two boys responded, rushing out the door and racing away. They shouldered each other roughly as they went, and I didn't know how a mother could live in such a place and not fear every moment that her children would fall over the edge and be killed.

Near the Crawleys' front door, several long boards had been laid over trestles, and crude wooden benches had been aligned on either side of this makeshift communal table. One end was crowded with a stack of the same thick china that was in my kitchen, along with a heap of silver, tumblers, a pitcher, and several iron pots.

"This china pattern is charming," I said. Where I came from, it was the sort of comment a woman might use to extend herself to another.

"Really?" Mrs. Crawley said. She narrowed her eyes at the plate I'd held up, as if something she hadn't noticed might appear. "It's the same at every lighthouse. Keeps people from stealing it." She gave a brief laugh. "Small chance of that here."

The meal was more stirred together than cooked, a stew of milk, salt pork, and the enormous fish we'd brought—ling cod, Mr. Crawley said it was—along with beans and cornbread, all swimming together on one plate. We were obviously expected to bow our heads while Mr. Crawley said grace, but it was hard to keep from raising my face to the wind, which seemed on this precipice to be sent directly from God Himself.

"Will there be fruit after?" Edward asked, rather too close on the heels of the prayer.

"Have we opened the barrels?" Mrs. Crawley countered.

Since this led to no further conversation, I introduced a topic of my own. "Where do the children go to school?"

"Oh, there's no school at this post," Mrs. Crawley said almost blithely.

"Closest school's in Monterey," Mr. Crawley said, removing a fish bone from between his lips. The plates were accumulating little piles of white needles. "That'd be a couple days' ride on a horse. Each way. Assuming we had a horse. Which, at present, we do not."

"What do they need with school?" Oskar said affably. He threw his arm out in a wide sweep, nearly knocking Mrs. Crawley's tumbler off the table. "Nature herself should be their teacher. They should look up, like Whitman, 'in perfect silence at the stars.'"

I thought of how very unstarlike was the nature the children had piled in our house.

"Did you learn from nature, Mr. Swann?" Mrs. Crawley asked, pinning a large chunk of cod to her plate with her fork.

"Judging from the number of books Mrs. Swann has seen fit to heave as far as this rock," Mr. Johnston put in as he rose to his feet, "I would guess she's the educated sort. Maybe she could play school-teacher."

Everyone, including the children, turned to look at me with new interest.

"Are you a teacher, Mrs. Swann?" Mrs. Crawley asked.

"Oh, no. I'm afraid I have no experience. I doubt I would be much good." My tongue tested the bit of salt pork in my mouth; it seemed to be mostly gristle.

"But you've had enough schooling to be a teacher?" Mrs. Crawley persisted.

"Well, I haven't been to normal school, if that's—"

Oskar interrupted me. "Trudy would be an excellent teacher!"

"You think it likely you know more than the children do?" Mrs. Crawley said.

"Well, I wouldn't—"

"Oh, for heaven's sakes, Trudy. You've been to college!" Oskar said.

"That should be adequate," Mrs. Crawley said, nodding. She wiped the milk that remained on her plate with a sponge of cornbread. And so the matter was apparently settled.

Perceiving the irony of having traveled thousands of miles only to do what I might have done in a more elevated way in Milwaukee, I quietly swallowed my gristle.

Oskar's mood, however, continued to be expansive. He waved a hand at the golden and green flanks that rose so abruptly to the east. "There's no one in those mountains?"

Mrs. Crawley nodded her approval. "You've read the Service booklet, I see."

"Lighthouse Service don't know everything," Archie Johnston said. His sister gave him a stern look.

"There's that crazy Yale fellow," Mr. Crawley put in, trying to lift the conversation again. "Lives in a hollowed-out tree."

"Do you enjoy living up here, Mrs. Crawley?" I was flustered by what had turned out to be my employment interview, but this was the sort of polite question I'd been taught so well to ask that I didn't need to think about the words.

"It's a decent post," she said, lifting her chin. "A good deal of work about the place, and no Chinese servant to do it, I can tell you that. With the animals, the children, the men, and the boiler, someone or something's always demanding to be fed."

"Euphemia's been keeping lights with me for over a dozen years," Mr. Crawley said. "She knows the job well as I do."

"Two for the price of one," Mrs. Crawley said dryly.

By now the sun had grown weary of us and turned a cold shoulder on our gathering. The children, who'd bolted their food, had already slipped away, and the boys brought a banjo and a guitar out onto the front steps and began to pick some old tunes. I thought I might join them with my violin.

Mrs. Crawley stood and began to reach around the table, stacking the dirty plates on top of her own. "Mrs. Swann and I will clean this mess up," she said, reminding me that I wasn't among the children here.

In the dark scullery, Mrs. Crawley instructed me not unkindly but firmly, and I found myself nodding, eager to please. I must not waste water; I must not chip china (or the inspector would dock Oskar's wages); soda crystals didn't grow on trees.

"Even if they did," I said, "there are no trees."

My mother would have laughed at this, but Mrs. Crawley did not. When we'd finished, however, she invited me into her parlor to see her "collection." Did everyone here have a such a thing?

"Our father was a whaler," Mrs. Crawley explained, stroking with one finger half a set of wooden teeth displayed on a length of red satin. "Archie and I grew up at a station up the coast. It was a treacherous stretch. Well, so many of 'em are. And the storms! You'll see," she said ominously, moving from the teeth to a swollen book that had obviously been soaked through, its pages printed in an alphabet I didn't recognize. There was a length of black fringe from a lady's shawl or a table covering; a knife with a wooden handle; a string of blue beads; a whole brown earthenware jug; shards of glass in every color; a basket of the sort a housewife might carry over her arm to go to market; a dented cigar tin and a coconut shell. "Sometimes we didn't even see the ship go down, but Archie and I would walk the beach with my mother, and we'd find things. You'd be surprised at what makes its way back to shore. There's not so much of it nowadays," she added wistfully, "now that we've got so many lighthouses."

As Mrs. Crawley touched her precious items with a smile as shy and proud as her daughters', I thought of my mother, pressing a fold of our drapes to her cheek as she shut them against the early darkness of a northern winter evening. She was proud to have good velvet, not, as she would say, the stiff stuff they sold over on Clybourn. I understood that the draperies' rich blue conjured for her the well-appointed rooms of her own childhood, with their gilt-legged tables and ceramic shepherdesses, rooms so faraway and foreign that when she told me stories about them, they sounded as magical and impossible as a fairy tale.

"Ma! We're ready!" One of the children—I couldn't yet tell their voices apart—had opened the front door and was shouting into the parlor.

They'd piled driftwood winched up from the beach, along with staves from broken barrels and any other combustible stuff they could gather, and the men must have gone down for the new barrels, for they stood nearby. Mrs. Crawley brought out rugs and invited me to sit beside her as Mr. Crawley lit the heap, and Mr. Johnston, to my surprise, delighted the children by pretending that he had no notion how to open the barrels. Finally, though, the lids were off, and the children, reaching inside to pull out whatever their hands grasped, behaved as though it were Christmas morning. Their "gifts" were mostly things like nails and canned produce. They squealed over fruit—pineapples, blueberries, blackberries, plums, and applesauce—groaned at peas and carrots, and were indifferent to green corn.

"This is excellent," Mrs. Crawley said, passing a can of roast veal and gravy for my inspection. "These cans are about the greatest invention of mankind, although they're the dickens to open."

I made a little pyramid of oysters and beef stew, remembering my mother's disappointment—"But it tastes so gray!"—when she'd sampled some canned good my father had brought home as a novelty.

There were boxes and boxes of a sort of cracker they called pilot bread, bottles of vinegar, jars of molasses and pickles, sacks of green coffee, onions and potatoes and dried apples. At the bottom of the barrels, too heavy for the children to fish out, were sacks of rice, flour, sugar, beans, and cornmeal, and salted cod, wrapped in waxed paper. There were newspapers, too—several months' worth of old news—and then the men pulled out a large wooden box.

"There's for your school," Mrs. Crawley said cryptically.

They set the box on one end and opened its wooden flaps. It became a bookcase with four shelves, each tightly packed with volumes.

"We get a new one of these every time the tender comes," Mr. Crawley said, running his oil-stained finger along the spines. "It's our library."

It was fully, almost densely dark now, and I had to stand close to catch the titles of the books in the glow of the fire. Whoever had collected them must have assumed that lighthouse keepers were partial to accounts of men on water, for the titles—*A Christmas at Sea, Memoir of Commodore David Porter, The Battle of Mobile Bay,* a translation of *The French Lighthouse Service*—leaned heavily that way. While I studied the shelves, Mrs. Crawley organized the new supplies according to which house or shed they ought to be stored in.

"Ready for the wagon," she said at last, but the children had stolen away.

"Mary! Edward! Nicholas! Jane!" Her voice thundered over the morro, and she peered sharply in the direction of the ocean, although, as nothing was there but black air and, far below, black water, it seemed an unlikely place for the children to be.

They did seem somehow to emerge from that place, however. We heard them running up the dirt path from the lighthouse, and they came panting into the firelight. Something swinging around the little girl's neck glinted silver, pink, and blue.

"Janie," Mrs. Crawley admonished. She looked quickly around as she pulled the girl to her. "How many times must I tell you?"

I stepped toward them for a closer look. The necklace was made of shells or bits of shell, like nothing I'd ever seen. "What is it?"

Deftly, Mrs. Crawley pulled the loop over her child's head. "It's not for her."

Jane let out a shriek to wake the dead, but Mrs. Crawley ignored it. She marched with the necklace into the darkness at the edge of the mountain and flung it in a wide arc, releasing it over the ocean.

"It was mine." The girl was crying softly but heartbreakingly. "It was my turn."

I stepped uncertainly toward the girl, wanting to soothe her but worried that I might interfere. Archie Johnston reached her first. He squatted beside her and opened his arms to offer her comfort.

CHAPTER 4

W HEN THE BONFIRE had been doused and Oskar and I came into our own rooms, I went directly for my writing paper and pen. I didn't know when I might have a chance to send letters, but I longed to talk with the people I'd left, if only in my head. I elevated our situation in a letter to Lucy, describing the vista as being what Mr. Edmund Burke would call sublime, exciting terror and admiration in equal measure, although I felt far more terror than admiration that night. And I wasn't sure what was more disquieting, the emptiness in all directions or the people who shared my isolation.

The closed windows dampened the crash of the waves far below us, but the sounds of life at the top of the rock remained distinct. There were footsteps on the path; someone heading toward the light, then someone coming back. Archie Johnston, that must be. Yes, I could hear him climbing the steps to his front door and coughing as he passed through his sitting room to his kitchen. On the opposite side, the children's feet pounded up the stairs to their bedrooms; doors slammed exuberantly.

I let Oskar show himself around our house. The noises he made as he galloped through the place, opening the cupboards and windows to peer in and out, were similar to the children's banging.

"Jesus! What's this mess?" he shouted down.

"It belongs to the children. I . . . they'll . . . we'll get rid of it."

"Looks like they dragged half the beach up there," he said, seating himself beside me at last.

"Their mother has a collection, too. It's awful! Some poor sailor's teeth!"

He'd put his hand in my lap and was beginning to stroke my thigh, but I stopped his fingers and held his hand firmly between my own. "Up here, I feel so . . . exposed."

"What do you mean?"

"Everyone can hear us. Mr. Johnston. Listen." The cough came again from the apartment next door. "The Crawleys. God."

"Oh, God!" He laughed. "I'm not worried about Him. But I agree that Mrs. Crawley is a different matter. She's daunting, isn't she? And the way she enlisted you to teach her children. I wouldn't like to cross her."

"You were on her side! Telling her what a wonderful teacher I would be!"

"You would!"

"I suppose I must try."

"Well, what else are you to do?"

"There's a good deal of work about this place," I mimicked, "and no Chinese servant to do it."

But he was right. Who was I here? Not Trudy Schroeder, pampered daughter, lively friend, bright student, all but affianced to steady Ernst Dettweiler. Here I would be a disappointment because I didn't know how to make butter.

"Will you like *your* work?" I asked.

"It'll be easy enough." He imitated Mr. Crawley's slightly nasal tones. "Scrape the rust, clean the lenses, keep the rollers and the air compressor running at the proper speed. Paint and polish. Check the boiler. Reset the pendulum every six hours, so the foghorn sounds on schedule. It's only maintaining machinery," he concluded. "I could do it in my sleep."

"If you don't like it, maybe we could go back. Maybe not to Milwaukee, but to Chicago or Cincinnati. Somewhere not at the edge of the earth."

"Go back? No! This place is exactly as I'd hoped it would be." He rose from the sofa and began to range about as he spoke, testing the slide of the windows, studying the pattern of the wallpaper. "I'll be able to do some real work here. When we go back, it'll be in triumph."

"Work on your electric engine, you mean?"

Oskar was among those who thought that electricity might be an efficient alternative to steam power. He'd built a small electric engine in Milwaukee and attached it to a canoe, which attracted a good deal of attention on the river. The problem, as he'd explained it to me, was how to make such a machine large enough to move a craft as heavy as a ship. When we'd learned that we'd be going to a lighthouse, he'd hoped it would provide a useful place for experiments in this line, but halfway here he'd stopped talking about such plans. I was pleased to hear them revived, although to me such work seemed impracticable in this setting. It was far more isolated than we'd imagined.

"You know, I don't believe that interests me anymore," he said. "So many others are already beavering away at electric engines. I'm going to do something new here. Something no one else has got hold of yet."

"That's wonderful, Oskar. What is it?"

He shrugged. "I'm not sure yet, but something will present itself. For a curious person, the world is full of opportunities." He threw open the large parlor window with a bang and leaned out of it, drawing the air loudly into his lungs. "Don't you think this place is inspiring?"

"No," I admitted, wrapping my shawl tightly around my shoulders. The temperature seemed to have dropped twenty degrees since the afternoon. "It frightens me. I don't think people are meant to be here."

"What's to be afraid of?"

"Everything! The wind that's trying to blow us off, the rocks that are waiting to spear us! If we were to step off this mountain one night, how would anyone even know what had happened to us? Being here, it's like we've disappeared."

At last, he turned and focused his disconcertingly bright blue eyes on me. "But don't you see? It's not we who've disappeared. It's they. We've got rid of all those people who would tell us what to do, who to be. Except," he added slyly, "for Mrs. Crawley. Now, if she were to step off this mountain . . ."

"Oskar!" But he'd made me laugh, and I was grateful for it.

"And now, Mrs. Swann," he said, extending his hand, "if it would please you to accompany me to our own bed in our own house, we'll do whatever we like."

It may have been our own bed in our own house, but when I awoke later in the night, it was nevertheless an unfamiliar place, full of unfamiliar shadows and, aside from the sheets that smelled comfortingly of home, strange odors. Oskar had opened the bedroom window, and in the dark, the ocean seemed to rise to me. I could smell it, its greenish, half-growing, half-decaying scent laced with salt and an unwashed animal stink. Or perhaps the smell was coming from the children's collection. I got up and closed the door to the second bedroom and our door and the window as well.

Except for the bed, our room was empty, so different from the fullness of my parents' house. I thought of the vanity in my mother's room at home—no, not at home, this was home now—where she'd brushed my hair not so very long ago and eons ago in preparation for my wedding. I thought of the silver-backed brush and mirror engraved with the swooping initials of the mother my own mother had left behind in Hamburg, a set surrendered to a dusty pawnshop in San Francisco.

I sniffed. The smell had been coming not from the open window nor from the next room but from Oskar. The sea had marked him with its briny green odor and its underlying scent of rot.

CHAPTER 5

IT HAD BEEN only a casual comment at an everyday meal, a small thing, that had caused my life to change course. But any sailor knows that an alteration of a few degrees, uncorrected, is enough to put a ship on a wildly different trajectory.

The meal that night had also been fish, carp boiled in wine, a dish recently popular with the members of the Milwaukee Women's Club. It had been prepared with more care than the ling cod.

"You see, girls," my mother said, measuring herbs she'd dried the previous summer and dropping them into the pot of simmering, sweet-smelling liquid, "you must pay as much attention to the poaching broth as you do to the sauce."

Gustina, our hired girl, nodded, but my attention had wandered to the window where the sky was alive with snow. It was two weeks before Christmas, 1897.

"All right, Trudy," my mother said, misinterpreting my distraction. "I know you have your essay to finish. And I've got letters to answer. Gustina can watch over this. Don't forget the potatoes," she called over her shoulder as she accompanied me to the parlor.

From my little writing table some portion of an hour later, I watched the lamplighter mount his ladder beside the post outside. There! Thick snow appeared in the sudden circle of light when his pole touched the wick. With the tip of my pen, I pulled spider legs of ink from the rich black blot that had dripped onto my copybook page just after Napoleon had set off for Moscow. I sighed. So far to go. Two more rays, and the spider became a sun. I tapped the pen with my index finger, and a miniature storm of dark droplets splattered the little general.

"Trudy," my mother said reproachfullly. She was seated at her own desk, covering pages with an irritating ease. "Don't make it so hard, *liebchen*. It's only a composition." She rose with a rustle of apricot silk. "I need to check on Gustina." On her way out of the room, she laid her hand on my shoulder. "You will finish before supper, yes?"

I sat up, sighed again, and pushed my fingers deep into my hair. Pins sprang from my coif, and I enjoyed the bit of drama and the little mess they made on her Turkish carpet. "Yes, yes, I'll try." I was too uncertain of myself and the source of my malaise to make any sort of stand; the best I could do was bend over the page in an exaggerated attitude of application. She deftly collected the pins without comment, gathered my hair, and twisted it neatly, resettling it like a sweet roll on top of my head.

When I could no longer hear the whisper of silk, I rose and went to her desk and slipped the unfinished letter from under the blotter. It was to her sister in Hamburg.

Trudy has lost her passion for her studies. It's not that she doesn't know her history and philosophy. The way she argues Kant with Felix! Papa would be pleased. They go until the candles gutter and the cloth is covered in nutshells. It's like living among chattering squirrels. But when she must compose her thoughts on paper, the rattle of the coals in the stove, the pattern of the snowflakes dropping from the ashen sky, even such little nothings distract her. There, she frowns at me, offended by my own prodigious pen scratchings.

She practices her music but without conviction. To be sure, her talent is not so great as your Johann's—I don't expect ever to hear her études at the Pabst—but she used to play with profound expression. I would wish music to be a greater pleasure to her. What makes

my heart weep most, however, is her poor, neglected drawing.
Remember those droll cartoons? Pages of them! But she doesn't prize
her skill and hurries through the exercises her master sets for her. All
slapdash, as they say here. Such a waste!

Latin and Greek she claims are useless. Her translations come
back covered in red. She proceeds tolerably with mathematics and
biology but complains that they, too, can have no place in her life.
She taunts me. How have I put to use my knowledge of chemistry,
my studies with Professor Von Rhein? "Oh, that's right," she says.
"You have instructed the laundress not to put too much bleach in the
bedsheets and told Gustina to add more vinegar to the kartoffel-
salat. *That is what you've done with your fine education."*

Be thankful you have only sons, Lilian. You cannot expect them
to be like you. But a daughter, naturally so similar to her mother,
can be a reproach in every way she is different. Of course, my
liebchen *is sorry when she is cruel. She throws her arms around my*
neck and cries. I know her hardness is only a fleeting expression of
her own frustration; to absorb it is part of a mother's role.

The poor thing is infected with the notion that all of her educa-
tion is "bourgeois trappings," as she puts it. "I must create my own
destiny!" she insists. How foolish children are to believe themselves
wise!

And now here she is, lying along her arm on the desk like a little
girl. To have them little again, just for an hour or two now and
then, what wouldn't we give for it? I must wind her up to finish this
composition or she will be wretched.

In so many ways, this assessment stung, though I couldn't deny the
truth of it. I had been hateful to her. Still, I couldn't agree that my frustration was a childish emotion I'd outgrow. For three years, I'd been exhilarated by the classes Milwaukee College had offered me. The history,
the science, the philosophy, all went far past what I'd learned in high

school. Here, I'd believed, were complex but satisfying ways of making sense of events and nature and ideas. I'd felt I was being given a glimpse of the world beyond me and the tools I'd need to explore it further. But now that commencement approached, I'd begun to perceive graduation more as a finish than as a beginning. I'd ingested all the material I'd been fed, but I was a goose plumped for others' consumption. My parents, Ernst, President McAdams, Miss Dodson, and even Lucy seemed to have a definite vision of how my life should proceed.

"But the goose will not have it!" I said aloud. And sighed. The trouble was that the goose, being a goose, had no idea what she *would* have.

Still, failing history would hardly help me. In any case, I'd been brought up to finish what I'd started. I sat myself straight in my chair again, resolved to push Napoleon smartly on.

I was fully engrossed in my essay at last when the bell rang. Absently, I capped my pen, wiped my inky fingers, and thinking of the troops pursuing the elusive Russian army and drawn inexorably toward Moscow, I wandered into the hallway and opened the door.

"Ernst!"

He had a cheerful, open face, neat white teeth, apple cheeks above his pale brown mustache, and gold-rimmed spectacles that fogged the moment he stepped into the warm house.

"You're surprised?" he asked, pulling off his gloves and pushing them into his pocket. He removed his glasses and handed them to me, and I polished them in a wifely manner while he slipped off his coat.

"Yes . . . I mean, no, of course not. Come in, Ernst. Here, let me take your coat and hat." I *had* forgotten that my father had invited Ernst to supper, but no matter.

My mother hurried from the kitchen, shedding her apron onto a hall chair as she came. She glanced critically at me. "I'll entertain Ernst while you run upstairs and make yourself presentable."

"Oh, Mother, Ernst doesn't mind a little ink."

"No, I like to see the evidence of Trudy's work. Especially here." He touched the tip of my nose with a blunt index finger. "It's very becoming. Like the nose of a little woodland animal."

"All right, all right. I'll wash my face."

I ran up the stairs on my toes, eschewing the banister, conscious that I was making my mother sigh by not planting my whole foot on each step as she'd taught me.

As always in the winter, my room was icy, the porcelain doorknob a cold stone in my palm. Unless someone was ill, there was no cause to light the stoves upstairs. Once inside that private space, I was snagged almost immediately by a sort of inarticulated dream and drifted to the window. The light of the newly risen moon reflected faintly off the whitened yard below. A wooden bench and a patch of red currant bushes in the summertime were amorphous mounds now; the former might be a man reclining under a blanket, the latter a flock of quiet sheep. Even the iron supports for the clothesline were softened by a thick sheath of clinging snow. I clouded the pane with my breath and traced a meandering path with my fingertip.

Ernst's laughter boomed up the stairs, recalling me to my purpose. "Say," he announced when I came back into the parlor, "I noticed that Winn and Hewitt is selling some Sociables. I'd consider buying one if I could be sure of a partner. It's not good for your health, you know, to read so long and neglect physical exercise."

"Sociables?"

"You know, Mama," I explained, "those bicycles that let you ride side by side, two people on the same machine. We saw one at Green Lake last summer."

"Bicycles in the middle of winter?" my mother said. Distracted, she pulled back the edge of a drapery to look out the window. "What I can't understand," she said, "is why anyone should work only eight hours a day when your father works far more than that. Always he is late. If the fish is dry tonight, you will know whom to blame, Ernst."

Just then the heavy outer door closed with a thump.

"Ah!" My mother nearly sprang for the door. "There he is."

Ernst and I followed her into the hall, where she was tutting and brushing snow from my father's collar. "You are a snowman," she fussed affectionately.

"And you"—he kissed her lightly on the forehead—"are a hot cross bun."

My father was a large man, tall and broad, with cheeks leathered from Lake Michigan's winds. He'd worked his way up from mechanic in a shipyard to captain of a tug barge to owner of his own barge, which he continued most days to captain himself. He pulled off his fur-lined gloves and flexed his fingers.

"Your fingers are hurting you again, Papa?"

"It's nothing. Only the cold."

"You must allow Gerhart to do more of the work, Felix," my mother scolded. "For what are you paying him?"

"Ach! You girls! Always fussing!" He winked at Ernst. "You see what you are in for, Ernst, don't you? And double the trouble if you have a daughter. Did you say the supper was ready, my dear?" He put an arm around the waist of each of his "girls" and led the way down the hall to the dining room.

"So, I hear you have a new carpenter," my father said, bending over his plate but raising his eyes to Ernst.

"Yes, my cousin Oskar."

"Little O!"

Oskar had stayed with the Dettweilers years before. I'd gathered at the time, eavesdropping from behind the blue velvet drapes, that because a red flower had died, his mother found herself unable to look at him without weeping. Afraid of being banished myself, I vowed to be more careful around my own mother's tulip beds. Oskar was a year or two older than Ernst, but a shorter and slighter boy with long girlish curls. He boasted a great deal about his father, who, he said, knew all there was to know about trains and kept beside his desk a big knife from Mexico for stabbing "like that!"—he'd thrust his arm suddenly forward like a fencer scoring a touch—"anyone who bothered him." He also bragged about his older brother, who had skipped several grades in school. He refused to be amused by any of our games, declaring them "too childish," but cried to Ernst's mother when we hid the flannel duck with which he slept. I'm ashamed to admit that we'd meant to make him cry, because when he did, he said, "Oh, oh, oh!" which was odd and amusing and therefore to be provoked. During the scolding we endured afterward, I discovered that the flower had been a younger sister who succumbed to scarlet fever.

"He isn't little any longer, but yes, that's the one. From Cincinnati. You'll like him now, Trudy. He's like you, always with his nose in a book."

"He's working as a carpenter?" My mother was quick to spot the seams where the pattern didn't quite match up.

Ernst understood her meaning. He shrugged. "He left college, you know. He says he wants to follow his own path, although it's a dead end, as far as I can see."

We laughed, and Ernst smiled shyly at his own cleverness.

My mother pushed on. "Peter must be beside himself."

Ernst's uncle Peter did something that required him to wear spats and travel to Washington a great deal.

"I think Uncle Peter resigned himself to Oskar's ways long ago. He has Manfred, you know." Oskar's brother, Manfred, I'd been led to believe, controlled all the shipping on Lake Erie. Admittedly, my understanding of business and finance was vague. "Oskar's the artistic personality, more Aunt Bertha's boy."

My mother sighed. "Poor Bertha."

My mother had lost children, too. Two infant boys before my parents had come to America, hoping for better luck. I knew that she and Ernst's mother—whom I called Aunt Martha, although we had no blood relation—often clucked over Martha's sister, Bertha, who, after her little daughter's death, had closed the kindergarten she'd founded and in many other ways allowed, as they saw it, despair to steer her life.

"Gustina!" My mother leaned back in her chair to direct her voice down the hallway.

"Coming!"

"I'm sure your papa will see that Oskar does very well as a ship-builder," my mother said, turning back to Ernst.

"As a matter or fact, he's been talking a lot about steam engines," Ernst said. "Says he might like to learn to run a tug."

"Is that so?" my father said. "You bring him to the dock tomorrow afternoon, and I'll take him out with me."

"Papa!" I set my glass with such force upon the table that wine sloshed dark red onto the bleached white cloth.

My mother reached quickly for the salt and poured it over what was sure to be a stain. "Trudy! *Was ist los?*"

"I've asked at least a dozen times to learn to run the *Anna P.*," I said, ostentatiously addressing my father alone.

"Oh, well . . ." My father looked helplessly at my mother.

My mother closed her eyes and gave her head a little shake, as if to dislodge the whole scene from her consciousness. "You're not going to become a tugboat captain, Trudy. For heaven's sake."

I couldn't honestly argue otherwise, but this seemed to be beside the point. "You don't object that my other studies have no practical consequence," I said triumphantly.

"Perhaps in July it might be pleasant—" my father began.

I interrupted him. "I'm not asking for pleasant. I'm just asking to broaden my experience. My own papa refuses me but is more than will-ing to teach some boy he's not laid eyes on for a dozen years."

My father looked to my mother again. It was her job to stand firm.

"It's not that I mean to become a sailor," I went on, "only that I want to feel and see something other than my path to school and home again, something other than well-appointed rooms, if only for a little time. I want to see what it's like to freeze in the open air and buck upon the wild water. I want a few hours in which I don't know precisely what will happen next!" Frustratingly, I knew that my words were only dramatic gestures at a feeling I couldn't articulate. "You came across an entire ocean to a new world," I reminded my mother. "All I'm asking is an afternoon on a tugboat."

"Trudy," she said, giving me a look. "You will help me clear, please. Gustina must be having trouble with the dessert."

While she lifted the platter with the fish carcass off the sideboard, I collected four wineglasses from the table, although I knew she preferred that those remain until last and that, to be safe, I carry only two at a time. The fragile material pinged with every step.

In the hallway, she stopped and leaned close to my ear. The platter and the near-empty glasses and even her breath carried the scent of sweet wine as she whispered, "You might try going to the dock tomorrow afternoon. You never know."

"I know, Trudy." Ernst's voice followed us down the hall. "Let's go and buy our bicycle tomorrow, what do you say?"

"All right," I called, then walked with exquisite care to the kitchen.

The next day I learned to stuff a hen in Domestic Sciences.

"Now, girls," Miss Emerson said, "you must take your twine, thus, and wrap it several times around the feet. Tie it off tightly but neatly. Even the operations that the diner will never see must be executed with care."

The bones were slippery, and I had a harder time than I'd expected, tussling with the headless bird, its insides plumped with onions and tarragon. I was relieved when the midday class ended at last and I was free to take a streetcar from the college to the docks.

But the journey was long enough and interrupted with jarring stops and starts frequently enough to encourage doubt, and by the time I stepped off the car onto the icy bricked road, my conviction had begun to ebb along with the day's pale light. My feet were numb in their thin boots and stockings, well suited to the college's heated classrooms but impractical for much time in the out-of-doors. I flexed my toes as I climbed the stairs to my father's office. For the first time it struck me that I'd likely missed the boat—after all, my father spent most of his time out on the lake—and I felt some relief at the thought.

No, I could hear Papa's voice before I'd reached the top of the stairs. ". . . didn't put all of my sweat and capital into this business to fork it over to men too lazy to make their own way."

"Come now." Ernst was there. "Gerhart Keffer can hardly be called lazy."

"Oh, Gerhart would never ask me for an extra penny. He knows I pay a fair wage."

"Of course you do." Even with the closed door between us, I could see Ernst nodding. He and my father were in perfect agreement.

I was reaching for the doorknob when another male voice pushed its way forward. "But who decides what's fair? The tug owners. What say do the workers have?"

I knocked, and the room behind the door fell silent. They were wondering. Well, they would be surprised, I thought stoutly.

"Trudy?" My father, one hand on the doorknob, had to use the other to take his meerschaum pipe from his mouth. He coughed a bit, startled to see me. "Trudy, come in. Come in." He stepped back to let me through. "Are you all right? Is your mother all right?"

"Don't worry. As far as I know, there's nothing the matter with either of us."

"Trudy," Ernst said, coming to stand beside me. "It's good of you to meet me here. Are you ready to pick out our bicycle?"

"Our bicycle . . . ?"

"First here's my cousin Oskar," Ernst went on. "You see that he's changed."

"Yes, Ernst has produced the cousin, as promised." My father gestured with the pipe's stem toward the man in the far corner of the room. "He's become a man of high ideals."

Oskar *had* changed. He was still not tall, but he was no longer slight, and his girlish curls had become thick, wild waves, the sort that must often break the teeth of a comb. I could discern no family resemblance between him and Ernst; his features were molded of a heavier, darker clay, his forehead more massive, his nose sharper and wider, his lips fuller. It was almost unseemly, I thought, how much of his face there was. He dipped his large head in the gesture of a bow. When he raised his eyes to meet mine, his bright gaze, a blue unsoftened by gray or green, struck me as somehow rude, intrusive.

"Trudy is an agitator, too," my father was saying. "She marched for the eight-hour day with her Miss Dodson."

"Her Miss Dodson?" Oskar frowned and turned his eyes to me again.

To my consternation, I felt my cheeks grow hot under his intense regard. "One of my teachers," I managed. "A woman of high ideals."

"Who nearly lost her position, in consequence," Ernst said, shaking his head. "A very foolish woman, really."

"It doesn't sound that way to me," Oskar said.

My father swept a hand through the air. "Enough politics! We've got to catch a schooner before she goes right on to Kenosha."

I said my piece then, firmly, knowing the condescending look with which Papa would answer me, a look I couldn't fight the way I could my mother's sharp words; knowing, too, that Ernst would add concern to that look, and that they would unite against me, tying my feet with their twine. "Papa, I hope you'll take me along today."

"Trudy, we've already discussed this," my father said. "No papa would put his daughter in such discomfort, not to mention danger, and no captain would allow it."

"What about our bicycle, Trudy?"

"No one buys a bicycle in the winter!"

Ernst looked hurt.

"I'm sorry, Ernst, but I don't think you or my father are looking at this fairly. I'm not suggesting that I'll be a help, but I'm not a child. I do know enough not to fall in, you know, and I can keep myself out of the way. Why can't I see, just like Oskar here, how it works, what my own father does every day? Please, Papa."

"Another time, Trudy. In the summer, perhaps," my father said absently. He was studying a chart he'd drawn from his desk.

"I think you ought to let her go," Oskar said.

My father and Ernst stared at him. I stared, too. I'd certainly not expected any help from Little O.

"Let her sit in the pilothouse," he went on. "She'll be cold and bored and miserable, and that will be that."

As if I were a spoiled infant. I was so outraged that I didn't know what to say.

"Keffer won't like it," Ernst said.

"I'm not entirely against annoying Gerhart," my father said.

"You might come, too, Ernst," Oskar said. "Keep her company."

"No, thank you." Ernst was angry with me, though because I'd been short about the bicycle or because I'd gotten my way, I couldn't tell.

My father, rejecting my overcoat as too fitted about the arms for easy movement and too loose in the skirt for safety, had me dress in old clothing of his: a suit of gray woolen underwear, a wool shirt, and navy trousers that flapped ridiculously around my legs.

"And this." He held out a mass of green so dark that it was almost black, the sweater his own mother had knit for him when he'd left Hamburg. He'd told me this story so many times that the garment, with its prickly fibers, its engulfing darkness, its soapy lanolin smell, had come to embody for me the grandmother Gertrude for whom I'd been named but had never met. When I pulled it over my head, I felt the weight of her sorrow at her son's defection to a distant country dragging my shoulders down.

The sweater had caught in my combs. While I regathered my toppled hair in a girl's braid down my back, my father stuffed a pair of his old boots with newspaper. He opened a large oilskin coat big enough to wrap around me twice, tied an oilskin hat on my head, and held out huge three-fingered leather mittens, lined with fleece, for me to push my hands into up to my elbows, dressing me as he had years ago when he'd taken me down toboggan runs.

"Now, don't let the mermaids find you," he said, chucking me under the chin.

In summer, we'd often gone to the beach under the low bluffs of Juneau Park to enjoy the sun and the water. Once, when I was a very little girl, I'd filled my pinafore pockets with stones, in the way of children, then climbed up on a pier and run to the end of it for no reason that I could remember. I'd been following a bird or the light on the waves or maybe only listening to the sound of my own feet thumping hollowly on the wood.

Suddenly, my father had stood huge over me, his face contorted, his fingers pinching my wrist. "Never!" he'd spat. "You must never run out on the pier alone!" He'd bent close and pointed at the waves shimmering—I did remember that, the sun bouncing off the facets of the water. "The mermaids live under there," he'd said darkly in German, the language of anger as well as affection in our house. "They take little girls like you, especially little girls with heavy stones in their pockets. They will snatch you with their long, wet fingers and drag you to the bottom of the sea."

"But you would save me," I'd protested.

"Sometimes, *liebchen,*" he'd said, softening, "you must also do your best to save yourself."

I'd been duly afraid, but as he walked me back toward safety, my hand in his, I'd peeked down at the spaces of shadowed water visible between the boards of the pier, trying to glimpse the world his warning promised.

While we'd been inside the building, the snow-swollen clouds had begun to leak. The flakes were heavy, clumping even in the air, and when they settled on the men's dark coats, their intricate fretwork glowed in sharp relief. Swaddled like a doll in so many layers that I could barely move my limbs, I followed my father and Oskar over the railroad tracks and across the road. A layer of white had already covered the boards of the dock. Our footprints, the two men's definite and mine slightly blurred from the shuffle of my too-large boots, were the first to mar it.

In the boiler room—which my father called the guts of the boat and which, with its shiny metal valves and pipes and cylinders, did indeed look like a mechanical version of what Miss Dodson had exposed when she lifted the flap of skin that covered a frog's belly—the men examined joints and pressures and had some words with the boilerman while I stood waiting, absurd in my oversized trousers and sweater and coat. Then we climbed the ladder to the pilothouse, a crystal perch, the upper half of all four walls being windows that admitted a clear view of the endless green-gray water. The lower half of the walls was paneled in a glowing birch, and in the center, like a varnished wooden sun, stood the wheel. As we came in, Gerhart Keffer turned from the chart he'd been examining at a small table in the corner.

He acknowledged my father's introductions with a curt nod. "Cold day for a boat ride."

"They're here to learn the trade," my father joked.

Keffer removed a tin from his pocket and put a dip of tobacco under his lip as he looked at me. He said nothing. I blushed.

"Trudy could be on watch," Oskar suggested. "Wouldn't hurt to have an extra pair of eyes on a day like this."

He and my father left me, their feet clanging down the metal rails of the ladder. In a minute or two, the engine began to thrum and the floor to vibrate.

"She's free!" I heard my father shout.

Keffer, a small man whose head barely cleared the top of the wheel, seemed to be listening for a certain pitch in the sound of the engine. Apparently hearing it, he eased a long lever forward. The tug slid away from the dock.

For a long while I did nothing but stare at the sky, gauzy and gray as a dirty bandage and filled with frenzied flakes, which seemed to dive straight at me, bits of the sky made solid. The effect, together with the roll of the floor as the tug alternately crested the waves and sank between them, was mesmerizing and dizzying. When I was young, I'd wished that my father captained a schooner rather than a tug. Tugs were prosaic, workmanlike ducks; schooners, with their sharp sails aligned and their sleek prows, were gulls. At every moment, I half imagined I could see the wings of a birdlike schooner emerging from the snow.

A glob of Keffer's spit clanged into the brass cuspidor at his feet, making me jump.

"It's snug in here," I said, partly to steady myself, partly to be polite.

"Huh," Keffer grunted. He worked the tin of Red Indian from his pocket and dipped again.

"In all of this water," I went on—my mother had trained me to be friendly, to draw people out—"how do you know which way to go to find the schooner?"

He shrugged.

"And in weather like this, it must be nearly impossible. Won't you tell me how it's done?"

"What for?"

"Well," I said, taken aback, "because I want to know." My parents and my teachers had always applauded my curiosity. Even my friends professed to admire it.

"Waste of time," he said, his eyes fixed on the water through which we were plowing. "Begging your pardon," he added superciliously.

Chastened, I trained my eyes on the receding shoreline, which now slipped and slid beyond a film of tears. I was cold, bored, and miserable, as Oskar had predicted.

My father clanked up the ladder again. Fresh, freezing air surrounded his body like a halo. "So, Tru," he said jovially, taking the wheel from Keffer and dismissing him with a nod, "maybe you'd like to drive?"

I saw Keffer frown, and I waited until he'd left the room before I moved to stand behind the wheel. It was a lovely thing, varnished so thickly it seemed to be encased in amber. Though I was nervous, it was easy enough steering in open water; all it required was resting my palms on the smooth pegs. Keffer needn't think he'd been doing anything so remarkable.

We went on a long while, until I could no longer make out the shore. For all I knew, we might be about to run aground in Michigan. We were sheltered from the wind in the pilothouse, but it was cold enough that our breath rose in clouds around us. My father frowned and trained his telescope through each of the windows in turn.

"May I go out on the deck to watch? I think I could see more clearly," I said.

"You'll get too cold."

"Papa. I'll be all right."

He sighed and opened a trunk that was built against one of the walls. "If you put this on first." He held out a life jacket. Grudgingly, I let him settle yet another layer around me, but I didn't stop to tie the vest closed before I hurried down the ladder to the deck.

I was too cold almost instantly. The bullying, frigid wind bored through all my layers of fabric, and a steady wash of biting spray stung my face. I tried to look into the storm, northeast, the direction from which the *Maria Theresa* should be running toward us, but the snow seemed to be driving with fixed purpose directly into my eyes. The flakes stuck to my lashes, blurring my view. I felt dizzy again, staring on and on so hard at nothing. I was beginning to feel sick, too, with the incessant rise and fall of the deck, the numbness in my fingers and toes, and the flakes rushing at me so relentlessly. Although I wouldn't have admitted it, I wished the job were done and I safely home, drinking chocolate, even writing about Napoleon. Finally, I lost my breath, as if the wind had stolen the very air from my mouth, and I had to turn away and cover my face with my mitten.

"Get inside, why don't ya?"

Oskar and Mr. Keffer had just emerged from the engine room. Keffer's tone was more than dismissive; it was mean. I bridled at it, lifting my face from my hands defiantly. It was that movement that allowed my eye to catch a fillip of red where there should have been only gray. It disappeared, and I thought for a moment that it might have been a trick of my mind, like water in the desert, but there it was again. I hesitated, not wanting to excite Keffer's impatience, but then I took myself firmly in hand. "Mr. Keffer!"

He paused, halfway up the ladder.

"What is that?" I asked. Now that my eyes knew where to focus, I could see it clearly. It looked like a red string dancing on the wind.

"There won't be no schooner there, at any rate. That direction's the shore. If you're seeing anything at all, it'll be the low sun catching on a roof. Waste of a man's time," he muttered, his feet ringing on the iron crossbars.

Oskar had broken from Keffer and came to stand beside me at the rail. He glanced at my face and turned toward the shore, following my gaze.

I couldn't look away until I'd determined for myself what I was seeing, for it certainly was not the reflection of the sun. It had nothing to do with light. There was a denseness about it, several densenesses. Later, when I thought about how it had happened, I realized that it was my willingness to accept what should not be there that allowed me to make out what was. People were hanging in the air! From one of them waved the bit of red.

"Look, there!" I pointed, pinning the sight to the sky. "Papa!" I ran to the ladder. "Look at this! You must look at this!"

Through his glass, it was obvious. The schooner, probably trying to stay within sight of land, had caught on the rocks just north of White-fish Bay and was sinking there. Already the foredeck was underwater, the masts pitched at an angle. The crew was clinging to the rigging, six men and a woman. "The cook, probably," my father said. It was the woman who'd been waving the red muffler that had attracted my attention.

We steamed toward the wreck with the engine at full throttle. I clanged back down the ladder and stood at the rail, watching my strange vision become more and more distinct and real. Now, although the cold was intensified by our speed, I didn't feel it.

Through the telescope, we'd seen the people shouting, but when the tug was near enough that their voices could be heard, they were quiet, watching, waiting to see how they might be saved. One man was slumped sideways, his eyes closed. Though one of his arms was hooked through the rigging, he seemed to be held aloft mostly by means of a rope wrapped around his waist. The rest of the men were alert but grim, their beards rimed with snow and ice. The woman's long hair swirled above her head in the wild currents of air. She'd let loose her red scarf; I'd seen it fly out and disappear when it settled on the water.

When they were a good way off, collecting these people from the schooner had seemed to me to be a simple task: the tug would sidle in close under the rigging, and the crew would climb down onto our deck. When we drew near, I could see that would be impossible. First of all, the rocks that the *Maria Theresa* had foundered on would wreck the *Anna P.*, too, given half a chance. Because of the rocks, and also because of the half-submerged *Maria Theresa*, large waves were continually springing up and dashing themselves down again in unpredictable directions. There was no way the tug could steam in close enough without swamping or worse.

To my right, the lifeboat hit the water with a smack. Oskar leaped into it just as my father came crashing out of the pilothouse.

"Oskar!" my father bawled into the wind.

Oskar was half standing in the boat, digging furiously with his oars to keep from capsizing, steering more than propelling the lifeboat toward the schooner. He didn't spare a moment's attention for the tug.

"Dammit! Now we'll have to rescue him, too!" my father roared. "Watch him, Trudy! Don't take your eyes off him!"

Even had staring threatened to blind me, I could not have looked away.

Over and over, a wave would lift Oskar to its crown and carry him forward while he pulled on the oars, trying to stay abreast of it, to ride it as long as possible. When the wave subsided, he would spill forward, the bow of the lifeboat plowing dangerously down, sometimes so far that it scooped below the surface and water poured in over the gunwales. Then he would hurl his weight back and dig again with the oars, resisting the lake's efforts to turn him sideways and tumble him over, to pick him up and pound him against the rocks.

I couldn't tell whether he was exceptionally skilled or foolhardy and lucky, but he managed to stay upright long enough for the waves to hurl him against the schooner with a force that might have cracked his boat in two but did not. Two of the crew of the *Maria Theresa* had eased themselves down the rigging in anticipation, and they somehow made the lifeboat fast to the wreck.

The tug itself was coming close to the rocks, and I could feel its engines protesting beneath me. I sensed that Gerhart Keffer and perhaps my father were turning away to see to our own safety, but I kept my eyes on Oskar, as if my steady and fervid gaze could form filaments that would pull the lifeboat out of danger. Already the crew was lowering the man who'd been tied to the rigging, and the woman, who'd scrambled up the highest, had picked her way halfway down.

When all were packed into the lifeboat, it sat far too low among the heaving waves, but it drifted well enough away so that at last the tug could do its work. My father ran neatly up alongside the little boat so that Keffer and the boilerman could snag its gunwales with their boat hooks. I was the one who made fast the bow line when Oskar threw it to me. Although the rope was frozen, I managed to bend it into the knot my father had taught me years before by pretending the rope was a rabbit.

My father helped Oskar climb last of all out of the lifeboat and embraced him roughly when he stood on the deck again. "My boy, I thought you were a goner. You can ask Trudy here. I was swearing to high heaven when I saw you jump into that boat."

"I guess I didn't think," Oskar admitted. "I just wanted to get there."

"Well, you got lucky. We all got lucky." My father drew his hand over his face to wipe his eyes and the ice from his mustache. "Trudy, *was ist los?*"

I'd burst into tears, overwhelmed by the strain and the cold and the idea that the man who had once been Little O might have been lost forever in the icy water.

CHAPTER 6

I T TURNED OUT that I'd not been weary of my studies after all; I'd only needed the right teacher. That Christmas, when my parents gave me a coral necklace in the hope, they said, that it would satisfy my craving for adventure on the high seas, Oskar gave me a small volume bound in green calf, the title, *Selected Poetical Works of G. Meredith*, stamped in gold.

Most of the poems celebrated man's connection with a grand and glorious Nature, a Nature that somehow lifted people above the stolid earth. But there was also a long group of sonnets that contained much about tasting and other physical features of amorousness that made me uncomfortable. They were dark and unromantic, a view of love and the loss of love that startled me. Though I didn't like them, I found myself turning to them again and again, gingerly, so that the fall of the book wouldn't reveal my interest to anyone who might casually open it. My mother, for instance. I was angry with Oskar for exposing me to such thoughts, but I couldn't chastise him without revealing that I'd read the poems, and I was far too embarrassed for that.

G. Meredith turned out to be the first flake in what soon became a flurry of books that drifted into piles on the end tables and the card table and the mantel in our parlor, as Oskar began to accompany Ernst to our house in the evenings. He didn't bother to change out of his rough work clothes, and I saw my mother more than once brush at the place where he'd sat, for fear he'd brought sawdust or worse onto our furniture. When Ernst hurried off to the Musikverein or one of his other clubs, Oskar would stay, producing from his leather satchel whatever he was currently reading, torn paper bookmarks sprouting from between the pages like the feathers of an Indian headdress. He claimed he wanted to talk over his ideas with me, and I was flattered and curious.

"I've read hardly any of this," I protested repeatedly, thumbing through Emerson and Whitman and William James, to name a few of the volumes he thrust at me.

"It doesn't matter," he said, shaking his head so that his wild hair lifted like wings. "You can think, can't you?"

When he got going, he seemed to leap from philosophy to literature to science, making connections that I could barely follow, let alone understand. Ernst had been wrong about his wishing to be a tugboat captain—not that it wasn't a noble profession, but Oskar had more cerebral ambitions. He wanted to improve the engines of watercraft and maybe the design of their hulls as well. Although he was wary of limiting himself. What he wanted most was to experiment and invent, "to discover something that will help the world." It didn't matter what.

"I would have thought you'd have found it worthwhile to finish college, then," I said. His attention had awakened feelings in me that frightened me a little, and I used an acid tongue to keep them at bay.

He wouldn't be put off. "Oh, Oberlin." He shrugged. "I milked all I could out of it. If you want to discover something new, you have to break from these institutions. As Emerson says, a man should walk on his own feet."

Trying to walk on his own feet was why Oskar had lived in so many places and worked at so many jobs. And it was why, in a few months, he was going to California, an exotic land where caballeros mingled with Orientals and people weren't afraid to strike out on their own.

He talked of throwing off the blinders of convention. "You were magnificent, spotting that schooner. You didn't let your mind convince you that it wasn't there."

"Of course," I admitted, "that's really because I didn't understand enough to know that it shouldn't have been there."

"You trusted yourself. That's the important thing."

He admired the Transcendentalists. They understood that Reason wasn't the be-all and end-all; there had to be a spark as well. Inspiration, they called it. Passion, even. God was a part of everyone, Oskar explained. Who knew what a person might be capable of with that Greatness in him? Or in her, he added, his eyes seeking my own.

Under his tutelage, I began to feel the ribbons of my small, trussed-up experience loosening. Through the force of his conviction and *his* spark, I saw the world, glistening and ripe, opening before me.

A visit to the panorama in March brought my feelings to a head, and my betrayal of Ernst at that place was particularly egregious, since he'd bought the tickets, five of them, as a treat for me and his cousin and our friends Lucy and Charles.

"We'll see Greece," he said, "and then we'll eat, and then we'll go to my concert—I have a solo, you know." (This was a joke on himself; he'd mentioned his solo so often in the past month that we'd begun to chaff him about it.) "And then we'll eat again. That's the way to spend a Saturday!"

We were to meet on Wisconsin Avenue at the entrance to the exhibit in the afternoon. The day was warm; snowbanks collapsed, revealing pure, clear crystals packed beneath the winter's crust of black soot pitted with horse urine. Although my mother had insisted I carry my muff, I left my coat open so as to show off my blue silk dress. I wore my Easter hat, a large fruited affair that slipped sideways, despite its pins, when I tossed my head.

I'd meant to wear my coral necklace, but it wasn't in the box where it belonged. My mother had surely picked it up from wherever I'd left it lying, but I didn't want to ruin my happy mood by asking and being scolded for not taking care of my things.

Ernst and Oskar were waiting, Ernst smiling, with a fan of tickets in his chestnut leather glove; Oskar frowning and stroking his mustache distractedly. I kissed Ernst lightly on the cheek in greeting, and then, on a whim, kissed Oskar, too. He started and furrowed his brow, looking quickly away.

"Are you in one of your moods," I teased, "or merely contemplating the riches of the classical world?"

"Hmph," he grunted. "Are those my only choices?"

By this time, a group of about thirty were chattering near the entrance, and the door to the panorama hall was opened by a man in an oxblood uniform with gold braid along the shoulders. He collected our tickets and directed us into a dark passageway; its novelty and air of mystery heightened our anticipation.

"When you emerge," a sonorous voice said from farther up the passage ("Our spirit guide," I whispered) "you will be transported to a different place, a different time. You will find yourself in Ancient Greece, land of poets and philosophers, of architecture and sculpture, of olive groves and wine-dark seas."

"Of cabbages and kings," I added to my group, resisting being swept away by this manufactured drama.

At the end of the passage, we remained in the dark, but the panorama was lit up before us. We seemed to be seeing the city—was it Athens?—from a roof or perhaps from the top of a high wall. To the left, a market bloomed and bustled, patterned fabrics were draped over lines, terra-cotta pots were strung on ropes, silver fish were packed head to tail in long, low baskets.

"Look," Ernst said, pointing to a wolflike dog that was running down an alley trailing links of sausages, "the Greeks had bratwurst!"

Fountains poured and gardens wound, each botanic specimen delineated. In an olive grove, men sat under the gray-green trees; near one of the fountains, women with hair braided and twisted into crowns stood talking, their earthenware water jugs resting at their feet. Interiors were visible as well: a hand plucked an olive from a dish; a woman played a small harp. The whole of it was so lovely, such an exquisite mixture of liveliness and tranquillity, that I instantly surrendered my ironic distance and wished that I could step into the scene, put my foot on the stone path that scarred one of the green hills, and simply run up it to the Acropolis, where the temples stood intact to welcome the gods. Just as the spirit voice had promised, I'd been transported to another place.

"Look here, Trudy!" Lucy tugged at my sleeve.

She was studying a green plain that became a yellow beach that became the sea, not wine-dark, as poetically promised, but a blue as brilliant as the sky. In the foreground, long black ships crowded the harbor, and in the background were more sails, sharp-edged and white, like the triangles of paper a child drops when she is cutting snowflakes.

"I don't believe there is any real sky that color," I said, attempting to break the spell that gripped me. "The sky must be the same wherever you go."

"I've read that it *is* different," Oskar assured me. "Something about the intensity of the sun and the dryness of the air, I suppose."

I turned and turned again, trying to take in every vista at once—the sea, the mountains, the olive groves, the gleaming white buildings under the marvelously warm sky—"Oh, don't you wish we really could go there? Just for an afternoon! It would be like stepping into a dream!" Spinning, I felt exhilarated and also slightly giddy, and my hand, when I put it out to catch myself, grasped an arm. It was not Ernst's. Had I known that?

Immediately, Oskar laid his hand over mine. I kept my eyes firmly fixed on Greece, though the whole of my being was focused much nearer to home. For seconds his long fingers encased the whole of my hand, his warm skin pressed against mine.

In those seconds, the lights dimmed, and the spirit voice descended on us again. "The time has come to bid farewell to Ancient Greece.

Please step down the passage to your left, so as not to collide with the incoming group."

By the time we reached the sidewalk, Lucy and Charles and I had been pushed by the crowd a little apart from Oskar and Ernst, and when Ernst came up to us a few seconds later, he was alone.

"So!" he said. "We'll get a snack and then off to our next bit of entertainment! My solo!"

"Shouldn't we wait for Oskar?" Lucy asked.

I'd thought the same but had not dared to voice it while I could still almost feel the pressure of his fingers.

"He had to go back to the boatyard," Ernst said. "Something to finish, he said. Off on another of his tangents, I guess."

"He's not going to the concert?" I brought out.

After what I'd felt at Oskar's touch, I'd not been prepared for him to take himself casually back to work. He'd not even bothered to tell me goodbye. The heightened senses I'd enjoyed that whole afternoon dulled, and the fruited hat that earlier had seemed to lift my chin now pressed heavily around my temples.

"That's all right," Ernst said. "As long as you're there." He gave my shoulder a squeeze to pull me toward him, and on top of my disappointment, I felt piercing shame. Without my willing them, my feet copied the rhythm of his as we walked toward the music hall.

I did my best to be bright in the seat near the front that Ernst's parents and my own had held for me. I caught his eye and smiled; I applauded energetically; but when it came time for the final number and the music master turned to announce that we were all to join in, I had to gird myself for what I knew was to come.

The popular "*Du, du liegst mir im Herzen*" swelled from the audience like a wave, and I sang, too, although my voice was only a whisper. "*Du, du liegst mir im Sinn.*" The words about pining for a lover who doesn't care enough bruised my throat, and I felt the push of tears behind my eyes. I allowed myself to be swayed back and forth in the waltz tempo, my shoulders locked with the shoulders of all in my row, but I knew I was alone.

At the restaurant afterward, Aunt Martha frowned at her liberally salted *hackfleisch*. "Oskar ought to have come. We're giving him a home, after all, even after what happened with Ida. And a job. The least he could do is show some gratitude and loyalty." She helped herself to a large forkful of the raw meat and paused to chew it before going on. "He failed half his classes at Oberlin, you know. He's in no position to act as if he can't be bothered."

"I'm sure he's had a hard time of it," my mother said kindly. "It must be very difficult to follow in Manfred's footsteps."

"You can hardly say he's done much following. Poor Peter despairs of his ever making a success of himself."

Stewing in my own mix of longing, disappointment, and shame, I said nothing about walking on one's own feet.

While we were out, a cheap envelope of the sort used to pay the iceman was pushed through the letter slot. It was addressed to me, so Gustina laid it on my bed. It contained my coral necklace, as well as a page torn roughly from one of Oskar's notebooks.

Dearest Trudy,

It is not my right to call you that, but you are my Dearest Trudy. I dare to say it because you have a good and true heart, the best I've ever known, and you won't laugh at my poor self but be sorry to have caused such feelings in me when of course you cannot return them. Believe me when I say I've fought against this idiocy—I've sat my feelings down and given them a stern talking-to and even licked 'em once or twice until they bled—but they only laugh at me. They

know what they want and will not be dissuaded by anyone so
trifling as me. And so I'm writing to tell you that I plan to leave for
California at once. I would not hurt my cousin nor cause you
embarrassment. I will, however, love you always.

    Yours without hope,

    Oskar

    P.S. I'm sorry that I took your necklace. I so desired the thing that
had lain against your beautiful skin that I couldn't help myself. I'm
sorry I stole your necklace, but you've done far worse. You've stolen
my heart.

I was powerfully moved by the idea that he planned to sacrifice himself. (Even while I recognized that his claim of hopelessness was merely proper modesty, for what was the letter itself if not hope?) I was enraptured by the notion of a love so fierce it would not be extinguished. I was nineteen, after all, too newly hatched into womanhood to have grown any protective carapace against the pressure of ardency. I don't accuse him of guile. I believe he produced these sentiments in the same spirit in which I craved them. That is ever the story of love.

I needed no more than the passion I saw in this letter to refine the clay he'd presented me into a finely molded figure. I admired his intensity of focus, his determination to do something in the world—qualities I wished for myself but feared I lacked either by virtue of my temperament or because I was not a man. The criticisms I'd heard of him were nothing except the fears of those who had neither dreams nor daring. I saw that he had superior understanding, and with it he saw me as no one else did, as someone different, even—dare I say?—better than others had supposed. I believed that he might make my life into something I couldn't even picture, because it was so far beyond my experience that I had not the imagination to conjure it.

And so, as my mother said, I ruined everything.

CHAPTER 7

OUR FIRST BREAKFAST at Point Lucia was pilot bread, which turned out to be hard enough to break a tooth on. Dipping it in coffee would have helped, but the beans Mrs. Crawley had given me were green, and even supposing I'd had the stove lit and could figure out which apparatus was meant to be a roaster, I'd not have had them browned, ground, and boiled before noon.

"I'm afraid it's not a very good first meal."

"Never mind." Oskar swallowed his down. "You'll figure it out." And then he was standing again, pushing his hat onto his head. "Best not be late."

I followed him to the door. I didn't want to call him back; I believed that I'd a duty not to, but I felt a sort of panic rise in my throat and couldn't help myself. "Oskar!"

"Yes?"

"But . . . well . . . what should I do today?"

"Oh." He smiled. "I'm sure you'll find something." He kissed me cheerfully, stepped into the cold, damp air, and was gone.

The dawn had just begun to gray the kitchen. I knew the place needed cleaning badly, but it was too dark to attempt it. I turned down the lamp and went back up the stairs, aware with every chilly step that I now lived in a pile of stone, perched at the top of a rock, hanging over the sea. The pulse of the ocean penetrated the windows—or it may have

65

been my heart sounding in my ears—and in time to it, I found myself repeating Mrs. Crawley's words: "No one comes here. No one comes here." How different this morning would have been on Tenth Street, I thought as I got back into bed. Gustina would have hulled strawberries at the sink while my mother set the table with the bone plates and the bird's-eye napkins embroidered with cherries. She would polish the silver forks with the hem of her apron before she laid them on, too. And then she would put her head into the back staircase—"Felix! *Was ist los?*"—because always he was slower to come down than she thought he ought to be, and I slower still, except that now I wasn't there at all. It seemed likely that I would never be there again, when I thought of the ships and trains, the many nights in unfamiliar beds, that intervened between that life and this.

The sheets, when I pressed my face to them, still smelled like home. Through the wall, I could hear Mr. Johnston calling gibberish in his sleep.

"Missus! Missus!" The children were clamoring for me. Was I expected to begin their schooling already?

The sun must have risen, but the sky remained gray. I scrambled from the blankets and hurried downstairs. All four stood at my door, mussed and grubby, as if it were the end of the day rather than the start. The oldest boy had a rucksack strapped on his back.

They stared at me. "Were you sleeping?"

"Yes," I admitted.

"But it's half past seven."

"Your milk and eggs have been here for ages."

"Did you sleep in your clothes?"

They were all talking at once, and I didn't know whom to answer or, in any case, what to say.

"We're going to the beach!" Jane said finally.

"We thought you might like to go with us," Mary added.

I hesitated. "Maybe we ought to begin your lessons."

"Not today!" the younger boy exclaimed with real dismay in his face. I remembered that his name was Nicholas.

"I suppose that can wait." I looked back over my shoulder. "But our house is so dirty. I ought to clean it."

To this they said nothing for a moment. Then Nicholas said again, boldly, "Not today!"

They looked at me, waiting to find out whether I would scold him for impudence and shoo them away. "All right, today I'll come with you. Why not?"

As a child, I'd cooled myself on many a hot summer's day by walking between the rows of heavy, wet sheets on the clothesline behind our house. Moving through the fog that hung around the rock felt much the same, though there was no freshly washed scent and no sun at the end to warm and dry us. The closest building, the workshop, was a dark, indistinct form. Possibly, the denser patch of gray beyond that was the barn. The lighthouse itself, farther down the path, was only a suggestion of something more solid than air. I expected the children to lead me to the little steam-driven platform on which Oskar and I had been carried up the morro the previous afternoon, but instead they launched themselves off the northern edge of the rock, directly into the clouds.

I shrank back. The descent was shockingly steep, although, perhaps mercifully, the extent of the slope beyond the first ten feet was so heavily shrouded that it was impossible to judge. What ground I could see consisted of sharp-edged brown and black rocks, each surface scored and cracked, as if some giant had attempted and failed to sculpt this matter into some graceful form. Hard and brutish as the materials were, however, the effect overall was not ugly. The rocks were covered with vegetation exotic to my eye. Orange and green lichens spread in a bright, haphazard patchwork, and plants in various greens and grays, even a few with flowers, clung defiantly to the cracks.

I picked my way cautiously, but at every few steps, my feet failed to find a purchase, and I slid until I could grab enough of the low, brittle plants to stop my fall.

"Is there a path?" I called into the grayness. "Should I be following a path?"

"No path." It was Edward who answered. "Best to zigzag."

"Yes, don't try to go straight down." That was Mary's voice.

"You'll kill yourself!" shouted Nicholas.

"Wait for me!" demanded Jane. "Ma says you have to wait for me!"

There was much sliding and scraping and clattering, and from time to time I spotted Jane's red sweater, but even that very little girl was moving faster than I was. I placed my feet with no notion of where I was going except down, fearing with every step that the ground might disappear entirely. Then, suddenly, the fog thinned. We'd come through the bottom of the cloud. I could see the children, Edward and Mary, sure-footed, in front; Nicholas, accepting the occasional slide on his bottom as the price of not falling behind; and Jane, who just then lost her footing and began sliding fast, rolling onto her stomach, but otherwise abandoning herself to the force of the slope.

I nearly screamed and let myself slide as fast as I dared without completely losing control, my feet turned sideways to the mountain. The older children looked up and moved to stop the little one's fall, but in the end, it wasn't necessary. A dense shrub caught her, and she lay until I could reach her and pull her onto my lap. I let her cry and dabbed at her scrapes with my sleeve.

"She's all right," I called down, but the others had gone on already.

I sat for a while, the child snuffling in my skirt, and wondered how we would manage to climb up again. Now that I was sitting still and could raise my eyes from the rough ground, and now that the sound of scraping shoes against the crumbling dirt no longer filled my ears, I became aware of the breaking waves. They were more violent today than yesterday, and they hurled themselves toward the rocks that shattered them into a million droplets. The waters I knew, the Great Lake and the Milwaukee River, were gray and stately, green and sluggish, respectively. This was wild, churning stuff, its turquoise color as extravagant as its movements.

The three older children had shed their shoes and stockings by the time Jane and I reached the bottom. Mary was tucking her skirt into her bloomers. I admired their unself-consciousness and their ease with the rough surf. They ventured in as the sea gathered itself and then ran, shrieking, from the tongues of cold water, like the quick-legged shore birds, although the birds were silent and serious. I followed the children onto an outcropping of rock and watched them squat over a clear saltwater pool, their shadows frightening crabs, which ducked nimbly under rocks. The bottom of the pool was lined with bright orange and brick-red starfish and even one of brilliant blue; small dark shells, whorled into points, like the budding flowers of an apple tree; tiny volcanoes from which waved frondlike tongues; pale green anemones that curled around the children's insistent poking fingers; columns of black mussels.

"Look!" Nicholas cried. With a bit of shell, he was teasing a bright pink blob off a rock. "I've never seen one like this!"

The others crowded around, squinting critically.

"I have," Edward boasted.

"You have not!"

"I have, too."

"Don't touch it!" I cried.

They all turned to look at me in astonishment.

"Why not?" Nicholas asked at last.

"It might bite or sting. It might be poisonous."

"It's not. See?" Nicholas had loosened the animal's grip on the rock. He plucked it off and held it up. Without its base to support it, it hung limply between his finger and thumb.

"What is it?" I asked. "Some sort of slug?"

"It's not a slug! It's a nudibranch!" Nicholas said, affronted. "And we've never found one this color before."

"Nicholas is right, Edward," Mary said. "I think we ought to keep it."

"What's a . . . what did you call it?" I asked.

"A nudibranch," Mary said.

"Is that a name you made up?"

"Of course not!" Edward said indignantly. "It's in the book."

"Some Species of the Pacific Coast," Mary explained.

"Mary stole it out of the library!" Jane said gleefully.

"I didn't *steal* it," Mary said. "I put something else in its place. That's allowed."

"Well, I'm keeping this!" Nicholas took a jar out of the rucksack, filled it with seawater, and dropped the animal inside it.

They splashed about in the water, sometimes scooping other animals into jars, sometimes dropping items straight into the rucksack—a bit of bone, for instance, and several rocks imprinted with ancient shells and bored through by worms. They pointed out dolphins' fins cutting through the waves and the dark bodies of seals lolling on the rocks.

It *was* tempting to pick up bits of sea life and look at them more closely once I saw they were harmless. The water itself seemed to bite my feet, however, as I stepped into the icy pool, reaching for a mother-of-pearl shell and a bright red star. I peeled off my boots and stockings and picked my way over the rocks and sand in my naked feet, no different from the children.

In an hour or two, we were eating pilot bread, thickly sugared with sand, that Edward had fished out of the bottom of the rucksack for our lunch. Although the air was clear enough immediately around us, a haze obscured everything beyond a hundred yards. One minute I was looking at nothing, and the next a dark shape emerged from the north, striding vigorously. The children followed my gaze.

"Mama!" Janie cried, jumping up and running toward the woman. Indeed, it was Mrs. Crawley.

"What are you doing down here?" she said when she was near enough for normal conversation. Her voice was sharp, although she allowed Jane to swing her arm playfully.

I'd thought to ask the same of her, although I certainly wouldn't have used that tone. "The children were showing me—" I began.

"They know better than to go down to the beach without permission, Mrs. Swann."

"But you never give permission," Edward complained.

"That's because there's plenty for you to do up top. I doubt any of you have finished your chores. And I'm quite sure," she added, "that Mrs. Swann has a great deal of work to do around her own house."

In a moment, the children had tossed their shoes into the rucksack and were scrambling straight up the forbidding, rocky wall, using both hands and feet; even Edward, dragging the full pack, moved quickly. I struggled awkwardly to pull my stockings over my own sandy feet and to thrust my feet into my shoes while Mrs. Crawley stood over me. Somewhat composed at last, I took a few steps toward the path the children had taken, keenly aware of my constricting corset and heavy skirt.

"*We* can take the steam donkey," Mrs. Crawley said.

It was a long, silent walk to the platform on the east side of the morro, and soon enough I wished that I'd scrambled after the children. I tried to make conversation, although I was rather breathless from having to keep up a near trot to match Mrs. Crawley's pace.

"Did you walk far?" I asked.

"What do you consider far?"

Her tone wasn't friendly, and I faltered in my answer. "Oh, more than a mile, I suppose."

"Then yes."

"It must be an excellent means of exercise," I chirped.

Since we'd begun our walk, she hadn't turned her face in my direction. Now she stared at me. "I don't require exercise."

Clearly, I'd gone wrong and I tried to explain myself. "It's so different here from Milwaukee." There you could take a streetcar to the beach and buy lemonade from a stand with a striped awning.

"Yes," she said. "Obviously."

"The children showed me so many interesting things," I pressed on. "They have a wonderful sense of curiosity, you know."

Finally, we reached the steam donkey. She threw a log or two into its boiler and reached out a hand to help me aboard. The car began to move before I had my footing, and her fingers closed around mine as she pulled me toward her to keep me from tipping off the platform.

"Curiosity," she said, her voice near my ear so I could hear her over the chugging engine, "isn't necessarily a virtue here."

At the top, she whisked away, and there was nothing left for me but to go into my dark house, where a dirty plate littered with the remains of Oskar's lunch—more pilot bread—lay on the kitchen table. There was a note beside it, written across a thick sheet of paper torn from my sketchbook.

Dear Mrs. Swann,
Will you have dinner with me tonight?
Your love,
Mr. Swann

CHAPTER 8

THE MONTHS BETWEEN Oskar's declaration and my becoming Mrs. Swann were riddled with the anger of those whom we'd disappointed with our plans, but this served only to heighten our passion and resolve. Like countless others before us, we believed that we alone understood the dictates of love.

Though Oskar was perhaps none too delicate when he announced his reason for moving out of the Dettweilers' house and into a Polish boarding establishment on the south side of town, I admired his courage and purposefulness.

Less stalwart, I wept at the hurt I caused my childhood friend.

"It's only a fancy," Ernst repeated several times. "I'm sure of it." He turned his back on me and set his face toward the rain-soaked street outside his parents' parlor. His fingers worked so ferociously, polishing the lenses of his spectacles, that I feared his handkerchief would fill with broken glass.

In the end, he clasped me to him, and I briefly yearned to belong in that snug space between his broad chest and pinioning arms, for my sake as well as his, but at last I couldn't draw breath with my face pressed against the soft wool of his jacket, and I pushed myself free.

"I must go. I'm so sorry, Ernst."

"You *must* go?" His voice was mocking as he sniffed and curled the earpieces of his glasses into place in a gesture I knew as well as the shape of my own thumb. "You're not compelled to do anything. You're choosing this, and you're an ingrate and a fool to do it."

I was grateful to him for this, because being angry in return was easier than feeling sorry. Even more assuaging to my emotions was the black eye Ernst gave Oskar the following day.

"I didn't put up any fight," Oskar assured me. "I owed it to him to stand still and take whatever he wanted to give me."

"I understand that you love him," my mother said. She was sitting at her vanity table, letting me brush out her hair with her silver-backed brush, a task that had always encouraged our confidences, perhaps because we didn't have to look directly at each other as we spoke or because the gentle stroking silently communicated some necessary reassurance. "I understand that you love him," she repeated, underlining the sentence with her finger on the burled wood of the tabletop. "And there is nothing to be done about that. But your father and I worry that he seems to care so much about what he'll do, what he'll achieve, no matter what it might cost someone else."

"Why do you say that?" I sought her eyes in the glass.

"Martha told me that he nearly ruined her sister."

"His mother?" I was used to hearing about Martha's sister's delicate emotions.

"No, they have an older sister, a maiden lady. Her name is Ida."

"I don't see how he could have harmed her," I said indignantly.

As my mother told me the story that Martha had told her, I studied her hair, which gently resisted the boar's bristles I was pulling through it. Gray strands stood out among the brown.

"It seems Oskar had the idea a few years ago to extend the life of the electric lightbulb. Or maybe to make it brighter. Something like that. Anyway, Ida had lent Oskar's brother some money for a project of his, so it seemed only fair to do the same for Oskar, especially when he seemed so sure of this scheme. That's what upset Martha, that he behaved as if he knew what he was doing, when he'd had hardly any training at all for that sort of thing. A class on mechanical science at Oberlin. A conversation with some visiting so-and-so. He got carried away, Martha says. He convinced Ida to give him more and more money, a great deal in the end, and then he gave it all up as a failure. Martha says her sister is greatly reduced and she believes worry over money has affected Ida's health."

This wasn't pleasant to hear, but I wasn't dismayed. The Dettweilers were understandably angry with Oskar—and with me—for disappointing Ernst. It wasn't surprising that they looked for ways to judge him harshly.

"I've no doubt that Ida did lose money," I said, meeting my mother's gaze squarely in the glass again, "but from all you say, it's clear that it was freely given and that Oskar used it sincerely for his work. All scientists fail far more often than they succeed. That's the nature of experimentation. Such things must have happened often to your Professor Von Rhein."

She shook her head. "Professor Von Rhein knew what he was about. This boy seems only to know what he wants."

Which, I thought with a thrill, was me.

I told Oskar the gist of my mother's complaint. He ought to know, I said, the way they were twisting things. And I suppose I hoped that he might defend himself with an explanation I could carry home.

"It would have worked," he said, "in time. My aunt understood that perfectly well. She wanted to give me more support, because she knew I'd pay her everything I owed her and more. It was my father who made us fail. He wouldn't allow her to give me the backing I needed to see it through. Originality frightens him."

My mother, I suspected, might take Oskar's father's side, but I believed that I, like Oskar and Ida, was unafraid of bold ideas. I would help Oskar to see his plans through.

I suspected, too, that much of my parents' unhappiness derived less from disquiet over Oskar's character and more from the loss of their long-nurtured vision of the happy Schroeder-Dettweiler family. And if Oskar were only going to replace Ernst, we all might have foreseen a time when the Schroeder-Swann family might have been equally happy; however, the house in the newish neighborhood and the peony garden were lost as well. For it turned out that marrying me wasn't going to change Oskar's plans to go to California. We were wedding with what might have appeared to be almost unseemly haste on the twelfth of July, because Oskar's father had arranged a job for him in the West. He'd contacted the son of a friend who was doing research at the University of California in Berkeley.

Of course, there's nothing for you at the university, Mr. Swann had written. *But Philip, being a responsible young man, supports his studies clerking part-time at the customs office in San Francisco, and in that capacity he's heard of a lighthouse keeper in need of an assistant. You'll have to take a test to prove you can read and write, and there'll be an interview, but I would think you would do all right with that.*

Oskar had been bitter at this letter's condescending tone and resentful, too, that his father presumed that he required help. He'd scoffed at the job for a day or so, but he understood, now that he was taking a wife to California, that he needed something more definite than a vague and glowing sense of opportunity there. Soon enough, he'd decided that working at a lighthouse might provide a chance for some truly independent trials with the engines he'd been working on in an environment, as he put it, "untainted by everyone else's ideas," and he was quite cheerful about his prospects.

"My father thinks to teach me a lesson with this. He wants to make me into the sort of plodding person who dutifully does his rounds, seeing no farther than the end of his nose. I'm sorry to be dragging you to who knows where. But I'll make gold of this, you'll see. An isolated setting will help me to focus. The lighthouse will be like an incubator, and in a year or two, we'll come back with something that'll surprise them all."

I protested that I needed no apology and didn't care whether the lighthouse would be an incubator or merely a means of earning a living. From the safe and dully familiar perspective of my room on Tenth Street, the notion of going someplace as unusual and romantic as a lighthouse was enticement enough. It would be a grand adventure, I told my mother, and after all, we'd not be gone forever.

My mother couldn't hide her despair or contempt. "A lighthouse! In California! An enterprising young man would find far better opportunities here in Milwaukee."

She was chopping citron and candied cherries for a stollen during one of these not infrequent outbursts, in her distraction uncharacteristically allowing bits of the fruit to escape onto the floor.

I collected them as I answered, feeling that I was the cool woman and she the frustrated girl. "Oskar says there's too much complacency in this city. People care only for cleanliness and order."

This was a sharp comment, since we were both well aware that she valued cleanliness and order a great deal. "They're complacent," she said, marshaling her dice with the blade of her knife, "because this is a good place to live. Most people I know here have no reason to complain about their lives."

"I suppose we're not like most people, then." I brushed the errant sticky stuff from my hand into the dustbin, thinking with secret scorn of my parents' smug friends, the men with their whiskers and beer, the women with their curls and playing cards.

Our wedding day was gray and cloud-clotted, and my hair, alert to the threatening storm, rose from my head like wires to meet the silver brush as my mother struggled to make the strands lie flat and neat under the wreath of rosebuds Lucy had fashioned for me. The wreath was reproach as well as ornament; Lucy and I had long planned a double wedding, and I'd ruined that, too.

As penance for the upset we'd caused, I'd refused a new dress, but Gustina, who had a talent for decorative needlework, had festooned the bodice of my gray silk with a rope of embroidered pink blossoms and sewn a pink gather inside the kick pleat to match. In this, I stepped across the parlor carpet to the mantel at eleven o'clock. When Oskar touched my hand to slip on the ring, a jolt of static made me gasp.

"Of course, your mother wasn't up to the trip," said Oskar's father—whom I thought of privately as "the great man"—over luncheon. "Given the state you've put your aunt Martha in." He himself had come all the way from Washington, where he was advising some committee. "And you know the demands on your brother."

My mother had set the table with the delicate blue Haviland, reserved for the finest occasions, and I feared it would break under the pressure of the great man's knife, with such firmness did he attack his cutlet.

"Yes," Oskar said. "I understand."

"What I'm not sure that you understand," Mr. Swann continued, a triangle of pale meat quivering on the end of his fork, "is that henceforth you must be different."

Oskar opened his mouth to object, but his father didn't need to raise his hand to indicate that interruption wouldn't be tolerated.

"Thus far in your life," he went on, "you've behaved largely like a child on Christmas morning, running from one shiny object to the next." He paused to insert the meat into his mouth, work his jaws, and swallow. "Given that this is your nature, I would not have advised you to marry, but you didn't ask for my advice. You never do." Hurt momentarily muddied his stern expression. "This young girl," he went on, "isn't to be cast aside when you lose interest in her."

"Sir!" I broke in. "Oskar will not lose interest in me!"

Mr. Swann turned his large head in my direction. "You misapprehend, if you believe I'm belittling your charms. Whether he turns his attention elsewhere or not will have nothing to do with you. To be flighty is his way."

"It is not!" I exclaimed, although I was aware that it was I who sounded childish now.

"I'm not going to be like Manfred," Oskar said petulantly, "plodding along the conventional path."

"I'd be the first to agree that you're not like Manfred. I would point out, however, that the occasion of your marriage affords an ideal opportunity to recognize that there's a good deal of worthy and profitable work to be done by all sorts of people. Not everyone can dazzle."

Oskar didn't look at his father; he glowered at the pale blue rosebuds on his plate instead.

"In any case," the great man went on, "I'm not here to argue about your path, as you call it. Only to satisfy my conscience that I've done all I could for a girl my sister-in-law tells me is a very fine person, which I'm sure you comprehend"—he turned to me—"means a great deal, given the bitterness you two have caused."

"Surely we need not speak of such things today," my own father put in.

After this, although the great man went on eating with gusto, the rest of us could swallow only a bite or two of the fruitcake and whipped cream that followed.

When I went to my bedroom to change into my traveling suit, I discovered my mother checking again the contents of the trunk she'd so carefully packed and which could hold so much less than she wanted to send with me, especially since the railway charged by the pound. In keeping with the local disapproval of our plans, there were few gifts, and in any case, we would not have taken many. The idea, Oskar had reminded me, was not to re-create my parents' parlor in the West. So the ginger jar and the cake plate depicting city hall, the cut-glass water jug and matching glasses would have to remain in Milwaukee. I could bring the silver pickle fork.

Had Gustina starched the linen waists? my mother wanted to know. Did I have my belt and a good supply of cloths? Oughtn't I to bring my old silk chemise as well as the new one? After all, it had some wear left, and it took up very little room. We'd been through all of this several times already, but the trunk—the very one that had accompanied my mother from Hamburg—was a cord between her and me, and she was terrified lest she forget to supply it with some essential item.

"I don't see your button box. Did we put it in?"

"Mother!" My emotions had reached a point of exquisite tautness, like the E string on my violin, and the tuning knob kept turning. "I'm sure the West is well supplied with buttons!"

"We don't know that," my mother sobbed. "We don't know anything!"

And then I was in her arms and we cried a bit together, which did much to relieve us both.

"Oh!" my mother said, wiping her eyes. "There's something else you must have!"

She hurried into her room and returned with the toilet set from her vanity. The silver pieces, engraved with monograms, flowers, and insects, were old-fashioned and heavy, beautiful in their way, but clearly the taste of another era. Among them was a pair of nail scissors, and she used these to cut a lock of my hair, which she'd so often brushed. She curled it around her finger to make a loop. I knew it would go into her locket, along with the silken curls of her sons.

She wrapped the toilet articles in a length of flannel and pushed them into my valise. "You'll have a grand adventure," she said tearily, "as I did." At her words, I remembered that she'd never returned to the home she'd left, and I felt a prickle of regret and fear. We repeated the assurances we'd given each other concerning frequent letters and a journey for my parents to San Francisco before too long, and we gripped each promise as tightly as we would the rungs of a ladder.

Despite our careful preparations, there was a scramble in the end. A wagon had been hired to carry us to the depot, and the four of us rode to the train, my parents unconsciously seating themselves on either side of me so that Oskar was obliged to take the bench opposite. The rain held off, sulking, and the water in the air brought out the city's summer smells: the yeast and malt of the breweries, the blood and fat from the meat-packers and the tanneries, and the general effluvia that rose from the river.

"I think there must be some way to post letters," my mother said, "even from a lighthouse. Don't you think there must, Felix?" It was not the first time she'd worried this issue. My father took her hand.

Our leave-taking seemed to stretch me fine as a thread of pulled taffy, and I longed for the train to arrive, to board it and be away, so that I could gather myself and turn my attention fully one direction, toward my new married life in the West. At the same time, I wished that the minutes on the platform would never end.

Without regard for my feelings either way, the train arrived from St. Paul, puffing and sighing in huge clouds of steam, its wheels shrieking against the tracks as it stopped. My mother lifted the gray grenadine veil from my face to kiss me one final time. There was a confusion of porters and ticket stubs, and at last Oskar and I were seated side by side on a velvet bench inside one of the cars. I knelt on the seat like a child and leaned out of the window, and my mother and father came and stood below. We were finished with wishes and promises, and we waited without speaking for the train to pull us apart. At the first lurch, I reached down my hands and my parents took one each, but I felt their fingers only for a moment because the wheels were rolling. As the train drew away, I saw my mother cross her hands over her heart, her gaze directed upward as if in supplication, and tears came to my eyes.

Then Oskar put his hand on my shoulder and coaxed me with gentle pressure into the car. "I'm sorry I'm taking you away."

I put my own hand over his, which was warm and firm and helped hold back the loneliness that had begun to fill me like cold water rushing into a cistern. "No," I said, "you aren't taking me. We're going together."

When we'd first sat down, he'd put our case awkwardly on the seat between us, and he rose to push it onto the rack overhead. I was acutely aware of its contents. More than the wedding ceremony or the leave-taking, the intimacy with which, inside that valise, his wooden-handled hairbrush lay beside my silver one and my bleached and ironed night-dress nestled against his striped muslin shirt, arms and tails tangling, made me know that I was now married and so a different person from the girl I'd been that morning. I was yoked to him.

CHAPTER 9

I CHANGED INTO MY duster, and for the rest of the afternoon, I laid claim to our narrow stone house, teasing cobwebs out of the corners of the ceiling, chipping hardened grease off the stovetop, washing the floors until the water in the bucket was no longer black.

I saved the second bedroom for last and then went at it with a broom and dustpan and a length of dirty oilcloth I'd found stuffed in a kitchen cupboard, intending to wrap up the whole mess and fling it into the ocean, jars and all. As I began to sweep, however, I thought of the children, their eagerness and sincere interest in their collection. I abandoned my broom and searched the outbuildings until I found a number of empty crates. These I filled with everything that didn't smell, and I lined them up along one wall. Only the things that reeked did I fold in the oilcloth and bury at sea.

By early evening, I was pleased with my work and pleasantly exhausted. Face washed, hair neatly coiled, and duster exchanged for corset, shirtwaist, and skirt again, with a smart black bow tied around my neck, I thought myself a charming picture of domesticity as I stoked the fire in the cooker, arranged potatoes to simmer in a pan with some milk, and coated a pot with lard in readiness to shirr some eggs.

I heard clanging from the kitchen next door as Archie Johnston prepared his own meal and the bang of a door as he went out, presumably to cover his shift at the light. I closed a letter to Lucy and inked an address on the envelope. Expecting Oskar every moment, I set the table with the lighthouse china and the linen napkins my mother had stashed in the trunk. I slid the potatoes from stovetop to oven, selected a can of peas and one of pineapple from my colorful store of canned goods, and pounded them open with a chisel and hammer I'd found in a drawer. Oskar didn't come. I read from *The Prisoner of Zenda,* the novel I'd chosen from among the books in the "library."

The potatoes browned. The peas warmed and cooled again. The eggs and pineapple beamed up at me from their bowls. The crown prince lay drugged or drunk in Ruritania. Still Oskar didn't come.

Exasperated and unable to sit any longer, I wandered through the parlor and upstairs to the bedroom. Eventually, I found myself in the "nursery," where I began examining one by one the items I'd stored in the crates. A few things—a bit of pressed seaweed, a mussel shell—resembled the plants and animals of Lake Michigan, but most were entirely foreign to me. I touched their surfaces, some sticky, some rough, others as smooth as the water itself.

A few items clearly hadn't come straight from the sea. There was a cracker tin, for instance. Its contents rattled. I hadn't peeked in earlier; after all, it belonged to the children. Now, with nothing pressing to do, I couldn't resist opening it. Inside were a tiny, intricately woven basket painted with black slashes that suggested diving birds; a bone with a well-sharpened point at one end and a small hole at the other; a piece of green rock cunningly carved in the shape of a fish; and a length of leather with feathers worked through it. I knew at once that the children hadn't fashioned these things. How had they come by them, then?

I was fully absorbed by these treasures when I finally heard Oskar's footfall on the path outside. It wasn't hurried or even brisk. In fact, he stopped for some minutes before climbing the steps to our door. Doing what, I couldn't imagine.

I went down the stairs, sure that at any moment the door would open. Finally, I pulled it open myself and looked out.

"Look at the moon." He pointed, not shifting his eyes from the sky.

I would not. "Where have you been? Your dinner has been ready for two hours!" I'd not allowed myself to feel angry while I waited, but now my impatience burst forth. I understood why my mother fretted about my father coming home on time. I'd organized a tableau that was to have established us, husband and wife, in our cozy home, but he'd not played his part.

"Oh!" He looked sincerely surprised and puzzled. "You shouldn't have waited for me. If you were hungry, you should have eaten."

"Should have eaten!" I stopped myself. He'd not promised me the rituals of home, a Milwaukee bourgeois existence transplanted to a new world.

He didn't notice my indignation. He went to the sink and began washing his hands industriously. "I was just going through the workshop, seeing what tools we've got. It's astonishingly well equipped. I suppose it would have to be—you can't run to the neighbors if you need a drill or a handful of nails. And there's plenty of wood to work with." He put his arms around my waist and drew me to him in an obvious effort to appease me. "I could easily make a chest of drawers or a night table, a vanity, whatever you'd like."

I weakened. It was not that I wished for any carpentry, only that I didn't want to be angry with him. "How about some shelves?" I suggested. "For the children's rocks and things. That would be useful."

"The children's rocks? I thought we were getting rid of that stuff."

"No," I said. "I guess not."

"Shelves are too easy," he protested. "I could do something much more elaborate than shelves." He sat down at the table and speared a cold potato with his fork.

"I'm sure you could," I said indulgently, ladling peas first onto his plate, then onto mine. I felt better now that at least some version of my domestic picture was taking shape. "Nevertheless, shelves are what I want."

CHAPTER 10

IN A FEW days, when Oskar had learned his tasks, he was assigned a shift of his own. Just as we, the last to arrive, got the dark house in the middle, so he was given the least convenient hours, eleven at night to seven in the morning. I went along, wanting to be with him, wanting to see the light, wanting, in a general sort of way, not to be left out. We became accustomed to that unnatural, upside-down feeling that comes from being up all night and sleeping through much of the day.

Tending a lighthouse turned out to be not so different from tending the lamps at home, although the wicks and the oil reservoirs were of a scale fit for a giant. They needed trimming and filling every four hours, and if you fell asleep and let the light go out, it might mean ships on the rocks, men dead, and profits spilled. The fog signal worked like the mechanism that ran the grandfather clock in my parents' parlor, though obviously much bigger and more important; the chain was as long as the light tower.

We spent most of our time waiting for the wicks to burn down or the oil to get low or the chain to drop to the bottom so we could race to the top of the stairs and rectify the situation. With the night pressing in from all sides, it was a close space, but not that different from any of the other confined places that Oskar and I had experienced together so far—the train's parlor car and the hotel room in San Francisco—and we were far from tired of each other. This was a honeymoon of sorts.

To amuse ourselves, I'm afraid we spent some of our time mocking the adults on the rock, especially Mrs. Crawley, whom Oskar called "The Dragon." We played Authors. We tried on the black spectacles that keepers wear to protect their eyes and groped around, pretending to be blind. We read the rest of *The Prisoner of Zenda* aloud. We told each other more about the lives we'd had before we'd known each other.

Along about the fifth night, Oskar brought a book into which he kept stealing glances as we talked. At last, in exasperation, I snatched it from his hand and examined the title page: *Electric Waves: Being Researches on the Propagation of Electric Action with Finite Velocity Through Space.*

"You've decided to work on your engine again." I was relieved at this notion, not that I cared so much about electric engines, but because it had been his ambition as long as I'd known him. His newly declared lack of interest in the subject on the night we'd arrived had disturbed me a little. It made him seem . . . well, flighty.

He dismissed my remark with a wave of his hand. "That's only a practical application. This is much bigger. It explains the behavior of electrical waves themselves. Listen."

He began to read, and I did my best to follow, but though these were clearly only introductory statements, I was almost instantly lost in a maze of polarizations and oscillations, insulators, conductors, and dielectric efficiency.

"It's intriguing, isn't it?" he said, pausing at last.

"What is?" I asked hopelessly.

He laughed. "The idea that electromagnetic current can be transmitted without wires from one point to another."

"Is that what it said?" To be honest, I hardly understood his translation better than I'd understood the original.

"Of course, it can't compete with *The Prisoner of Zenda*."

"You're right about that." I was vaguely disappointed in myself and annoyed with him for creating the circumstances that made me feel so. "I'm afraid I'd rather read the logbooks."

I meant that he should set his book aside, but he seemed to think that I intended sincerely to pursue this course, and that he was therefore free to devote himself without inhibition to the behavior of electrical waves.

With nothing else to occupy myself, I did go to the logbooks, which were arranged by year along an oily shelf on the boiler room wall. They contained a record, if not of all the work done at the light station, at least of each day's major task, along with the ships that had been sighted and often a description of the weather. Oskar had read aloud from one of them on a previous night, imitating Mr. Crawley's gentle drawl, Mrs. Crawley's imperious tones, and Mr. Johnston's sneer, depending on the hand in which the entry had been written and delivering phrases like "changed burners" and "repaired boiler gauge" in dramatic tones that made me laugh.

I selected a year at random and wandered haphazardly through the matter-of-fact lines. "Weather fine. Replaced screw set in valve. Two ships, one schooner, one steam." "Cleaned clock machinery. Rain: four inches." "Mixed whitewash. Russian schooner, three masts." "Packed south siren with sheet lead and canvas. Repaired blown gasket. Sun." "Stacked wood." "Stacked wood." "Stacked wood." After some ten pages, I believed I had a good sense of the Sisyphean life of the place; nearly every day something broke or became dirty. Keeping a light station was like running a house, albeit with a fine view of the sea. "Repaired broken window. Morning fog. Scrubbed floors." Buried among the mundane was an occasional momentous event. Here were a dozen whales and here the purchase of the cow. An inspection went well; I thought I could see the satisfaction in the dot of ink that closed Henry Crawley's sentence. I skimmed pages and pages, gobbling the bits of human interest strewn among them as if I were a bird pecking up seeds. "Assistant under the weather with piles." "First batch of whitewash ruined by curious hands." "Baby Johnston born and buried."

"Oh!" I must have exclaimed aloud, for Oskar looked up from his *Electric Waves*. I brought it to him and put my finger on the entry. "What do you think it means?"

"I guess he had a baby and it died, poor fellow."

"If he had a baby, then he had a wife."

"I suppose." His eyes were straying back to his book, to which his mind had returned already.

"But where is she?"

He shrugged. "Maybe the Dragon ate her. Or maybe she ran off. If I were a wife of Archie Johnston's, that's what I'd do."

I paged haphazardly through a few more of the logs, but it was tedious going. A month or so before the Johnstons' loss, I discovered the birth of a baby who completed the Crawley family, but I could find no mention of a Mrs. Johnston taking ill or leaving the light station among the pages of lens cleanings and lamp burner repairings.

Finally, Oskar pulled his watch from his pocket, stretched, and set his book aside. "Time to trim the wicks."

We tromped around and around the circular stairs in our black spectacles, and when we'd finished this simple task—actually, when he'd finished; I only stood companionably about—we stepped onto the catwalk, where we hung our heads back to admire the brilliant, glittering sky. Unlike in Milwaukee, the night air here retained none of the heat of the day, and I shivered and pressed my body against his.

He put his arm around me, but he did so absently, and he didn't turn his face to mine but toward the impersonal spangle that dominated the sky. So I looked up, too. The stars seemed to throb at me, and soon I had to turn away.

He quit the heavens and peered down at the heaving blackness that was the sea, leaning so far out over the spindly iron railing that I couldn't help putting my hand on his back, as if he were a child. "Oskar! Be careful, please!"

"I'm not going to fall," he said impatiently. When he stood up again, he softened. "I'm sorry," he said, and this time, when he put his arms around me, it was I who commanded his attention.

The next night I brought two new books of my own, *Some Species of the Pacific Coast*, which Mary had lent me, and *Voyage of the Paper Canoe: A Geographical Journey of 2500 Miles from Quebec to the Gulf of Mexico*, which I'd found in the library, and when Oskar settled into his *Electric Waves*, I had my own reading.

In the background, the surf threw itself against the rocks and the foghorn's clockwork clicked. Both sounds were lulling, and the paper canoe traveled slowly, so I was half asleep when, from upstairs in the lamproom, a crash sounded. I thought first of Gustina dropping a tray of wineglasses, but of course there were no wineglasses in the lamproom, only windows all the way around. We ran up the stairs, Oskar first and me after him, forgetting our black glasses.

We kept our eyes on the floor, away from the turning light. Knifelike shards glittered there.

"A spontaneous explosion," Oskar said. "It must have been the heat of the light on the window, meeting the coldness of the air. Or maybe a bird smashed into it."

"No, it was this." I picked up from the floor a jagged brown rock the size of my fist.

"Come down," he said, tugging my arm. "It's too dangerous without the glasses."

Mrs. Crawley confirmed that it had been a bird. "It's the light that attracts 'em, although why they want to fly straight into the sun is beyond me. Some twist of your precious Nature, I suppose. Generally, they're just stunned, although you'll find dead ones now and again on the catwalk in the mornings."

"But what about the stone?" I insisted. "How could it have come there?"

"Oh, the children are always leaving stones and the like lying about. It's time you start those lessons and give them something more constructive to do than forever collecting things that would better remain where nature left them. They slipped down to the beach again this morning, you know."

"All right," I said meekly. To the extent that I'd thought about the teaching, I'd expected it not to begin until the summer was well over.

"I'll send them to you tomorrow morning. Eight sharp." She stepped back inside her house and closed the door.

Clearly, I had work to do. I resolved to make a teacher of myself by breakfast time.

CHAPTER 11

Bᴜᴛ ᴡʜᴇʀᴇ ᴡᴀs I to teach them? I assessed the possibilities of the sitting room. Our furnishings, supplied by the Lighthouse Service, were scant: a brown velvet settee, a chair with a wine-colored back and seat, two occasional tables, each supporting a kerosene lamp. Should I line the children up on the sofa and make them use one another's backs as desks? The kitchen had advantages; I could perform some domestic tasks—bake bread, make soup, clean the ash from the cookstove, perhaps even learn to churn butter—while the children did sums and recited Longfellow. But I could hear my mother admonishing me to do one thing at a time. A schoolroom in the kitchen would make me both a poor teacher and a poor cook.

The nursery was the obvious choice. Except for the children's collection of marine life, the room was entirely bare, which appealed to me, for I could make of it what I would. Oskar had carried the trunk to our bedroom, where it was serving as a bureau; I dragged it across the landing to use as a writing table. I would ask the children to bring the pillows from their beds to sit on. I took a few precious sheets from my store of writing paper, along with my sketchpad, and placed them at the center of the trunk. How long would my pencils last when four children were scraping away with them? Were writing implements ever in the barrels?

From the books in the traveling library, I selected a volume of Stevenson's poems, a book written expressly for children called *The Five Little*

93

Peppers and How They Grew, and *The Battle of Mobile Bay*, thinking it might be a means of introducing some study of history. I had pulled up in my reading of *Voyage of the Paper Canoe* at the Great Dismal Swamp, but I thought I might begin again and read it aloud to give the children some sense of the geography and communities of the eastern United States.

I didn't go with Oskar to the light that night but slept instead, so as to be ready for my students in the morning. But they were not at my door at eight sharp nor even at nine. Maybe they'd gone to the beach again and hadn't asked me along this time. Probably they'd gone to escape me and my lessons. To my surprise, this idea hurt me.

I decided to scan the beach from the lighthouse. If I spotted them, I would wash my hands of them for the day. Surely there were other tasks worth my while. I ought, for instance, to figure out how to remove the salt that coated the windows. It was nearly impossible to see through the panes that faced the ocean.

Mr. Crawley was stuffing the boiler at the base of the tower. He shrugged amiably when I asked about the children, although whether to indicate that he didn't know their whereabouts or that he hadn't heard my question was not clear.

At the top, I saw that the shattered pane had already been replaced and fresh paint industriously applied to all the frames, so you couldn't tell which window had been broken. I stepped to the rail, which was no more than a narrow iron band about waist-high, intended more to suggest safety than to provide it. The sun was fiercely hot; the air seemed thinner here in the West than in Milwaukee, a substance too weak to intercede between the earth and that ball of fire. Far to the north, a steamship was churning through the waves, plying its way from one port to another and staying well clear of our treacherous rocks. As I watched its slow progress, the heaving ocean caught the sunbeams and threw them back at my eyes as white-hot needles. I wished I were wearing the black spectacles.

Yes, they were on the beach. Or at least some dark little forms moved along the far reaches of the sand. From here, they looked more like shorebirds or crabs than children. As before, they were venturing to the edge of the water and racing away when the waves came in to lick their toes. It would take me nearly an hour to reach them, and I wouldn't have the heart to drag them back. I would have to occupy this day in some other fashion.

I was beginning to make my way around the catwalk to the bridge when a shape on the mountainside almost directly below the tower caught my eye. Hanging over the rail, I determined that it was a small pile of stones. Smooth and white, they almost glowed against the sharp brown and black rock upon which they lay. Baby Johnston born and buried, I thought. The idea of that fragile, helpless little being suspended in a place so grand and desolate made my eyes fill.

The cairn was clearly tended. An ornament lay on the stones, a sort of disk made of green-black feathers. Who had placed it there? The children? It was difficult to imagine Archie Johnston with a such a feathered bauble in his hands.

Oskar had come home while I'd been out, and I found him in bed—he had to rest in the afternoon, so as to be awake for his shift. He wasn't sleeping, however, but taking notes on *Electric Waves* in a shorthand he'd developed years before, when he was a child bedridden with rheumatic fever and needed to amuse himself. Spread over the blanket and drifting onto the floor were pages covered with what were to me incomprehensible, frenzied, and somewhat juvenile lines of squiggles and arrows, pistols and stars, exclamation points, tiny tornadoes, and other symbols and designs that had once come readily to his ten-year-old brain, along with equations equally baffling to me.

As I gathered his papers, I told him about the cairn of smooth stones and the feathery thing on top of it.

"Poor Johnstons," he said.

"I wonder what happened to the mother." I imagined a woman boarding the tender on which we'd come, turning a bonneted head away from this place.

Oskar was finished with the subject. "Come here." He lifted the blanket, inviting me in. "Let me tell you what I've learned about electric waves today."

Long after Oskar had gone to his work, my afternoon in bed kept me awake. I sat for a while at the kitchen table, foolishly sipping coffee as though it were morning. I wrote some passages of a letter to my mother, not mentioning the cans, and several paragraphs to Lucy describing the cans in detail. Then I paged desultorily through *The Battle of Mobile Bay*. The room grew steadily colder, and I began to be aware of the darkness pressing around me. Through the wall, I could hear Mr. Johnston moving stealthily about his kitchen.

Restless, I lit our Aladdin lamp and roamed the house. I held the glow to the spines of the books we'd stacked on the occasional table, but none of the titles held my interest. I stood before the stove and considered emptying the ash. I went upstairs and studied our bedroom window. Perhaps I should look for some fabric to make a set of curtains that would block the setting sun. I decided that I might at least make a list of these tasks, so I sat down at the kitchen table again and pushed my hand into my apron pocket, feeling for a stub of pencil I remembered depositing there. When I removed my hand, it contained the bits from the sea I'd collected on that first day, when the children had taken me to the beach: the red sea star, its arms stiffened and its color slightly faded; a small black turban of a shell; a chip of mother-of-pearl colored with the gentle pinks, blues, and silvers of the sunrise; a rubbery splay of vegetation, like the horns of a tiny green reindeer. I went up to the schoolroom for *Some Species of the Pacific Coast* and turned its pages, searching for pictures of my specimens.

Somewhere between abalone and periwinkle, I came upon a spread of seabirds, their plumage brilliantly rendered in twelve colored plates. On the cormorant—"widespread marine bird, known for its dark, lustrous feathers"—I recognized the black feathers with the iridescent green undertone that made up the ornament I'd seen on the cairn.

I wanted a closer look at that feathered thing. I knew it was a foolish thought, but it gnawed at me, the way ideas will in the deep of the night. Silently, I carried my lamp out of the house. By now I'd wrapped myself in a shawl; nevertheless, the cold, damp air startled me. That the blazing heat could have been eradicated so completely in such a short time made me uneasy. It was almost as if the season had changed from summer to winter in a matter of hours. The sound of the water at the base of the rock had changed as well. It was far louder than it had been in the daylight. Even from so high above, I could hear the waves tumble the stones and claw them back, like gamblers raking coins.

A long streak of yellow shot across the black water; that would be Oskar, sending the signal into the dizzying void that was the endless churning water and the endless spangled sky. The gibbous moon washed rock and water in a ghostly light, inviting me to walk right off the morro into the air. As I made my way to the lighthouse, I stayed well back from the brink.

In a short time, I was standing at the base of the light tower, peering down toward the place where I knew the stones must be glowing. They were hardly visible from this vantage point, tucked under an outcrop of black rock, the hard edges of which the moonlight threw into relief. Perhaps I ought to have read this as a warning, but I chose to interpret it as evidence of solid ground on which I could plant my feet. I began to circle the tower, searching for a path or at least a gentler stretch of slope.

Yes, under the northern wall, where that structure met the side of the mountain, hidden from the usual entrances and exits one might make from the lighthouse, was a scraped bit of earth. I plunged right and snaked left, following the same sort of zigzag pattern the children had demonstrated for me a few days before, when we'd slid all the way to the beach. I didn't want to go to the beach this time. Instead of allowing the slope to pull me down, I began to work my way west, to the part of the morro that extended far out over the water.

I wouldn't have thought anything could have been more difficult to cling to than the slippery slope the children and I had negotiated, but soon enough, the way—for it could not be called a path—that I'd put myself on proved to be so. In only a few steps, I needed to use my hands to keep from falling. This ought to have been my cue to turn back, but I abandoned my lamp and crept on, away from its comforting flame, feeling more than seeing the texture of the rocks and brittle plants. How far I would have gotten, whether I would have reached the stones at last or given up or overshot them or lost my footing and handholds and fallen to my death, I will never know, because at this delicate point I was interrupted by a sharp voice coming from somewhere over my head.

"What are you doing there?"

It was Mr. Johnston. His voice roused Oskar, and I heard the upper door of the light tower, the one leading to the catwalk I'd been standing on that morning, bang open. "What's going on?" Oskar called.

What *was* going on? How had I come to be nearly hanging by my fingertips over the crashing ocean, my skirt tangled about my legs, my face and arms scratched and bruised? It occurred to me to suggest that I'd been sleepwalking. There could hardly be another plausible explanation.

I said nothing while I picked my way back as well as I could. The two men had gotten as far as my lamp and were standing together in its feeble light, their faces as craggy and shadowed as the mountainside.

Oskar reached for me, his face a worried question. "Trudy, what . . . ?"

"What are you doing here?" Mr. Johnston repeated.

"I saw . . ." I hesitated, not wanting to be blunt. "Some stones," I finished lamely. I turned my head to indicate them, but even that slight movement served to unbalance me, and I had to bend and grab for the rocks to steady myself.

"What were you going to do with them?"

"Nothing. I—"

"You were just curious," Mr. Johnston said mockingly.

I stood silent. What he said was true.

"Those stones are our business. Not yours."

"You needn't be rude to my wife," Oskar said. "She meant no harm."

"Well, she might have come to plenty. It's a very long way down and no good once you get there."

CHAPTER 12

Mrs. CRAWLEY MUST have admonished the children, for they began to appear at our front door every morning, their pillows clutched to their chests. In the first week or so, we looked at one another with trepidation, and our steps on the narrow stairs to the schoolroom sounded a doleful and dutiful march. They were forced to make various accommodations with their legs to sit beside the trunk—the top, for instance, came to the chins of the littler ones if they sat fully on their pillows—and then we addressed ourselves to the unnatural tasks that make up the usual school day.

They were shockingly uneducated. None of them could read more than his or her name, and only the two eldest could add and subtract and that not beyond what they could count on their fingers. They knew nothing of history or geography, not to mention science, art, and music. The two youngest didn't even know how to hold a pencil properly.

My mother had taught me all of these rudimentary skills. I struggled to remember how she'd done it. It had helped, I'm sure, that she'd had a great deal of authority over me. Jane, in this regard, being the littlest, was the most tractable and receptive, but she looked to her older siblings for her models, and they didn't see the point.

"We know how to keep the light," Mary objected.

"And I can fix the steam donkey," Edward added. "I've done it thousands of times."

"Don't you want to know about other places?"

101

"You mean like Cuba?" Edward asked.

"Yes, I suppose Cuba would be good to know about."

"That's where Mr. Finnegan's gone!" Nicholas put in. "He's going to kill the Butcher!"

This seemed to be a signal to aim imagined guns at each other and make explosive noises. I told them about the troops I'd seen massing in the Presidio and used several sheets of my sketchbook to draw a map first of the line of coast along which Oskar and I had come on the tender—were they not curious to know where the tender came from?—and then of the whole of North America, adding a broken line from Milwaukee to San Francisco to indicate our train journey. By placing some pebbles Nicholas took from his pockets on the trunk at some distances from the map, I showed them where the Philippines and Cuba lay in relation to the rest, although, truth be told, my own grasp of world geography was rather loose.

Then we used pebbles to mark all of the places we—really, I—could think of: Paris, London, New York, Peking. I wondered how I might procure a globe.

"Where is Salinas?" Mary wanted to know. I couldn't even pretend to guess.

I printed the word HORSE in large letters—there went another piece of paper—and taught them to read it. But then I had to draw a horse as well, for they'd never seen one, or at least couldn't remember doing so. They were amazed that the steam donkey had the name of an animal like a horse. I tried writing DONKEY then, but it was clear by the avidity with which Edward tried to capture a fly under his cupped hand and by the fact that Jane had laid her head upon her pillow seat that they'd already learned plenty for one day.

"They're entirely ignorant," I marveled to Oskar.

We were kneeling before our store cupboards, which were stuffed so full of cans that I'd had to tie the doors closed with bits of ribbon to keep them from popping open.

"You choose and then I'll choose," he said.

I selected oysters in cream, and he pulled out venison cooked in port wine, as well as sweet potatoes, green beans, and cherries in thick syrup.

"No." I laughed, but I was serious. Some quality of the air here had increased Oskar's appetite, and we were consuming far more than was prudent. "Really, we must put at least one of these away. You don't seem to realize that this is all we'll have until the next tender. That's months away."

"Oh, please. I'm so hungry today. Tomorrow I promise I'll make it up. I'll eat stones and cornbread. Or I'll get Crawley to go down and catch us a whale."

Against my better judgment, I gave in and built up the fire in the stove. Then, while I held each can firm, Oskar set the chisel as close to the edge as he dared and gave it sharp taps with the hammer.

It was difficult to keep from pulling away. "What if you slip?"

He grinned. "Maybe you'd best use your left hand."

Watching translucent gravy melt around chunks of meat and a froth of white bubble up around the oysters, I knew my mother would frown at this method of "cooking." The food did not taste good, but the novelty charmed us both. I made him close his eyes and held a bit out to him on my fork—oyster or venison?

"Tomorrow," he declared, "we try the goose and the plum pudding."

He was increasingly excited about *Electric Waves*, and he tried to get me to apply equivalent enthusiasm, as well as the scientific method, to my own work.

"Don't you see that the children's ignorance is wonderful? They're like a primitive people. You could do all kinds of experiments to find out how they think. Let's ask them to explain things—how far the ocean goes, say—and see what stories they've devised for themselves."

As he embroidered these ideas, he reached to push his fork into my bowl; he'd already eaten all of his portion.

"But Oskar," I protested, "they're children. They're not aborigines. They know how to fix the steam donkey, for heaven's sake."

Nevertheless, he remained convinced that the children presented a rare opportunity for study and if I were not to mine it, he would. Every few days, he set aside his research into "electrical transference," as he'd begun to call it, and came bounding up the steps to the schoolroom with a lesson he thought we ought to try.

"Never mind those letters," he announced one day, pushing aside the pages on which the children had been laboring for at least a quarter of an hour. "Here, Trudy, give them fresh sheets. Now," he went on when each had a new piece of my creamy writing paper before him or her, "I would like you to write a message without words."

They stared at him uncertainly.

"I see that already some damage has been done." He shook his head, but he was smiling, his expression kindly and patient. "We can undo it. Listen to me. Pretend you've never been taught a word of English. You possess no worn-out, conventional, mindless phrases. You've just come into this world," he went on, entrancing them, "and now you must sort it out on your own. You will experience it directly with your senses without intervention from teachers." He paused and looked around our schoolroom. "No, wait. I have a better idea. There's too much distraction here. These books . . . and what is this? A map? No, no, this won't help. What we'll do is go outside. We'll go into nature itself and get away from these sullying influences. Come on."

"Oskar—" I began to protest. It had been so difficult to collect and keep the children in this room, and he was working against all I'd accomplished. Also, I'd done my best with very little in choosing those books and drawing that map; I didn't like him to say they were sullying.

He held up his hand and shook his head. "Trudy, don't interrupt. Let's try a real experiment. We might all learn something."

And so, Pied Piper–like, he led them down the stairs, out the door, and from one spot to another around the top of the morro. He had them brush their palms over the bright lichens and press the soles of their bare feet into the sharp rock. He took them to the boiler room and told them to smell the oil. He filled a bucket with water and had them plunge their heads into it one by one. He encouraged them to lie on their stomachs at the very edge of the mountain, with their heads nearly hanging into the air, and then he told them to close their eyes. "Imbibe the rhythm of the ocean!" he ordered, while I surreptitiously clutched the hem of Jane's pinafore with one hand and Nicholas's heel with the other.

When we trooped back to our little schoolroom at last, he said he wanted them to show him on paper what they'd experienced, though he cautioned them again not to use words.

"If you didn't know the words 'ocean,' or 'sea,' or even 'water,' for instance," he said, "how would you tell me what lies out there?" He gestured toward the west.

They obediently scrubbed away at their pages until Euphemia began to ring the bell that stood outside her door, signaling them to abandon their studies in favor of lunch and chores.

Oskar was disappointed in the results. "I thought they'd draw pictographs," he said after glancing at the well-covered pages. "Like the ancient Egyptians. These are only pictures."

"They're revealing, though. Look." Mary's was an orderly landscape with everything in proportion. She'd even thought to include the clothesline and the steam donkey. Edward appeared in his own picture, looking as if he'd just conquered the morro and was using it as a vantage point from which to further command troops. Nicholas had filled a sky with birds and an ocean with creatures of all forms. Jane's sketch resembled Impressionist paintings, all shades and strokes and feeling, the boundaries between water, mountain and air indistinct. Perhaps she was too young to, as Oskar had said, "sort it out."

"Mmm," Oskar agreed, although he wasn't really looking. "I was hoping for something else. These are all so . . . idiosyncratic. We can't extrapolate anything from them about the way primitive man perceived the world. Maybe mathematics would reveal something more basic and universal. Next time let's see what they do if we give them a mathematical problem and some dry beans to help them with the numbers."

I admired the way Oskar seemed able to translate the most mundane circumstances into opportunities for study, and the children were clearly delighted with his methods, but I saw that he was more interested in what he could learn from the children than he was in teaching them, so I was relieved that he was often too busy with his electrical investigations to bother with us.

My sheaf of writing paper was disappearing quickly, eaten up by the children's scratches and smudges. Oskar was also using a great deal, even pinning sheets together to give himself room for extended diagrams.

"Imagine," he said one afternoon, chiseling open some rhubarb and spooning it right from the can, "if I were the one who figured out how to send a signal on an electrical wave."

"You mean like a telegraph?"

"A telegraph uses wires. I'm talking about a signal that could reach where no wires will ever come, to a place like this. Or out to sea, to a moving ship. Right through the air."

"Do you really think you could manage something so . . . ambitious? I mean, you've only just learned about these waves, haven't you? From that book?"

"You have to be ambitious," he said, "or you'll never get anywhere. But I am going to start with something more limited." He tipped the can so the last of the juices could run into his mouth. "I'm going to send a signal from our parlor to the light tower."

"Was that in the book?"

"The book?" He shook his head. "I'm finished with that. The real work is in the brain, considering what's known and determining how to pursue what's not." With that, he helped himself to several sheets of paper, tapped the stack smartly on the tabletop, and settled down to form the squiggles and arrows of his brainwork.

Our schedules had become unmatched, now that I had the children in the morning and the housework in the afternoon, while he still manned the night shift. When he stood up from the table and took my wrist, pulling me away from the story about eels that I'd begun to print in large block letters for Nicholas and Jane, I felt slightly irritated at the interruption of the rhythm of my daytime life. From our bed, while he moved his hands around my body as if testing for holds on the face of a cliff, I could hear the children's shouts, Mr. Crawley talking to Mr. Johnston as they passed on the path, Mrs. Crawley shooing the chickens aside.

"Ma! I can't find any blackberry jam!" Jane's voice penetrated the membrane between their world and ours.

I opened my eyes to smile at Oskar in collusion, but his face was turned toward the window, his gaze focused beyond the horizon.

When he fell asleep, I got up again. After all, there were windows to rub with vinegar and floors to be scrubbed with a rough brush and a cake of lye soap; Mrs. Crawley had shown me the trick of such tasks by now. And the woman herself might come to the door with a job that demanded the two of us, rug beating, for instance, or linen boiling. There were always the stories to write as well. Even *The Five Little Peppers* had turned out to be too difficult for the children, so I'd begun composing tales for them myself, full of oversized letters and jaunty illustrations. Along with the eels, I'd done one about a crab who wore a bowler hat and slid down the rock canyons on a broken cigar box; one about a starfish who took a train to Indiana (prompting much map drawing and some disjointed discussion of Lewis and Clark); and one about a mermaid who untangled her hair with a silver-backed brush.

"She lives in a cave," Jane said.

"All right," I agreed.

Drawing was Jane's particular pleasure, so I let her sketch the mer-maid's house and wished that I had watercolors for her to paint with, so lavishly did she decorate her picture with ropes of kelp and abalone shells larger than soup bowls.

CHAPTER 13

THE AUTUMN PICNIC on the beach, Mr. Crawley explained, was an annual treat. "Before the rain begins," he said. I assumed he was joking. Not a drop had fallen since we'd arrived at Point Lucia, and what was a day or two or even a week of rain?

"When does it start to snow?" I asked, and Mrs. Crawley admitted that she'd never seen the stuff.

Oskar and I, thinking of the ice and freezing winds that would soon be assailing the East, laughed at the idea of a final hurrah before a little wetting. Nevertheless, we were happy to picnic. On the designated Sunday, the sky was a rich, saturated blue, and the sun promised to bake the beach all day.

We were to grill abalone and whatever else Mr. Crawley, who loved to fish in the surf, might catch, as well as boil mussels, and Mrs. Crawley set a hamper in the yard so that we could all contribute from our own stores the most delicious foods we could spare. Oskar made several trips from kitchen to hamper with cans labeled California Fruit and Boston Baked Beans and squares of chocolate.

We adults all rode decorously down on the platform. The tide was very low; the sea, as I was mildly scandalized to hear Mr. Crawley say in a soft voice to his wife, had "hitched up her skirts," and an undulating surface of dark, treacherous rock was exposed a good way out. The three older children followed their father onto it with sharp sticks to pry abalone from their beds.

While Mrs. Crawley and Mr. Johnston collected dry wood—Mrs. Crawley energetically; Mr. Johnston pausing often for long, scrutinizing looks up the shoreline as if he expected someone or something to appear out of that endless, rocky wilderness—Jane and I were sent along the beach with a sack to hunt mussels. Our progress was slow; we had to pause often for Jane to bend and poke at the sand with her miniature finger, examining pebbles and the like. We were in such an attitude, her hand clasped in mine, pulling me down to her level, when a dark shadow rushed up behind us. I was frightened for a moment, but it was only Oskar. He tapped me lightly on the shoulder.

"You're it!" he cried, running on, his bare feet slapping the wet sand.

I began running, too, Janie shrieking with excitement beside me, and we went perhaps twenty steps at a speed nearly fast enough to catch him, although only because he'd turned and was running backward. That was as far as I could go with the shallow breaths my corset allowed.

"I thought you could keep up." He smiled and shook his head. "You disappoint me."

"You try running in this thing." I pressed my hand to the garment that constricted my ribs.

"For heaven's sake! Why are you wearing it?"

"Because," I said, "it's what one wears! I would look . . . peculiar . . . without it."

"That's ridiculous! You would not look peculiar. In any case, who's here to see? Janie? Mrs. Crawley?"

"There's you," I said in a small voice.

"I've seen you without your corset, Mrs. Swann, and I assure you that you do not look peculiar."

I glanced away, embarrassed to show that this pleased me.

"Mr. Swann! Come and help us!" the older children called from the rocks, and he dashed off like a kitten after a tail of yarn.

"He's right," I said to Jane, knowing she couldn't understand. "It's a ridiculous vanity. I renounce it!"

There were caves of a sort at the south end of the beach, almost directly below the lighthouse, abscesses where the ocean had licked away the black rock. They filled with water at high tide but were empty now, and in the dimness of one of these natural cabanas, I unbuttoned my dress and released the clasps of my Chicago waist. Putting my clothes back together without the undergarment was a struggle, for when my torso was uncinched, the buttons at the bottom of my rib cage would no longer meet. "I'll simply fold my hands, so," I said to Jane, covering the spot through which my petticoat peeked. She giggled, but I sighed, knowing that if I didn't put the corset back on, I'd have to drape my shawl around my waist when we joined the others, and then I would indeed look peculiar. I ran a few steps in the wet sand, testing my power now that I was free to draw full breaths.

"Look! A mermaid baby!" Jane squealed.

The girl was crouching in the far corner of the cave beside a bundle of kelp that was the size and shape of an infant. I bent close, unable at first to make sense of the tangle of slick green ribbon and rubbery tubes. With horror, I saw misshapen arms and legs, dark brown and clawed, and then a flat black nose.

"Is it sleeping?" Jane asked.

The creature's eyes were closed. Its smell was astounding, a ripe combination of animal, vegetable, and salt, the smell of sea beings exposed too long to the harsh air, but I picked it up and held as tightly as I could to its slippery covering. And then I ran.

"We found a mermaid!" Janie shrieked, and I must have been screaming, too, for the two men and the children began to move across the rocks back toward the beach, and Mrs. Crawley and Mr. Johnston looked up from the scant pile of driftwood they'd been arranging.

"Oh, why do they just stand there? Why aren't they coming?" I whispered, my heart louder in my ears than my voice.

I held the bundle out to Mrs. Crawley, but she didn't take it. With one hand, she gently moved a rope of kelp away from the brown face. "Ah, poor little thing."

"What is it?" I gasped. My breath burned down my throat and in my chest.

"A baby otter," Mrs. Crawley said. "A killer whale probably got its mother."

"A whale would be more likely to take the baby," her brother said. "I'd guess one of them Portuguese smugglers clubbed the mother. A load of furs'll be headed for Russia."

"What should we do?" I asked.

"There's nothing we can do about smugglers," Mr. Johnston said. "They'll be long gone."

"No. About the otter."

"You can see it's hurt," he said. "Best to kill it fast."

"Kill it! Oh, no!"

"I'm afraid it's nearly dead already," Mrs. Crawley said. "Look, it's struggling to breathe, and it can hardly open its eyes."

Its eyes *were* open slightly, enough for me to glimpse the living being in their bright darkness. "I'll take care of it," I said, pulling it closer to my chest. Without my corset, I could feel through my clothes its still-warm body under the wet fur.

"Unless you're planning to hit it over the head with a rock, you won't. You'll just make it suffer," Mr. Johnston said.

"He's right," Mr. Crawley said from behind his wife's shoulder, his pale eyes pinked from the wind or from emotion. "You'll only hurt it."

Oskar had come up, and I looked pleadingly at him. "What's the harm in letting her try?" he said stoutly.

"The harm, in my experience," Mrs. Crawley said, emphasizing the last word, "is a slow and painful death. It's cruelty, and I won't allow it."

Archie Johnston's hard hands closed around the little bundle and I felt him tug at it. "I'll take care of it," he said in a strange echo of my own words. I held on.

"Let go, Archie," Mrs. Crawley said, shouldering him aside. "Here." Her large, capable hands slid between the baby and my breasts. Tenderly, she lifted the animal in its weedy bunting from my arms.

"Where are you taking the mermaid, Mama?" Janie asked anxiously as Mrs. Crawley began to step away from the rest of us.

"Back to the ocean just down here. Where it belongs," Mrs. Crawley answered. "You take Jane now," she added, nodding at me. "Go on. All of you children. We'll have nothing to eat if you don't hurry up with those abalones." She motioned with her head toward the edge of the beach, where they'd dropped their sacks and sticks.

"Come on!" Oskar called. He began to run, sweeping the children up with the force of his exuberant motion. They followed like birds behind their leader.

I trailed after them, grateful to be dismissed with the children. But I couldn't help looking back. Mr. Crawley had taken a few tentative steps after his wife, then had stopped and stood still, rubbing his hands helplessly against his trousers. Mrs. Crawley went on some distance across the sand and then knelt beside a log of driftwood. She laid the bundle on it, slowly taking her hands away.

"Don't look," a low voice, surprisingly gentle and solicitous, said beside me.

Startled, I stumbled, and Mr. Johnston caught my arm. "She's used to it," he said. "But you needn't be."

Although I let him lead me away, I glanced back through slitted eyes. Mrs. Crawley's arm was high in the air, and her hand clutched a thick driftwood club. I did not, thank God, hear the thump, but the sound of her retching was plain.

*   *   *

I didn't give a thought to my corset until late that night, and the next morning I couldn't bring myself to go down to that place again to find it. In any case, I was sure the waves would have dragged it away. Another piece of my old life lost. Until I fashioned something new with which to bind myself, I would have to give up wearing my cinched skirts and dresses and rely on the loose-fitting duster that until now I'd worn only for the dirtiest work.

CHAPTER 14

IF THE CHILDREN were not apt pupils, they were good company, and I began to appreciate their distinctions. Mary thrived on organization. She anticipated the materials we'd need and kept an eye on her siblings to be sure they were paying strict attention. She had a small silver pocketknife of which she was proud, and she was forever sharpening pencils with it and polishing the blade with her apron. She ordered by species the items we continued to collect from the beach, using the book she'd kept from the traveling library, and of all the items in the Sears catalog, she coveted most a spice cupboard with eighteen cunning drawers. She wasn't quick, but she was dogged and would worry a problem or a passage until satisfied that she understood its meaning perfectly. If this tended to make her literal and somewhat humorless, it also made her careful and thorough, and I admired her for it.

As so often happens with siblings, Edward, quick, restless, and impatient, was nearly Mary's opposite. She blamed him for breaking the points of his pencils on purpose to annoy her. Edward was confident and outgoing; it was no accident that he was the first person we'd met when we landed at the light station. He loved machines, either because he associated them with his father, who had taught him their workings, or from a natural proclivity, and he was fascinated by Oskar's electrical contraptions. I liked to see them together, their heads bent over some mysterious bit of wire. Edward was protective of his siblings, always shouldering the heaviest burdens and stepping forward to test anything that appeared questionable or dangerous.

Nicholas was prone to daydreaming. He spent hours charging back and forth over the bridge to the light tower, waving a stick and mouthing encouragement to his troops. (I was gratified that some of his commands echoed those I'd read to him from *The Battle of Mobile Bay*). He was the most avid collector; he gave Christian names to nearly all of the items he picked up, including the stones and the weeds, and then told Jane little stories in which these creatures and objects figured as characters. He had a keen sense of fun and was the only one who dared to tease the formidable Mrs. Crawley. You could see that she was pleased to be allowed relief sometimes from her strictness.

Jane was the most curious and forward. She seemed to suspect that information was being kept from her—perhaps it was; she was the youngest, after all—and she questioned vigilantly and exhaustively. She tried out roles for herself, sometimes aping her mother, sometimes her sister or brothers. I was flattered the day she tried looping the two front locks of her hair to the back, the way I did mine. But her own strong personality—inquisitive, willful, and self-assured—overwhelmed any she might copy. I saw something of myself in her, and while I'd quickly become fond of all the children, I believed that she and I had a special sympathy. I sensed that she'd chosen me as a model much the way I'd chosen Miss Dodson.

With Miss Dodson in mind, I gradually decided that, given our unusual situation and my students' interest in aquatic life, I ought to become more of a real teacher of science. The children had recently found a sea urchin freshly expired on the beach. *Some Species* contained a picture of that creature's insides with the parts labeled, and I thought it would be instructive to open the animal and observe the complex structures beneath the shell. I'd not expected its outside to be so hard, however. Because of the roundness and the spines, it was difficult to hold the thing steady enough to plunge a knife in safely.

"Edward, run and get your mother's big shears, or we'll never open it."

While we waited, the others pretended to prick their fingers on the bright purple poisonous needles.

When Edward returned, I fitted the jaws of the shears around the middle of the urchin and squeezed until the shell broke with a snap. With dish towels to protect my hands, I pulled the halves apart. The children leaned forward for a better view. Inside were soft twists and folds, glistening clusters of red and gray ribbon, and drifts of yellow seed pearls.

"There"—I pointed triumphantly, feeling quite like Miss Dodson—"is Aristotle's lantern!"

The whole looked like a tulip. Nature repeating her patterns, I thought, remembering Miss Dodson quoting Mr. Emerson. There was an important idea in this somewhere if I could figure out how to articulate it. Oskar, I was sure, would be able to explain it. The lesson, I believed, had been a great success.

Then Janie reached with her fork—utensils were our only dissecting tools—and poked at the soft ocher flesh. The briny smell of the sea rose from it, and suddenly, the tangle of innards, which a moment before had been a gorgeous arrangement of colors and shapes, stood out to me as what they were, a cup of guts, some small measure of which had tipped out onto my kitchen table. What had possessed me to take the thing apart?

"I'm sorry," I said. With great effort, I forced a feeling of sickness down, as cold sweat rose on my neck.

The children clamored for my attention.

"He spilled!"

"Can we open another?"

"Ow! Don't poke me!"

Their voices scraped at me unendurably. My collar was so close about my neck; it seemed to restrict my breathing. When the bell clanged at last, calling the children to their lunch, I fled the kitchen and stumbled up the stairs to lie down.

I slept for an hour or so, waking when Oskar slipped into the bed beside me for his "night." Feeling better, I went back to the kitchen. Oskar had left his lunch plate of sardines and pilot bread atop the gore. I scraped the violated urchin into a pail and carried it to the edge of the rock to hurl the mess into the sea. Mrs. Crawley was there, disposing of her family's garbage in the same way. I confessed my weakness.

"I'm surprised," I concluded. "I've never been squeamish before."

She gave me an appraising look. "Some women have these episodes when they're with child, although I never did."

My mother had admonished me to keep careful track of my bleeding, so as to avoid stained sheets and undergarments, but that was another instruction I'd resisted. I had no need of calendars and notebooks; I could tell by the tightening and the ache when the blood was due. My lax habits meant that I didn't know how many weeks had passed since I'd last bled, although I'd been vaguely aware that more than the usual had gone by. I'd attributed this irregularity to the strangeness of the place, of the diet, of the entire life here. In reality, nothing extraordinary had occurred; the simplest, most obvious explanation was the truth.

I pressed my hand against my abdomen as if to hold the incipient child back. "I can't have a baby here!"

Mrs. Crawley laughed. "Of course you can. I've had two in this very place, and if the good Lord sees fit to send me more, I'll have them here as well."

"How?"

"The same way you would have it anyplace else. It's you who has to do it, you and the baby, not anyone or anything else."

"What about Oskar?" I hardly knew what I meant, but it seemed to me that he had to be included somehow.

"I'd say he's done his part. The rest is yours, I'm afraid."

"What if something goes wrong?"

She looked pensive, her eyes fixed on the milky water churning among the sharp black rocks far below us. "Babies don't always live, it's true. But something may just as easily go wrong in Monterey or San Francisco. Even in Milwaukee, I dare say."

I must have looked stricken, because Mrs. Crawley put a hand on my arm. Though it was cold as a fish, its pressure was firm. "I'll be here, you know. I do have a bit of experience. In the end, you'll see that there's little for you to do other than endure. Nature will take care of it one way or another. You needn't worry."

I attempted a smile, but it wouldn't stick on my lips.

"You'll want the nursery cleaned up," Mrs. Crawley said brightly. "Won't take more than an hour to pitch all that junk into the sea."

CHAPTER 15

Oskar was elated and confident. He convinced me that it was a sign—if one believed in such things; of course, we did not—that all was as it should be. After all, I was a young married woman; producing a child was what I was meant to do.

In a matter of minutes, it seemed, I changed from my mother's daughter, who might make any messes she pleased, because it wasn't really her job to keep order, to my own child's mother, who didn't want her baby born into any more disorder and chance than its own coming would create.

That night I roamed the house, straightening and scouring. I scrubbed the kitchen table with salt, wiped the soot from behind the stove in the parlor, and repaired a rent in a sofa cushion. I took my Aladdin lamp upstairs and surveyed the schoolroom. Oskar had never made shelves—the wood hadn't been to his liking, or Mr. Crawley had needed it for some other purpose; he'd been vague enough about the reason to make me understand that, in truth, the job no longer interested him once he'd found a more exciting pursuit. The trunk around which the children and I staggered forward with letters and numbers formed a sort of island, surrounded by a sea of dried creatures and weeds, along with various shells, sticks and stones, egg cases, teeth, and bones, which we'd gradually removed from the crates where I'd stored them, so that we could examine one thing or another. The

idea that Mrs. Crawley thought this ought to be cleared away wholesale disheartened me. Had we just been biding time while we waited
for Nature to organize her agenda? Unable to face such a thought, I
turned away.

Our bedroom was equally untidy, the blankets recklessly cast aside
as Oskar had left them when he'd risen from bed for his dinner. As
I reached to pull them up, I saw that the sheets were no longer the
creamy white they'd been when my mother folded and placed them in
the trunk, but pale brown. There were stiff circles where Oskar's spilled
seed had dried, rusty swipes of blood, even patches of actual mud. How
had I allowed this?

I yanked the sheets from the bed. On them I piled every towel and
handkerchief we owned, and every item of clothing we'd worn in this
place. Hardly an inch was fit to touch human skin.

I pushed it all down the stairs in a filthy mass.

For over an hour, partially clothed in one of the remnants of my
former life—a dress I'd dragged here, not realizing it would be too fine
to remove from the protection of my trunk—I spread a mixture of soda
crystals and water on all of our cuffs and collars and the worst of the
stains on the sheets and napkins. It seemed crucial to return everything
to the state in which it had been before we'd left Milwaukee.

The next morning, even though it wasn't the usual day, Mrs. Crawley
agreed to wash her family's clothes as well, so as to make heating the
copper worthwhile. She and Mary and Jane and I went to the cellar,
where we plunged shirts, trousers, petticoats, skirts, and linens of all
descriptions into fiercely boiling water, while the steam curled our hair
around our faces.

"It's to be expected," Mrs. Crawley said approvingly. "You're readying
the nest."

I was as much irritated as reassured by the idea that I might be acting
under the influence of some universal feminine instinct.

"That's enough, my girl!" Mrs. Crawley barked.

I snapped to, but it was Mary she was addressing. The girl was vigorously grating soap over the writhing clothes. A dark gray scum had gathered at the top of the copper.

"You'll scrape your fingers and get blood on the sheets if you're not careful," her mother said. "That's plenty of soap, anyway."

Jane had the safer job of dropping bluing into a tub of cold water. The globes of heavy color sank and stretched into jellyfish and then dissipated into wisps of indigo smoke before they disappeared into the clear water. "See? It's invisible, but you know it's there," she said. "Just like electricity. Mr. Swann says that everything and everybody's got electricity inside 'em. Did you know I had electricity in me, Ma? Mr. Swann says electricity is one of the invisible powers of nature. It's all over the place, even in the air."

Her last sentence made electricity sound less like the mysterious and beautiful bluing and more like the particles of dirt roiling around the copper.

"Mr. Swann has a great many ideas, doesn't he?" Mrs. Crawley said, handing me one end of a dripping sheet to wring.

"Oskar's designing some experiments involving electrical waves," I explained.

"Experiments? I didn't realize that Mr. Swann was a scientist." She began to twist the sheet.

"Well, anyone can be a scientist, don't you think?" I recoiled as icy water ran up my forearm. "I mean, it's just a matter of considering what's known and determining how to pursue what's not, isn't it?" But the words that Oskar had spoken so robustly sounded hollow when I delivered them. "He's going to build a machine," I tried, struggling to keep my grip on the sheet that Mrs. Crawley was fiercely twisting. "He's going to send messages from the parlor to the lighthouse using the electric waves in the air."

"Hmmph," she said, dropping what had essentially become a dry snake into the basket. "He might try shouting."

When we went outside to hang the clothes, Mrs. Crawley told the girls they could go and play; they'd helped enough.

"I wanted to tell you privately," she said when they'd run off, "that it's good to prepare, but it's better not to expect. You never know what might happen."

"You mean like Baby Johnston," I said.

She looked at me sharply.

"I read it in one of the logbooks. 'Baby Johnston born and buried.'"

"Oh. Yes, that's right."

"And his wife?"

"Gone, too, I'm afraid," she managed around a mouthful of pins.

"Poor Mr. Johnston. He practically threw me off the rock when I tried to look at the grave."

"You'll learn, Mrs. Swann, that privacy must be respected here." She gave the sheet she was about to hang a violent shake to discourage wrinkles. "When you're living this close to people, sometimes you have to look the other way. There'll be times you'll want them to look the other way, too."

"He left birds on the catwalk again." Mr. Johnston had crept silently up the path and was standing just behind us. I stiffened, worried that he'd heard our conversation. "And his mess was all over the place downstairs."

I had a fleeting image of some marauding animal before Johnston passed some familiar-looking papers to Mrs. Crawley. I imagined with chagrin the boiler room looking like our front room or kitchen after Oskar had spent hours working on his plans, the pages he'd carelessly let fall from the table drifting like autumn leaves against the legs of the chairs.

"I'll have Henry speak to him."

"Oh, Henry knows," Mr. Johnston muttered as he continued past. "Who do you think found the dead birds?"

"Dead birds? What can he mean?"

"I told you. They fly into the windows at night. Keeper's supposed to check for birds on the catwalk before he goes off duty." She handed me the sheaf of papers. "More about that invisible power, I daresay."

We were finished by noon, and I was home in time to make lunch, but Oskar was late, as usual, and when he came in, he was preoccupied and shuffled through the piles of papers that he'd heaped on the kitchen table over the last few weeks. Having exhausted these, he went into the parlor and thumbed through the pages he'd spread across the sofa. I watched as he held *Electric Waves* by its spine and shook it.

"What are you looking for?" Yes, I was disingenuous. I was annoyed about the embarrassment he'd put me through.

"Some papers," he said. "Some drawings. I had a sort of inspiration last night, but now I can't find my notes."

"You left them in the lighthouse."

"Oh!" Relieved, he turned to the door, obviously intending to retrieve them from the tower.

"They aren't there now. Mr. Johnston picked them up. He said they were a mess all over the boiler room. And that you didn't clean up the birds. You left dead birds lying on the catwalk. You're spending too much time on this electricity business. You're not paying attention to what's important, Oskar. The lighthouse is your job, your real work."

"The lighthouse is hardly what I'd call real work."

"Oskar, you must do it properly. It was embarrassing, listening to Mr. Johnston say those things in front of Mrs. Crawley."

"Forgive me for embarrassing you in front of the All-Powerful Crawley. If you understood what it meant to have real work, you would know that occasionally it might come before a dead bird. Now, please, give me those papers."

"Yes, of course, I'll give them to you. But really, Oskar, you can't let the light go out. That would be very serious."

"Oh, for God's sake, I'm not letting the light go out!" He'd followed me into the kitchen, and I looked beside the stove, where I believed I'd set the papers.

"Where are they?" His voice had a hard edge.

"I thought I'd left them here. Mr. Johnston gave them to Mrs. Crawley, and she gave them to me." I went back into the parlor, where I hopelessly lifted the cushion of the armchair and peered beneath it. "Where could I have put them?"

"You must find them."

"I understand. I'm looking."

"No, you don't understand. You must find them. They're very important."

"Oskar, you left them flying around the boiler room!"

"Where they'd be now, if that busybody hadn't taken them! Idiot!"

"You can't call him an idiot for picking up papers that you left behind."

"He's an idiot, and you are a stupid girl! What have you done with them?"

At that I stared at him and then ran from the door. I'd set the papers on the ground while I pinned the last of the clothes. I remembered it clearly now. I ran to the lines on which the shirts and trousers and underthings frolicked and the sheets billowed like sails. Of course, by this time the papers had blown away. Nothing light and loose could stay put on that mountain. I started back to the house to confess what I'd done, but when I came to the bottom of the stairs, I kept on down the path, my feet moving faster and faster, until I stepped off the edge and began to slide.

I took myself all the way down to the beach and walked fast, fast and north, where there was nothing to stop me.

CHAPTER 16

I T WAS NOT the first time I'd wanted to run away from my husband. Only three days after we'd been married, halfway to California, I had almost turned back.

The train from Milwaukee had taken us as far as Chicago, and from there we'd booked a Pullman sleeper. But at the station Oskar changed the tickets for a parlor car, a tiny private room furnished with a sofa and two armchairs that transformed into beds at night. The walls were hung with looking glasses, the curtain rods plated with silver, the spittoon shining brass—the effect of the whole was all brightness and light. We had a table on which to spread our books and pencils—Oskar was determined to spend the journey developing his electrical engine designs. Cases of books were set into the walls, and many of them, including a guide to San Francisco, had been chosen with the Western traveler in mind.

In the dining car, where the linens and silver were marked with the Union Pacific's own crest, we were seated opposite a handsome couple, a little older than we. Mr. Hatch had a boyish look, and Mrs. Hatch wore her hair in a cascade of little curls in back—rather an old-fashioned style, but it suited her delicate face. They were from Muncie, Indiana, where the husband owned a machine shop and the wife kept ducks.

"I recommend the chicken," Mrs. Hatch said. "It's not as plump, certainly, as the hens we get from two or three farmers in Muncie, but it isn't too tough, and the gravy is acceptable. Don't you agree, dear?"

"It's decent enough," said Mr. Hatch, "although it's a shame this train doesn't buy its fowl in Muncie."

Oskar easily made himself the host of our little party, drawing Mr. Hatch out about his shop and ordering a bottle of wine for the table, which our new friends made a show of refusing at first—they claimed to be mostly teetotalers when they were at home in Muncie, where one can have "a perfectly pleasant time without strong spirits"—but then Mr. Hatch said, "When in Rome," and Mrs. Hatch agreed, and they both enjoyed themselves very much and became wonderfully pink in the cheeks.

"The Muncies," as Oskar and I referred to them privately, were to be met by the mister's older brother, who had gone West ten years before and had not had the benefit of anything Muncie since. They planned to tour Yo-semite, where, as Oskar said, the famous big trees would be grand but surely not so graceful as the elms and oaks of Muncie.

Oskar and I shared the larger of the two beds, the one made from the sofa. We were new to this, having spent only one night in Chicago acquainting our bodies, and my pleasure was still greatly tempered by anxiety, but Oskar was uninhibited in his delight, and I had to shush him more than once, so as not to disturb the lady schoolteachers from Albany with whom we shared a washcloset. In the middle of the night, it was I who was awakened, however, by the scratch of his pen on his sketchbook—my sketchbook, really, since he hadn't thought to pack one of his own.

"What are you doing?"

"You'll see," he said, smiling.

He went on with his scribbling, and I was obliged to put the pillow over my head to find my way back into my dreams.

At breakfast, Oskar didn't wait for the porter to show us to a seat but went straight to the table at which our new friends were already drinking their coffee. "Take a look at this," he said, laying his sketch before Mr. Hatch.

"What is it?" Mr. Hatch picked up the paper and squinted at it.

"It's a lathe powered by an electric engine. It'll transform your shop."

"Oh, I didn't realize you were a salesman," Mrs. Hatch said.

"I'm not a salesman!" Oskar was offended. "It's just that I've been working a good deal with electricity lately, and it seems to me that someone with an operation like yours ought to consider changing to a more efficient power source."

"Well," Mr. Hatch said, "thank you. Very nice." He folded the paper and pushed it under his plate.

"I doubt you've come across this sort of thing in Muncie," Oskar said. "You ought to take a closer look." He nodded encouragingly at the edge of paper that was visible under the rim of the plate. "I do know something about engines."

Mr. Hatch made a show of drawing the page out and carefully opening it, spreading it over his plate. "Paper's very nice." He looked the drawing over. "It's a pretty picture," he said at last, "but this thing wouldn't have the power to drill a hole in a doughnut. Make a darn clever toy, though." He refolded it neatly and handed it back to Oskar.

Just then the train pulled into a station where many Chinese men were strolling about the platform or squatting, the ends of their long braids brushing the wooden floor. At an earlier station, Oskar and I had bought glasses of buttermilk from a boy on the platform with a bucket and a dipper, and I'd seen other people selling cheeses and lengths of sausages, bottles of medicine, stationery and newspapers and books, but these Chinese weren't selling anything. They took no notice of the train and looked as if they'd been shipwrecked on that wooden island in the middle of a sea of wheat.

"Why are they here?" I asked. "What are they doing?"

"They're waiting for an emigrant train," Mr. Hatch explained. "Probably got put off the one they were on because the car was needed."

"You have to watch out for those in San Francisco," Mrs. Hatch said.

"Emigrant trains?" I said.

Mr. Hatch laughed. "No, Chinks, of course."

"William!" Mrs. Hatch said sharply. "You know I don't like such vulgar talk."

"Well, anyway, whatever you call 'em, you can't trust 'em. That's what Tom says, and he ought to know. They're thick as rats in a barn out there in San Francisco."

"Oh, William! You know you don't believe that. Those poor people, they're just trying to better themselves."

"You wouldn't like it much if they were all over Muncie, washing clothes and digging ditches."

"I suppose you're right. I wouldn't feel comfortable sending my pillowcases to a Chinaman, although you hear they do it in San Francisco all the time."

"What is that?"

Mr. Hatch was pointing at what I'd taken to be a heap of rags but which had begun to shift and shudder and now rose from the platform, supported unsteadily on two brown sticks. Above folded and flapping bits of cloth, a mat of hair took shape, half hiding a face brown and creased as damp leaves, split by a toothless red mouth. The Indian came at us, bending, swaying, dipping, reaching, spewing incomprehensible syllables in abject tones.

Mrs. Hatch shrank from the window in horror. "Don't look," Mr. Hatch commanded.

The creature's eyes, slits between swollen lids, were as unsteady as the legs. Its gaze wandered over the cars but returned to me. The thing held out its appendages. "Mun-nee! Mun-nee!" it beseeched. Someone threw an object—maybe a roll—from one of the windows; it landed well back on the platform. The creature turned, exposing its back to the train.

And there a baby rode. It was wrapped tight against a board, its round, dewy eyes in its dear new face gazing at us with confident dignity, as if we were its subjects, gathered to pay our respects.

"Hey! Give you greenbacks for the papoose!" some lout shouted. "Sell us the papoose!"

The rag creature looked back over her shoulder, but her aspect had changed. Contempt shaped her face, and derision sharpened her eyes. Her disdain—her loathing, even—raised her up. She was, after all, a woman. A mother.

The train, refreshed with coal, pulled away from the platform, and with relief, we welcomed eggs and toast and bacon to our table, busying ourselves longer than was strictly necessary spooning sugar and spreading jam. We'd all been debased, I suppose, by what we'd witnessed at the station and were shy of facing one another in such a state.

Finally, Oskar spoke. "You have to admit it wouldn't be altogether a bad thing."

"What wouldn't?" I asked, relieved that he'd shrugged off Mr. Hatch's dismissal of his drawing.

"For that unfortunate woman to sell her baby."

"What! Swann, that's ridiculous!" Mr. Hatch sputtered.

"When you think about it, it makes good sense," Oskar said. "How will she raise that baby? Obviously, she can't even take care of herself. He's bound to suffer, and he's likely to die."

"We're not slaveholders anymore," Mr. Hatch protested. "We don't sell people. We never did in Indiana."

"That's right," Mrs. Hatch put in. "Now, if you were to suggest that some responsible group assume care for the child, some church, perhaps, or the town . . ."

"Take him away and put him in an orphanage is what you're suggesting?"

"Yes, so some nice people can adopt him," Mrs. Hatch said. "I'm sure it's done all the time, when parents are drunk, for instance, or crazy."

"She isn't crazy," I said.

"No?" Mr. Hatch asked. "What makes you say that? She looked crazy enough to me."

"Didn't you see when she turned around?" I said. "She was disgusted with what she heard. With all of us, I'm afraid. She knew what she was about and what we'd done. That's not crazy."

Mr. Hatch was shaking his head. "I don't see why you say *we* did anything—"

"But," Oskar broke in, "if you just take him, then the mother is left with nothing, which isn't fair. Because right now she does have something dear, something that people want."

"An Indian baby?" Mrs. Hatch scoffed. "I doubt there'd be many who'd sincerely want that child."

"Even such a little prince as that?" Oskar sighed. "I suppose you're right. After all, we destroyed these people so that you Muncies can live wherever you please."

"Oskar!" I was shocked.

"What are you talking about? *We* haven't destroyed anyone!" Mr. Hatch said indignantly.

"At least some of us," Oskar went on, "are ashamed. We appreciate the horror of what's been done in our name."

"And yet," I said, determined to put my husband in his place, to pay him back for the discomfort he was causing me, "we ride the train, which, as I understand it, destroyed the Indian as much as anything."

"Yes," he said irritably. "Of course we ride the train. What would be the point of not doing so?"

I couldn't blame the Muncies for leaving the table in a huff. In our parlor, I remonstrated with Oskar. I averred that some of what he said was true—the child was precious, and the Muncies were benighted—but he ought not to have run roughshod over them, and he ought not to set himself above them. Did he not see that we were hardly different? He would not agree. He made fun of Mrs. Hatch's laugh and the way

Mr. Hatch held his fork. He declared that he wouldn't waste another minute on such people. I regretted this deeply, not so much because of any attachment to the Muncies themselves, although they'd been friendly to me, but for the fact that in breaking with them, Oskar had cut what I'd seen as our last tie to the East. It was strange to consider that, although all my life I'd lived in "the West," Wisconsin had become "the East."

In the afternoon, we stayed in our compartment and ate the remaining hard rolls, now worthy of their name. Then, unusually exhausted, Oskar attempted to convert our sofa into a bed without assistance from the porter. He was asleep before the sun had set.

We're climbing into the Black Hills, an accurate name for these dark, stunted pines and tortured rocks . . .

Unable to concentrate on my letter to my mother, I lifted my pen and stared at Oskar from my chair. He looked uncomfortable, his body contorted by the ill-constructed bed. Ernst never would have said what Oskar had said, any of it, anything like any of it. But then I hadn't married Ernst, had I?

The Union Pacific had furnished our parlor with a map of the nation's train tracks so that passengers could mark their progress. I unfolded it and spread the whole of the country across my lap. Tomorrow we would reach a large depot in Ogden where many eastbound trains must stop. I imagined myself climbing down from this train and getting on one of those. In a couple of days I could be far from this wild, unsettling landscape and back in the comfortable streets I knew. I thought of my parents' house—the blue velvet curtains, the kitchen worktable, the currant bushes in the backyard below my bedroom window, all dear and familiar. But if I returned to them, I would forever be the girl I'd always been.

I refolded the map. As well as I could, I slid into the half-made bed with my husband and allowed the motion of the train to rock me to sleep.

In the hours that remained of our journey, I wrote letters filled with descriptions of the Great Salt Lake and daylong sagebrush deserts and the mountains, all jagged rock and green pine pressing close and black gorges yawning open. I'd never seen anything remotely like any of it, and I wrote honestly of my pleasure in experiencing such variety and strangeness. But with each fresh stretch of landscape, I was more aware of how many new worlds imposed themselves between me and home, and when we came down into the valleys of California, I felt the Sierras close behind me like a door.

CHAPTER 17

WHEN I'D MARCHED a good distance up the beach, the steady rush and retreat of the surf, together with my own exhaustion, began to soothe me. I slowed my pace and took notice of my surroundings.

Almost at once a sea star presented itself, stranded on the sand by a wave. I picked it up and balanced it on my palm. It seemed alive, its body not light and stiff like the ones in our schoolroom, but heavy and surprisingly fleshy. Such a strange creature, and yet its five arms were so like my five fingers. Over a year before, I had dissected a starfish in Miss Dodson's biology class. I remembered the smell of the oiled wooden floors of Gruber Hall and the wash of the bright morning sun. I'd cut along the creature's underside, as Miss Dodson had indicated, and duly observed the means by which the animal took food directly into its stomach without the intermediary of throat or esophagus. Miss Dodson limped from girl to girl, a magnifying glass in a leather pouch at her hip, her gold locket tucked into her blouse so that it wouldn't swing and knock against the specimens.

"You see the madreporite, Miss Schroeder?" she'd asked, touching a small circle at the center of the star with her ink-stained finger, the place where the animal let seawater into its body. I'd nodded and noted all the structures, but the creature had been only the peculiar basis of an exercise to me; I couldn't conceive of it as a living being. And yet here it was, far more at home than I. I drew back my arm and hurled it as far into the ocean as I could, hoping to give it a chance to survive.

I wondered if Miss Dodson had ever seen a sea cradle or a nudibranch, the real live animals, not just pictures in a book.

The valleys and the soft hills of California had been thick with oats and fruits and, finally, humanity again. In Oakland, we were met by a good old steam tug and ferried across the bay to San Francisco. The dock at night was a confusion of shadows and shouts. Men stalked up and down, swinging lanterns, and women, terrified lest their children tumble into the bay, swatted little ones behind their skirts. Dazed by the people who seemed to swoop around me from all directions, I clung to Oskar's arm as he arranged with a Chinese pushing a wheelbarrow for the transportation of our trunk and consulted with a colored man about the location of our hotel.

I waited for a long time in a tin-ceilinged lobby while he talked to the man behind the desk. At last he turned to me, shaking his head. "We can't stay here."

Though Oskar spoke matter-of-factly, I was alarmed. "We wrote ahead. I'm sure we reserved a room."

He shrugged. "They say there's no place for us."

"But what should we do? Where should we go?"

"The porter says he'll store our trunk for us. I think we'd better do it. We can't afford to have it trundled all over the city, and who knows where we'll end up? We can come get it tomorrow."

Who knows where we'll end up? That wasn't encouraging, and, indeed, although we passed several other hotels, he barely glanced at them.

"What's wrong with these?" I asked, finally.

"We haven't got the money for these places. That parlor car wasn't free, you know!"

"You mean we couldn't afford it?"

"I paid for it, didn't I? I wouldn't say we couldn't afford it."

"Now we'll have to lie down on the street? I would far rather have used the sleeping berths and had something left over."

"Heavens, Trudy!" He put his arms around me. "We won't have to sleep in the street. We'll find a cheap room somewhere, and I'll pawn my pocketknife in the morning. It's only for a day or two, after all. In exchange for a little scrimping now, we had that wonderful parlor car all to ourselves. Wasn't it worth it?"

I felt foolish and cowardly. "I'm sure you're right."

In another two or three blocks, the hotels had become dark and shabby boardinghouses, and he said we might give one of them a try. The landlady, roused from her bed, came to the door without her teeth and with her hair tied up in rags. She led us up three flights of narrow stairs that smelled of damp and rodents to a room at the back. We wriggled out of our clothes in the tight space between the wall and the sagging rope bed and lay down on thin sheets turned edges to middle with a roughly sewn seam. Still, Oskar was merry, and I was easily infected with his optimism. He reached for me before my hair was properly undone, accidentally knocking my brush to the bare wooden floor in his impatience.

Breakfast—sour bread and weak coffee—was included. Even in the morning, the house was dark, although that was as much the fault of the weather as of the placement of the windows hardly three feet from the next building. Only one other lodger sat at the dining table, a man who stared in response to my "good morning" before going back to his newspaper. From my own seat, I glanced at the headlines—counts of troops boarding ships for Manila, a report of an opium raid.

Oskar nudged my arm and produced a little book from the pocket of his jacket. "Look what I found in our compartment."

It was the guide to San Francisco. "You stole it?" I was more shocked than accusing.

"I'm sure we were meant to take it. What good does it do on a train?"

Outside was nearly as dark as inside, the sky gray and heavy, as if before a snow. I could feel droplets of water thick on my skin and in the fabric of my dress.

Oskar was ecstatic. "Feel the sea! We're nearly walking in it!"

The landlady, who, once her teeth were in, had become a cheery woman with her gray hair in ringlets like a little girl's, had recommended a pawnshop on the next street. At first the ease with which Oskar walked into the place and presented his knife to the proprietor reassured me. Then I considered the significance of his being familiar with such procedures.

The pawnbroker didn't offer as much as Oskar had expected. "Pretty case, but out here," he said, pressing his thumb to the blade critically, "they're wanting something bigger. Not much call for apple paring and twig whittling." He sucked his teeth thoughtfully. "Maybe some woman will buy it."

"How about this?" Oskar said. He produced our silver pickle fork.

The man turned it over. "Good. No monogram."

He gave Oskar a few worn bills and pieces of silver. Oskar pushed the money deep into his pocket and looked carefully up and down the street before stepping out of the shop in a way that made me walk close to him until we reached Western Union.

We used some of the silver to send a telegram to my parents: ARRIVED SAN FRANCISCO.

"That's only three words," Oskar pointed out. "You could say three times as much for the same money."

I shook my head. Expressing my complicated feelings would require far more than six or seven extra words.

After much studying of the maps in the guide (I had to admit it was useful), we clambered onto a cable car—for which we had to spend more silver—and its thrilling, lurching ride, crawling up the hills and barreling down the other side, lifted my spirits again. Our stop was in a district of buildings made of shining white stone that were tiered like wedding cakes, but the address listed in Oskar's letter didn't correspond to any of the confections. His interview and exam—the means by which some unknown person or persons would determine whether he would suit as an assistant lighthouse keeper—would be in a low gray rectangle. I could see that whoever worked there would care for nothing but straight answers and strict adherence to rules.

The Customs Offices were just inside the door, as befitted their importance, and Philip spotted us at once. Since I knew no more about him than that Oskar's father approved of him, I expected a youthful version of the great man (if such a being were possible), but Philip, a rumpled young man with a beaky nose and a large smile, was warm and welcomed us with a charming, self-deprecating manner.

"But you won't be finished until five o'clock, you know," he said apologetically to Oskar.

"That's all right." Oskar pulled the guidebook from his jacket. "Trudy'll have a look at the city."

Philip frowned. "I don't think she should wander around on her own. I mean, she doesn't know the first thing about the place. The wharves are pretty rough, for instance, and you never know about Chinatown."

Oskar looked at me. "Stay off the wharves and away from Chinatown, all right?"

I giggled. "Yes, sir!"

Although I may have shared Philip's trepidation, I dared not express it. In any case, I had no desire to spend my time in the Paris of the West sitting in our dirty little boardinghouse room. "I have the guide," I said brightly.

"We'll meet at the house at half past six," Oskar said. "And we'll take Philip somewhere to celebrate."

The two of them went off down the corridor. I listened until their footsteps stopped and a door closed behind them. Then I took myself back out onto the street alone.

I spent the morning marching through the gloom on the most re-spectable, well-populated streets, gathering notes in my head for my letters, aware that I would enjoy the place more in the telling than in the somewhat tense experience. At the malodorous fishing docks, I turned west for a time and skirted the city, taking comfort in the water that was darker and greener but not so different from the water I knew well. Now that I wasn't climbing, I had to walk briskly to stay warm—so strange to feel cold in July—and soon I turned inland to escape the chill and was faced with another hill.

When I reached the top, the sun at last broke through, and suddenly, the day was blue and clear, the air fresher than I'd ever experienced. To the west, in a vast open space, I spotted soldiers massing, rows of tents, and whole herds of horses. With a thrill, I understood that they were readying themselves to board a ship to the Philippines. The events of the wide world were shaping themselves before my eyes.

I watched them for a time and then began to walk in what I knew must be the general direction of our boardinghouse. The neighborhoods I traversed were ordinary in their makeup—the bakeries and butcher shops, greengrocers and saloons not so different from those in Milwau-kee—but they seemed more interesting somehow, their signs more col-orful, their wares more vibrant, simply by virtue of being in this place.

I walked up and down more hills, past brightly painted, shingled, and sometimes turreted houses, and then through some neighborhoods without any paint at all. I heard people speaking a language I thought must be Spanish or Italian; maybe I heard both. Confident of my direc-tion and sure that I must be within a mile or so of our boardinghouse, I stopped consulting the guide. If I didn't happen upon the right street, I could always get my bearings again or inquire. I wasn't such a ninny that I couldn't find my way home. I was pleased with myself and eager to tell Oskar about all I'd seen.

Then I made a mistake. I didn't realize my error at first; the blocks along which I walked resembled those from which I'd come, the cobbled streets muddy, the houses two-story wooden structures. It was the writing on the signs that first caught my attention, slashing lines, jumbles of sticks and rods, more foreign to my eye than Spanish or Italian could ever be.

I resisted as too embarrassing turning tail and going back the way I'd come. I thought I might go around a block and make my way back more subtly, but the narrowness of the next street, a sort of alley, discouraged me from that course. Anyway, I wanted to see, so I walked on.

At first I was almost disappointed because the men—initially, I saw only men—might have been anyone, anywhere, at least when viewed from behind. They wore the same sack suits and bowlers as the men of Milwaukee or Chicago, although some had the flatter-crowned hat I'd grown used to seeing at the western depots. As I got deeper into the district, however, differences began to accumulate. More and more often, a long black pigtail hung down from under the hat brim, and sometimes the hat had no brim at all. And the women were wearing trousers! I began to see stiff black jackets, bright white stockings, old men in satin robes with fur collars, children with their heads shaved. I passed a table where two men sat drinking tea from little bowls; each had a nail on the fifth finger of his right hand several inches long, yellow and curved as a scimitar.

I saw a woman carrying a basket of curled eels, and a man shouldering a stick from which pairs of satin slippers hung like fish. I stopped to admire some bright globes, like miniature hot-air balloons, that dangled from under second-story balconies. How silly the Muncies were to fear these vivid people!

Someone bumped my shoulder. Stepping to catch my balance, I knocked against a woman carrying a bundle who scowled and spat syllables that hit me like slaps and made me blush. On my right was another dark, narrow lane, off of which a door opened, and I thought of the newspaper article I'd seen at breakfast about the raid on an opium den. Our teachers had frightened us with stories about those dim, foreign holes with their depraved and addled customers, lolling upon soiled mattresses and sucking at pipes, the mouthpieces of which, "you can be sure, are never properly sanitized." I realized with alarm that I might be standing beside such a place.

I became aware of words as harsh as crows' caws in the air, along with pungent smells: garlic and animal fat, fish and cabbage, spices I couldn't recognize, and something sweet and sharp at once.

A man smoking a thin cigarette smiled at me, and I looked quickly away to avoid meeting his eyes. How many Chinese there were! It was as if I'd entered Peking itself. How much farther did this district extend? Ought I to go on or go back? This time I did try a side street, but it led to a louder, more crowded, more Chinese street to the south. Or was it east? Although I turned over every page of the guidebook—as discreetly as I was able—I could find no mention of Chinatown.

When at last the signs above the shops began to appear in English, I hurried along for some blocks, anxiety pressing me on, and then, as my fear drained away, I wished I could stop somewhere and rest. I'd been walking all day with nothing to eat except that bit of bread at breakfast. There was no place suitable, however. There was no green park in which I might relax; nor, even had I the money—which I did not, Oskar had it all—was there a café in which to spend it. There were saloons, but I couldn't go into those alone, not even to ask directions.

I inquired at a cooperage, where, luckily, a man knew the neighborhood I wanted, if not the establishment, and when I turned onto the street, I chose the correct direction by luck. Finally, I was standing in front of the unpainted clapboards and half-shuttered windows of our boardinghouse again.

It occurred to me as I climbed the house's fusty staircase, in which hung the grease of years of frying sausages, that Oskar might not pass his tests. I carried a book with me to the empty parlor but found I couldn't read it. I should've helped him think of the questions they might ask, the answers he might give. What if we had to stay here more than a few nights, gradually pawning all there was in our trunk? We should have considered the consequences of this day—of everything—more seriously.

At seven o'clock, I heard the clatter of plates and the rise of voices from the dining room. I'd told the landlady we wouldn't be having dinner.

"Are you sure you won't take a little something?" she asked kindly when I, going back for a shawl, passed her on the stairs. "Mrs. Cartwright never touched her sausage. You could have it for two bits. And I won't charge a thing for the potato alongside."

"No, thank you," I said proudly. "My husband instructed me to keep my appetite up. We'll be going out for a celebration tonight."

"Ooo, a celebration!" she said mockingly. "Then you won't want my poor meal." She lifted her head and passed on.

They came in at last at eight o'clock.

It was Philip who apologized. "I'm sorry we've made you wait. I'm afraid we stopped for a quick bit of celebration along the way."

"So you passed the test?"

"Did you doubt my ability?" Oskar bowed low to me. "Second assistant keeper of the Point Lucia Lighthouse, at your service."

"Your husband," said Philip, "gave the most unusual answers I suspect anyone in the Lighthouse Service has heard, but he convinced them that he's, at the very least, overqualified for the job."

As we waited for our lamb chops and peas in the chophouse that Philip recommended, an electric buggy puttered down the street.

I nudged Oskar. "See? That's where you should be putting your engine."

"Thomas Alva Edison says gasoline is more economical," Philip said. "Electric storage batteries are too big and heavy to be practical."

"Do you study science at the university, Philip?" I asked.

"I was studying history, but now I'm more interested in archaeology and anthropology. I've been cataloging Mrs. Hearst's collection."

"The newspaperman?"

"No, *Mrs.* Hearst. His mother. She's got a collection of artifacts from all over the world, although what really interest me are the things from Indian tribes right here in California. Those people are on the verge of extinction, and we know practically nothing about them. I'd like to work in the field to record their languages, learn their customs, that sort of thing."

I feared that this would prompt Oskar to bring up our recent Indian experience, but he was thumbing through a booklet produced by the Lighthouse Service, each chapter of which was devoted to a coastal location on which a lighthouse stood.

"Here's where we're going, Trudy." He began to read:

"'One hundred and fifty miles south of San Francisco, the remote light station of Point Lucia was erected in 1890 on a promontory three hundred and sixty feet above the Pacific Ocean. The point is surrounded on three sides by the Santa Lucia Mountains, which rise abruptly from the sea to heights of nearly a mile. An overland journey to the nearest town is three days rough going in fair weather and the track is impassable during the rainy season. The rugged coast admits no harbors except for the beach below the light station to which supplies are delivered by sea three or four times a year. Temperatures range from mid-forties to mid-eighties Fahrenheit.

"'Because of Spanish land grants, Mexicans still control land to the north and south along the coast, although they do not occupy it. With the exception of some logging and a brief gold rush in 1891, no enterprises have induced humans to penetrate the interior. Last reported sightings of Indians native to the area were in 1875. Local fauna include cougar, bobcat, brown bear, beaver, sea otter, golden and bald eagle, cormorant, pelican, and red squirrel.'"

With what remained of the proceeds of the knife and pickle fork, Oskar paid for all of our dinners, and his high spirits continued in our room that night.

"I dazzled 'em," he said, describing his interview.

Between energetic ardor and the discomfort of the rope bed, we were awake late, so that I slept too long the following morning, long enough for the sun to eat through the fog, long enough for Oskar to pawn my silver-backed toilet set to pay the landlady, our passage to Point Lucia, and a Chinese porter to carry our trunk to the dock.

I cried at the thought of those implements lying lonely in a case in that dirty shop.

"I promise I'll get them back," he said, sitting beside me on the thin mattress, touching my tears with his sure fingers. "As soon as I'm paid, I promise I'll redeem them."

He seemed so desperate to make it up to me that I didn't remind him that he wouldn't be paid for months, and by then we would be far away.

CHAPTER 18

I HAD WALKED AS far north as the beach allowed, for here the rocks met the ocean in a wall that entirely blocked my path and my view of the coast beyond. However, the water was shallow, so, abandoning my shoes and stockings on the sand, I began to wade around the barrier. I needed to find out what lay past it. Perhaps we weren't so alone here as the Lighthouse Service booklet and the Crawleys claimed. Maybe there was a village tucked in the hills that I hadn't been able to see from the tender. The thought of finding a nest of Portuguese fishermen or even of Chinese shrimpers sustained me as I waded deeper into the cold water, wetting my skirt as far as my knees. Beyond the rock wall were more sharp black rocks, though these were low enough to climb. I picked my way over them and over and around the enormous tangles of bleached logs they'd snagged. The rocks bruised my feet, but I was determined to go as far as I could, to put the Crawleys and Mr. Johnston and even Oskar behind me, at least for a time.

A tide pool arrested me at last, a pool far more brilliant than any I'd seen before. It was wider and deeper, for one thing, and full of water almost clearer than the air, water that magnified the creatures beneath it. The colors were those of precious jewels, unnatural to an eye accustomed to the soft hues of the East. Violet balls of sea urchins, lustrous as Christmas ornaments, nestled in tufts of emerald algae. An orange crab, alarmed by my shadow, scuttled into hiding.

The pool was not only far removed from the light station physically, but also in tone. I remembered Mrs. Crawley marching out of the fog from this direction that first morning, but it was difficult to imagine her, brisk and businesslike, pausing to admire such treasure. I was sure I'd found a place that none of them knew.

The wind carried a dense animal smell as three seals heaved themselves onto a flat expanse of rock a short way out in the water. They joined two others that were already sunning themselves, their bodies like rolled rugs. And then all five of them abruptly, swiftly shimmied across the rock and poured themselves over the far side into the waves. They'd been startled by a new smaller black head that had surfaced nearby.

This animal didn't climb out on the rock; it remained bobbing among the waves. It wasn't, I determined, another seal but some other species with a nose less pointed and coloring more variegated. I couldn't decide whether I was looking at the back of the head or the front before it disappeared below the surface, and although I waited five minutes, at least, I got no second look.

I knew nothing about tides. Though I'd read about the ocean advancing and retreating according to the pull of the moon, I never considered that such rhythms might affect me. It hadn't occurred to me that the rocky stretches—slick with algae and crusted with mussels, periwinkles, and closed anemones—over which I'd walked would soon be under water. I did notice that the waves were beginning to reach close enough to throw their spray into the pool at my feet. I began to retrace my steps over the slippery rocks. There were stretches, I realized, where the water would eventually meet sheer walls. I might be trapped for hours—or worse.

I leaped when I dared, crawled when I had to, and slipped often enough to soak my dress and bruise and scrape my knees and elbows. At last, I reached a place where the rocks were too steep to climb, and I was forced to wade back into the water that now crashed in waves against them. When I'd started out, the water had merely tugged at my ankles, but now it rushed toward me, icy and unrelenting, wrapping around my waist. It shoved me toward the rocks, then dragged me into deeper water, first lifting my skirt and then trying to pull it from my body. I staggered around the bend and could see, far to the south, our morro with its cluster of doughty buildings upon it.

I pushed toward the beach, tripping in my haste so that for a moment even my head dipped into the brine. Streaming cold water, I regained the sand. The shoes and stockings that I'd left there were gone. Bitterly, I concluded that their loss did not matter, for they were nearly useless; there was nowhere for me to go. I'd verified what I'd already known to be true: the nothingness of rock, mountain, and sea stretched far, far beyond the distance my puny legs could travel.

The sun was setting by the time I staggered to the top of the morro. My feet were bleeding, and I was shivering so violently that my head ached, but most terrible of all was the fierceness with which I longed to be home, my mother calling for Gustina to bring hot water, my father shaking his head fondly at my rashness. My loneliness overwhelmed me like one of the waves, and I gasped and closed my eyes against it.

When I opened them, I saw Mrs. Crawley. I'd hoped to slink inside, unobserved by any of them, but there she was, swinging her arms mannishly as she came down the path toward me, preparing to bark a thing or two at me about lighthouse life.

She must have seen me from her window, for she'd brought a navy blanket, property of the Lighthouse Service. She wrapped it around my shoulders. "What's happened to you? We worried."

I sobbed then. I couldn't help myself. "I've ruined my dress." This was not at all my concern, but I couldn't bear to voice any other, truer sorrow.

"For heaven's sake, the dress will wash."

I blotted my tears on the blanket's rough wool.

"The husbands were afraid you'd fallen off the morro. I told them you weren't so stupid. You went for a swim, though, I see."

I told her how far I'd walked, about the purple pool and the relentless tide. "And I saw a strange animal. Not a fish, I don't think, and not a seal. Its head was small and black, but there was a little brown on it, too."

"An otter, I'll bet, like the other. There must be a community of them, then. Good."

We were quiet for a moment, remembering the pup.

"Go inside," she said, resuming her old briskness, but in a way that warmed me. "Tell that husband of yours to make you a good hot bath."

"Thank you, Mrs. Crawley."

"And now you'll know better than to go wandering off, won't you?" Although her voice was kind, I could hear the flint beneath it. "You have to think about protecting your baby. Don't forget, there are many things here that you don't yet understand. This isn't Minnesota."

"Wisconsin," I said weakly. She was right. I'd had no idea about the tide. I knew so little about this place. "I understand, Mrs. Crawley."

"Euphemia," she said. She gave me a little push toward our front steps, as if I were a child who needed direction, and then stepped to the bell outside her own door to summon her family to dinner.

Oskar was sorry. He begged me to forgive him in words that washed around me like a warm bath. He'd advised against the literal bath, instructing me to take off my clothes and lie beside him in bed, skin to skin. It was the best cure, he insisted, for hypothermia. I was sorry in return not to have been more careful with his pages.

He claimed that he couldn't re-create the diagrams. The solution to the wireless telegraph, the proper combination of magnet and mercury, wire and glass, he said, had come to him in a flash, almost in a dream; he couldn't call it back. Although I urged him to reapply himself, he refused. It was true that, having never felt inspiration myself, I didn't understand its fits and starts. Could he really have lost everything with those few pages? Or was it an excuse to jettison another project he feared would fail?

CHAPTER 19

OUR BABY CAME to nothing.

For some weeks, we'd lived in happy anticipation, expecting, despite Euphemia's warning. Without electrical experiments to distract him, Oskar was enthusiastic again about furnishing our house. He built a cradle and a night table. "So I can bring you coffee in bed," he said.

If it was a girl, he hoped we might name her Amelia, for his sister. He pressed his palm to my belly, which, in truth, had hardly grown. Had I felt it quicken? he wondered.

I had not. What I did feel one afternoon was a faint echo of the familiar tightening I'd known for a day or two every month since I'd been a high school girl. In an hour, I was gasping, holding my breath, curling myself into a crouch in a vain effort to push away the relentless, wringing grip.

"What is it?" Oskar asked desperately, standing over me as I rolled myself into a ball on our bed, trying to escape from my own insides.

"It's nothing," I said, my voice taut and small. "Nothing." It was, I believed, the old monthly pain making up with a vengeance for the time it had lost. "Only Euphemia was wrong after all."

I begged for it to release me, and after some hours it did, but Euphemia hadn't been wrong, for within the river of blood that gushed from between my legs was a miniature figure, unquickened but nevertheless human. Its few inches included a tiny head and limbs. It hung from me, attached to my insides by a cord so fine that I could and did pinch it in half with my fingers. Later I would wish that I'd held the being who was not to be more tenderly, and at the same time, I would wish that I'd not dared to look at its haunting form at all.

Oskar had fetched Euphemia, and she whisked it away and led me to the bed. She fitted folded cloth after folded cloth between my legs to stanch the blood.

"Poor dear," she said, and I didn't know whether she meant me or the other.

"Is it a boy or a girl?"

"It's nothing."

To buck me up, Euphemia told me that she herself had had three such experiences, one even further along. "If it's going to happen, the sooner the better. You're lucky."

Euphemia said I ought to stay in bed, but lying there thinking about nothing made me cry, so as soon as I was able, I took myself outside to tend the tubs.

Our collection had steadily swelled. Recognizing the cruelty and futility of trapping a living being in a few inches of dirty water, as the children had been doing with their jars, I'd asked Mr. Crawley to saw some empty barrels in half to make tubs in which the animals and plants we gathered might thrive. He'd hesitated. The barrels were Lighthouse Service property. We were required to return empty as many as we'd received full, unless we put them to another purpose. This was another purpose, I'd insisted.

"I'd not relish being the one to explain these shenanigans to Inspector Roberts," he'd said, but his saw had been poised for the first cut.

As best as we could, we created the world of the tide pools in the tubs, arranging rocks to which anemones and mussels clung, making caves in which crabs could hide. One of the key ingredients, naturally, was salt water. We carried several buckets up at a time on the steam donkey, refreshing the tubs every few days. Our aquariums attracted gulls, so we had to build a scarecrow beside them, which pleased Euphemia, since it also discouraged the eagles from swooping down on the chickens.

The tubs helped to make sense of what we found. We began to understand how some of these animals grew and changed, who ate whom, which preferred shade and which craved the sun, which liked to live near one another and which couldn't abide certain neighbors. I was impressed by the sheer range of life that the whole mess represented, but I was also beginning to recognize an order in it. Altogether, it was thoroughly satisfying work, even if some of the creatures, despite our best efforts, couldn't adapt to the artificial environment and died.

It was so satisfying that adding to and organizing the collection became pretty much the focus of our school. In the classroom, while dried specimens continued to cover the floor, they were no longer a jumble. Using *Some Species of the Pacific Coast*, as well as our own observations and reason, we'd arranged our finds into distinct categories, the pressed seaweeds in one portion of the room, the bivalves in another, and so on.

Prime real estate under the window was devoted to the unusual man-made objects, among them the cormorant-feather disk that I'd seen on the cairn. The children had recently added some new things: one morning when I'd opened the door, I'd found Mary standing with her two cupped hands before her, forming a nest for four little bundles. I thought they must be mice or fledglings, but they were not living creatures. Rather, they were little twists of the rubbery plant called kelp.

By this time I'd discovered kelp to be a fascinating substance, monstrously long and tough, but also beautiful if viewed in the right way, with its strange hollow stems, its pale green bulbs like enormous pearls, and its trailing leaves that rose and fell like hair on the undulating water. To the children, though, it was as unremarkable as grass, so I couldn't see why Mary cradled it with such care and why the rest gathered around so eagerly.

"We should each open one," Edward said. "Jane chooses first."

The kelp only served as a wrapper. "What are these things?" I asked. "Where did you get them?"

They didn't answer, only went on pulling at the leaves, which fell quickly away to reveal four objects carved of soft gray driftwood, each about two inches high: a crab, a pelican, a dolphin, and a seal, the last sitting cunningly on its own little rock.

"Where did these come from?" I asked again.

"From the mermaid," Jane said finally. "She left them on the stones for us."

Baby Johnston's grave. I felt a personal pain in thinking of it now that I'd experienced my own loss. Archie Johnston must have left the figures, I thought, as offerings for his dead child. Did he know that the living children took them for themselves? Remembering him giving Jane the worm shell on my first afternoon, I believed he did. Probably he guessed, and perhaps it gave him some comfort to play fairy godfather. Poor Mr. Johnston.

To be sure, we kept on with our sums and our passages. And we worked at our Latin—mostly to assign appropriate "scientific" names to beings we couldn't identify in *Some Species*. But we would hurry through these lessons, and often in the afternoons, instead of climbing into bed with Oskar, I would scour the beach with the children, searching for new species and fine examples of those with which we were already acquainted, with a good deal of larking about thrown in. I explained to Euphemia that on these afternoons I was teaching my students to observe astutely, to handle wildlife with respect, to understand natural history and scientific classification, and to draw. (Having long ago exhausted my sketchbook and all of my writing stock, we were filling blank logbooks that I'd pilfered from the lighthouse.)

"As long as their chores are done, I don't mind," Euphemia said. "But," she added, looking sternly at the children, "you must stay on the beach."

They nodded solemnly and promised. I wondered if she feared they would swim away or disappear into the mountains. Of course we'd stay on the beach. There was nowhere else.

CHAPTER 20

ONE AFTERNOON IN early November, I remained beside one of the tubs after I'd dismissed the children for lunch, sketching in a logbook a being that the children called a sea cradle and *Some Species* labeled a chiton. Had I noticed a chiton on my first day on the beach, I would have dismissed it as a small rough patch, not an animal but a defect of the rock. Now I understood it to be a single-footed creature whose simple plates of armor had served to protect its species since practically the beginning of the earth. Chitons came in different colors, and I wondered why some were red and some were brown and some were yellow or gray or green. I speculated as to whether the pigments in their food somehow tinted their skin and whether their colors camouflaged them from predators. They appeared to stay still, yet I knew from observing them in the tub that they somehow moved across the rock, leaving in their wake a path cleared of algae, which I supposed they must be eating. They were primitive creatures, but even so, they knew enough to curl their armor around their vulnerable undersides when they were pried away from their homes.

First I sketched the little creature as it flattened itself against a rock, and then I tried without success to tug it gently off its base, so as to make it roll up like a pill bug.

"What're you doing?" Oskar had come up behind me.

Hastily, I pulled my fingers from the water and wiped them on my duster. "I'm sorry. You must want your lunch."

"I'm all right. What were you doing?" he repeated.

"I was trying to get it to defend itself. The book only shows it flat." I pointed to its picture in *Some Species,* which lay open beside me.

He studied the page. "Are you sure it's the same? This says it's supposed to be brown."

As I described my own puzzlement over the colors, he slid his fingernail between the rock and the animal and, without hesitation, pulled it free, whereupon it gradually curled up, as I'd known it would.

"Perhaps you've discovered a new species. You ought to send one to your Miss Dodson. See what she makes of it." He dropped the tiny balled creature back into the water and turned his attention to the log in which I'd been drawing. "Yours is better than the one in the book." He touched my picture, leaving a wet circle on the page. Then he turned his intense gaze on me, as he'd not done in many weeks. "You should work up a catalog of your creatures. That'd be a real contribution to science."

"Oh, I don't know." I brushed futilely at the drop of water that had soaked into the page.

He shrugged. "If you're done, let's eat. I'm exhausted."

Since he'd given up electricity, Oskar had become the model of an assistant lighthouse keeper. He arrived at his shift on time and stayed late, meticulously if dully checking and cleaning the machinery and the building. He'd discovered, even before Mr. Crawley, that the mercury on which the Fresnel lens floated (without this lubricant, the massive glass prism would be far too heavy to turn) had evaporated dangerously. He'd put a new blowcock and pipe in the boiler without help from Mr. Crawley or Archie Johnston, and he'd tarred the smokestack in his free hours. He came home promptly for lunch and didn't complain about the monotonous fare that remained in our stores—mostly beans and sprouted, rubbery potatoes. Immediately after lunch, he would take himself to bed and lie there wearing the black spectacles he'd brought home from the light, so I couldn't tell whether his eyes were open or closed. He'd quit interrupting the children's lessons, and had there been any writing paper left, we would have had it to ourselves. At first I'd been relieved that he was no longer so overexcited and preoccupied by his "real" work, but now I was anxious and unhappy, for he wasn't himself, and though I tried to engage him with sprightly conversation and caresses, he rarely responded. It seemed we would not be returning in triumph after all.

I'd intended after lunch to see if Euphemia had some work for me, but today I stubbornly followed Oskar up to our bed. Although in the past, there had been plenty of afternoons when I'd wished he would leave me alone, I missed being the object of his desire. Admittedly, since I'd lost my corset, I hadn't attempted to constrict myself to fit into my attractive clothes but went around every day in my loose duster. I took the shapeless thing off and stood naked except for my shift while I combed out my hair, a pose sure to interest him in the past. To my chagrin, he was asleep before I'd slipped between the sheets.

Discouraged, I dressed and made my way back to the tubs. In one of them, a small green crab, *Pugettia producta*—or was it *Pugettia gracilis* or *Pugettia richii* or, as Oskar had suggested, some other, unidentified *Pugettia* altogether?—worked its way busily over a ribbon of kelp. Its round black eyes reminded me of Miss Dodson's—although hers were not on stalks. Perhaps I should send her a selection of starfish and crabs—they dried well—and a few nudibranches and chitons. Anemones would be nice, but without water in which to expose their tentacles, they were unimpressive, resembling wadded dirty rags.

I tore a page from my logbook:

Dear Miss Dodson,

I am sending you some dried specimens, along with drawings of some others that I fear would not make the journey well, in the hope that they might interest you. All of them can be found along the central coast of California, where I now live. They seem to me to be strange creatures, for the most part, but perhaps they are ordinary and strange just to me, who am not used to such things. I look forward to your response but can receive and send mail only every three or four months, so you'll understand when I'm slow to reply.

I considered explaining how I came to be in California and concluded that such personal details were not the purpose of my communication with my former teacher. I signed the letter with my maiden name, realizing that she wouldn't know me by any other. In a postscript, I mentioned the catalog and asked her advice. Did she think it might be a worthwhile pursuit?

I spent a great deal of time on my drawings, considering how to illustrate the distinctions among the crabs, for instance, and including detailed renderings of the claws. I pondered how best to show scale and habitat, in which the distinctions most vividly came into play. And I recorded habits—as far as the children and I had been able to observe them—thinking that would be valuable information, too.

It was difficult to package the specimens. Resilient in their saltwater baths, they were fragile as glass once they'd been dried. The children helped me to gather grass in the wide meadows between our morro and the mountains, and I made a little nest for each creature and then laid the nests in a crate, smothered them with more grass and crumpled newspapers, and nailed it shut. In a barrel, I made a bed of sawdust for the nailed crate, along with a couple of gauges that we couldn't repair by ourselves and were sending to San Francisco.

* * *

The Madrone, the same tender on which we'd come, arrived on a hot, clear morning late in November. It was our first contact with the world beyond the morro since we'd arrived in July, and I waited, nearly holding my breath, for Euphemia to dole out the contents of the yellow mail pouch that the steam donkey trundled up. In the end, I had a precious stack of envelopes: a long letter each from three of my school friends, including Lucy; two from my father; and six from my mother. We also got a share of a smattering of *San Francisco Examiners,* seemingly selected at random, and Oskar got a letter from his father.

At the barrel-opening ceremony that evening, Euphemia set aside a number of choice cans—sweet potatoes and currant jam and such—not to be opened until Christmas dinner, for the tender wouldn't return until after the New Year. I was pleased to discover Volume 3 of *The Complete Works of Shakespeare* in the fresh library and showed it to Oskar. He only nodded.

I'd paid to send a small package to Milwaukee College for Females in the same way I paid to send my letters, using credit drawn on Oskar's paycheck, which the Lighthouse Service deposited quarterly in a bank account in San Francisco. A few years earlier, a chief keeper at a light up the coast had sunk like lead when his skiff capsized as he returned from the tender with his pockets stuffed with gold coins, half a year's pay for himself and two assistants. That loss of both man and money had prompted the service to eliminate payment in cash. It was no great hardship to do without money at Point Lucia. There was nothing here on which to spend gold.

The following morning, I happened to see the letter from Oskar's father in the kitchen pail, and I couldn't help but skim the well-formed but anxious lines visible among the potato peels.

> . . . *understand that Philip was a help to you. I hope you were sufficiently grateful, for his time is no doubt very limited.*

A slight shake of the pail revealed:

> *. . . hope you're applying yourself steadily. I must say that I often*
> *envy those like you who have the satisfaction of practical work, work*
> *that dirties the hands and tires the back and forms the foundation*
> *upon which society—all societies—rest . . .*
> *Your mother sends her best.*
> *With sincere hopes for your happiness,*
> *Papa*

To make my own letters last, I allowed myself one per week and read very slowly, as if sucking a chocolate. Each began stiffly with good wishes for my journey and questions about my current life but soon began recounting activities that reminded me how far removed I was from my old world. Gustina was to have gone with me when I married Ernst, but my mother had promised that Lucy might have her, if Gustina agreed, which she surely would. My mother herself had already begun to train a new girl, Polish, somewhat fierce, and even more ignorant than Gustina had been. Also, Ernst had been spotted by a trustworthy source walking with a Miss Cynthia Davis on his arm. It was a relief but also a disappointment to learn that I wasn't so important after all.

I thought often in the next few weeks of my little package of Pacific creatures tracing the journey that I had taken, only backward; the boat trip to San Francisco, where the barrel in which I'd packed my crate would be split open, spilling sawdust onto the loading area of the post office; and then the train trip across the western states; and finally, the second train from the terminal in Chicago to Milwaukee. I hoped I'd padded the specimens well enough to keep them whole. I imagined Miss Dodson opening my letter with surprise and reading with affection; my teachers had always liked me. Having read, she would pry open the crate with the curiosity, if not quite the fervor, of the children when they attacked the fresh barrels. I could picture Miss Dodson drawing her magnifying glass from its leather pouch, and the notion of this tangible thread between my old life and my new was a comfort to me. She would compare the names I'd listed to the ones she could find in her own books; and she would be especially interested in the specimens I couldn't identify. I felt a shimmer of excitement at the thought that some might be new to her; that, as Oskar had suggested, the children and I might have found creatures unknown to the rest of the world.

CHAPTER 21

"Do you ever see the otters?"

The children and I were on the beach again, and I couldn't resist scanning the knobs of kelp—deceptively like heads—that rose and sank in the waves for the unusual creature I'd spotted when I'd lost myself among the rocks. And I couldn't keep from my mind the baby Jane and I had found. I imagined that the two belonged together, perhaps as mother and child.

"No." They shook their heads.

"I think I have. At least your mother thought that's what it was." I described the small black head that had frightened away the seals.

"Oh," Jane said, "that wasn't an otter. That was the mermaid. Want to see where she lives?"

"Ma says we're not to go there," Mary warned.

"Mama says mermaids are dangerous," Nicholas said. "She says they like children so much that they drag them down to their lairs under the water."

"Where they drown!" Edward finished.

"But her lair isn't under the water," Jane objected.

"I think it would be all right," I broke in, "if I'm with you." I smiled, wondering what sort of animal or make-believe the children would show me. "Only we must come back right away if I say so."

Immediately, they began to run, and they kept going with remarkable endurance, much farther than I'd anticipated, all the way to the end of the beach, where they splashed into the shallow water to make their way around the rocks.

"What about the tide?" I called.

"It's going out," Mary called back over her shoulder. "We have hours."

I didn't know whether to trust their judgment. I was much older and therefore should be the one responsible, but I had no idea what was wise and what was foolish here.

We reached the pool of violet-spiked urchins, which was obviously familiar to the children, for it seemed to serve as a sort of landmark where they turned inland. Soon they stepped into what, from a distance, appeared to be a rock wall but which was a passageway, so narrow in places that it was nearly closed at the top.

With a start, I realized that this must be the very place Euphemia had meant them to avoid when she'd warned them to stay on the beach. "Maybe we should go back," I said.

"Shhhh!" Edward whispered. He turned to me. "We don't want to frighten her."

Were otters like bears, animals that could be dangerous if they felt cornered?

"I think we should go back." This time I whispered. The passage was so tight in places that I had to turn sideways to slip through. Any animal at its far end would surely feel trapped.

The children pretended they hadn't heard me. Suddenly, they stopped and crowded against one another.

"See?" Jane breathed.

I had to push against the children to peer into the dark space, but once my eyes were accustomed to the low light, I recognized at once the cave Jane had drawn. It was a low-ceilinged room, obviously formed when one boulder had crashed down upon three others that refused to give way. I'd expected some sort of burrow or nest, but although an animal stink hung about it, it was clearly the home of a human being. It smelled of smoke and unwashed skin and skeins of seaweed that hung from a crude wooden rack. Piled higgledy-piggledy about the floor were enormous abalone shells, their mother-of-pearl bowls exposed. Heaped in some were what I took to be tools: mallets and scrapers and pointed sticks. One shell was brimming with acorns, another with sharpened yellowish bones, another with round shapes I first took to be ivory buttons or clasps and then realized were vertebrae. Here and there were baskets as well, some flat-bottomed and some rounded, one in the shape of a cone. Most were finely woven of some light-colored plant material I couldn't identify, into which dark patterns had been worked. Near the center of the cave was one piece of what might have been called furniture: skins stretched over a wooden frame to make a kind of platform that served, I supposed, as a couch or bed. Along the far wall, arranged in a pyramid, were brightly labeled cans of the kind I'd come to know well: green corn and tomatoes, sardines and plums, and at the apex, a hash made of beef and potatoes, its label bearing a large blue ribbon. The floor, covered in sealskins, was a lustrous brown. Folded in one corner was a navy wool blanket, Lighthouse Service–issue. Most astonishing of all was what was beside the blanket, arranged neatly side by side: my shoes and stockings.

"Who lives here?" I whispered, astounded.

"The mermaid!" Jane looked at me as if I were a simpleton. How many times did I need to be told?

"Well, we're not entirely sure." Edward looked to the others, as if uncertain how much he ought to reveal.

"She doesn't have a tail," Nicholas explained. "Just ordinary legs."

"But she *is* a mermaid," Jane said stoutly. "We saw her come out of the water."

"She had a spear and a big rockfish stabbed right through," Edward said.

I saw that the crevices between the rocks at the entrance were filled with fish vertebrae and that the stone surfaces were flecked with scales that shimmered like quartz.

Jane took a step into the cave, but Mary grabbed her crossed pinafore straps and pulled her back. "You know better, Janie," she said. "It's not polite to go in if she's not at home."

"Why isn't she here?" Jane asked, a little petulantly.

"Probably because of Mrs. Swann," Nicholas said. "It's only that she doesn't know you," he added kindly.

"The things in your collection, in the box," I said. "Did you steal them from her?"

"Steal them!" Edward was indignant. "Of course not!"

"They're meant for us," Nicholas said. "She puts them on the stones."

"I told you," Jane said.

"Ma doesn't like it," Mary said.

"It was my turn, and she threw it away," Jane complained.

Mary sighed. "I gave you the feathers, didn't I?"

"I wanted the necklace!"

"I told you not to wear it," Mary said. "I told you to put it straight in the box."

"She wanted me to wear it. She was sad when I didn't have it. You know she was."

I could hardly listen to them, caught as I was in my own conjectures about the creature who lived in this hole. Who was she, if, indeed, she was a woman at all?

I feared that a black-haired, seal-skinned banshee might come whirling down the narrow path, brandishing a spear. I glanced at the rock walls that rose high over our heads. There were dozens of crevices that, for all I knew, might hide a person.

"We'd better go." I didn't wait for arguments but turned and began to make my own way back. This time they accepted my authority and followed without protest.

They would have dawdled along the beach—to them, apparently, the idea that a wild woman lived in a cave not five miles from their home was only a bit of distraction to spark up an afternoon, something like going down to the river to watch the drawbridge open had once been to me—but I hurried them on like a hen pushing her chicks toward the roost. This time I kept up with them as we straggled up the steep morro—I had learned to crouch low and use my hands as well as my feet, as they did—and I went with them all the way to their parlor.

Through the doorway, I could see Mrs. Crawley—Euphemia—reaching into the oven for a pan. On the worktable beside her were two cans of the blue-ribbon hash that had been so artfully displayed in the cave.

"Wash," Mrs. Crawley called, and the children crowded past me and pushed into the kitchen.

"Mrs. Crawley. Euphemia."

"Oh!" Startled, she let the hot pan clatter onto the stove. "Why are you lurking there? Come in."

I stayed where I was. I wondered if she'd deliberately misled me about the otter, and I wasn't sure how she would respond.

She advanced through the kitchen doorway and came toward me, wiping her hands on a towel. "What is it?"

"It's a woman, I think. Or a person, at any rate. She lives in a cave in the rocks, not five miles from here."

"They took you there? I told them—I told *you*—to stay on the beach!" She directed an angry look toward the kitchen, where the children were laughing and clattering the china. "Be careful with those plates!" she snapped.

"Yes, I'm sorry. I didn't realize what you meant until . . . Is she dangerous?"

"She's mad," she said firmly. And then she softened. "I don't mean that she's a lunatic, exactly, but she's touched . . . different from you and me. She's . . . unpredictable." She paused, absently adjusting the wooden teeth and other items of wreckage on their lurid cloth. "It's not so unusual around here, you know. This is the kind of place that attracts people who can't get along in regular society."

"How does she live? Won't she starve? Or freeze? Isn't she lonely?"

"I wouldn't worry about that. She knows better than any of us how to live. She's been there for years, you know."

"Since before you came?"

"No. Not that long." She held me in her formidable gaze. "My children are not to go near her, you understand. And if I were you, I would stay away from her, too."

In my own kitchen, I pounded the chisel into two cans and poured their contents into a skillet, distractedly mixing oxtail and duck. Then I remembered that I'd neglected the stove all afternoon and let the fire go out. It would take at least an hour to warm it up again.

I set a plate of cold meat in congealed gravy in front of Oskar that night, and he began to eat without comment. I was too preoccupied to lift my own fork. I thought about the woman returning to her cave and wondered if she would smell us on the air and know we'd been there. I imagined her squatting on the rocks, scraping scales from a limp fish, or sitting on the sealskin floor, rolling acorns about. Who was she? How had she come to be there? Were there more like her?

"Oskar," I said abruptly.

He looked up, raising his eyebrows slightly at the intensity in my voice.

"I saw something strange today. A sort of hideout in the rocks. Euphemia says a madwoman lives there."

I was leaning forward, unconsciously heightening the intensity of my words, but he seemed unaffected. He continued chewing a cold oxtail for what seemed a long time. "It's not all that surprising," he said at last. "Didn't the Crawleys say there was some crazy old hermit around here? I can see how this place could drive you insane, the damn wind, the damn waves, the damn foghorn, the damn rust. It all keeps worrying at you until you're ready to do something desperate. You were right, Trudy; people aren't meant to be here." He pushed his plate away as he spoke and stood up from the table.

"Oskar, she doesn't seem crazy to me. I mean, not really. Her things are organized. And some of them are beautiful."

"Well." He sighed. He was already halfway down the hall so that the walls muffled his words. "I suppose you'll have to show me one of these days."

CHAPTER 22

THAT NIGHT THE rain began to fall so thickly and heavily, it seemed as though the bowl of the ocean had risen into the sky and upended itself. It went on for weeks, the deluge pausing only to reveal more vast columns of gray to the west, their winds screaming as they advanced, so that the chickens had to be staked to the ground with a bit of string around one leg to keep them from being blown right off the morro. I diverted the children by reading *The Tempest* to them, from the Shakespeare the tender had delivered, and together, we loosely adapted it into a piece they could perform at Christmas.

To my surprise, Euphemia abandoned an afternoon's work to help us fashion the costumes, and these delighted the children more than the story itself. As Ariel, Jane got two lace handkerchiefs tacked to the shoulders of her dress to suggest wings. Every few minutes she would jump into the air to make them flutter. Edward assumed a dignified expression in Oskar's wedding jacket and didn't look ridiculous with my muff tied over his chin as a beard. Archie Johnston donated a sheepskin rug for Nicholas to wear as Caliban, and Mr. Crawley's indigo nightshirt, together with a crown Euphemia constructed from empty tin cans, was his costume as the prince. I had the perfect dress for Mary's Miranda.

Though I'd not opened our steamer trunk since the day I'd feverishly collected laundry, now I stood it up on its end and parted its halves, allowing the colorful fabric of my former life to spill forward, crushed but still lovely.

"So pretty." Jane unself-consciously stroked the sleeve of the blue silk I'd worn to the panorama.

"Yes, that's the one." I held it up to Mary's scrawny chest.

"Not really!" Mary covered her mouth with her hand. She looked almost terrified at the thought.

I floated the dress over her head. The garnet buttons met far too easily at the front, and both girls giggled at the bustle, but when I'd loosened Mary's braids, I could glimpse the woman she would become.

"She'll trip over the thing," Euphemia said, shaking her head. As she combed her fingers through the girl's hair, I saw that her dismissal disguised both pride and sorrow at her daughter's maturation.

Little Jane insisted on trying the dress, too. She looked absurd, drowning in silk, but Euphemia indulged her, patiently arranging the folds of material around her feet, making her look as if she were standing in a pool of water.

"I'm a mermaid princess!" the little girl announced.

Our Christmas party, Euphemia hinted, would be an occasion worthy of the fine table linen stored in my trunk, unused since it had left Milwaukee. We would gather, we decided, in my parlor, since it was less crowded with furnishings and bric-a-brac than the Crawleys', and we would need space for the plank table and for the entertainment. From her hoard of provisions, Euphemia produced a bottle of tawny liquor. We would make rum balls and a large rum cake from her mother's recipes.

Early on the morning of Christmas Eve, the men rode the steam donkey down the morro in the rain, and by early afternoon, they returned with their quarry. Johnston dangled three ducks by the neck; Mr. Crawley had strung two large rockfish together through the gills; and Oskar had his arms around a sweet-smelling pine that he crowded into one corner of our parlor. Although popping corn was among our stores, Euphemia had never taught the children to string it nor to make paper chains out of strips of old catalog pages. I set them to work on these decorations while Euphemia and I erected the table, covering it with two of my mother's fine white cloths and laying out the full set of lighthouse china. It was a simple spread, without the niceties of compote dishes or pickle forks, but inviting nonetheless. A bottle of wine glowed in the center with a ruby luster.

At the other end of the room, the children and I strewed evidence of a shipwreck, courtesy of their mother's collection, and arranged some of the larger rocks and specimens, lengths of driftwood, and coils of dried kelp from our own stash to suggest the island. The players hid in the hall, whispering and giggling as the audience took their seats, while Mr. Crawley went around with the rum that remained after our baking.

"Must you pour so much, Henry?" Euphemia was wearing more than one petticoat under her skirt—she couldn't know that it was a style long out of date—and it made her appear even larger than usual.

She was right that the tumblers were overfull, given the strong nature of the drink. Mr. Crawley was clearly not in the habit of serving liquor.

"Now, Effie," Archie said placatingly. "It's only one night a year."

"Effie" was so incongruous a name for Euphemia Crawley that I didn't dare to meet Oskar's eye for fear I would burst out laughing.

The show itself was both charming and tedious, as children's performances must be, and as I'd hoped, it took the sting out of a Christmas so far from the ones I remembered. We dimmed the lights, and Janie and Nicholas made a fine storm, drumming with spoons on pots and running back and forth with my dark shawl held over their heads to suggest the tossing wind and the waves. Prospero relinquished his magic stoutly, if a bit stiffly. Miranda handled her gown with surprising grace. Ariel sucked on the strings of her long dark hair—though we'd tied it in rags overnight, it wouldn't hold a curl—while she delivered her song about coral bones and pearl eyes with only a few whispered prompts, and Caliban growled with delightful fierceness. I'd given Nicholas some lines from the famous speech about the sweet noises of the night, and he spoke them with an appropriately wistful air.

When he'd finished, Archie turned to me. "I see I was right about your being a good teacher," he said disarmingly. "Although," he added, glancing at his sister, "you chose the wrong one to play the wild thing."

Euphemia's face hardened. "You see, Henry?" she said, plucking the bottle of rum from the floor where it had wandered.

"I only gave him a glass, same as everyone," Mr. Crawley said.

"Why didn't you include 'Be not afraid of greatness'?" Oskar murmured.

"Wrong shipwreck play," Euphemia said with her usual efficiency.

I admit I was as surprised as Oskar that she would know such a thing. I hoped it didn't show on my face as it did on his.

"One reads," she said.

The players, luckily, took no notice of their audience's inattention, but entertained themselves to the finish, and then we all sat down to eat. Euphemia, with uncharacteristic attention to aesthetics, had added to the table a series of short candles whose flames dipped and straightened in the draft that seeped through the windows. This time it was she who took the bottle around, splashing a few dark drops of wine into each of our glasses.

"Now, Effie, don't deprive us of our Christmas cheer," Archie coaxed.

Euphemia frowned. "You don't always wear it well."

"I've been a good boy all year. Haven't I, Henry? Tell my sister how good I've been, now, c'mon."

"He hasn't caused any trouble, Euphemia," Mr. Crawley said. "It's true."

"And I'm entertaining," Archie said. "Look!" He'd hung his spoon from the end of his nose, and it dangled there ludicrously, making the children scream with laughter and begin applying their spoons to their own noses with clattering results.

"Well," Euphemia acquiesced, tipping the bottle, "I suppose if you must have it, now's the time."

She poured a bit more into each of our glasses while Mr. Crawley served the duck with a fairly steady hand and Oskar, Mr. Crawley, and I lavishly praised the meat and its currant glaze, to appease both brother and sister. Soon we were all festive, the men enjoying themselves by loudly reviling Spain as Euphemia and I peeled oranges and cracked walnuts for the children without insisting that they first finish their peas.

There were no curtains in our parlor windows, and happening to catch a glimpse of my reflection in the dripping glass, I was conscious of how we would appear if anyone—a passing angel, perhaps—could see us from the outside. Much like the lighthouse itself, we, gathered in this little room, were a warm and bright spot in a vast space of cold blackness. I scanned the flushed and happy faces of the people I'd come to know this half-year, grateful that I had a part in this family now that I could no longer be with my own.

Oskar must have been feeling much the same, for he raised his glass, which had been refilled a second or perhaps even a third time, since Mr. Crawley had produced a second bottle of wine, seemingly from under the table. "To Christmas!"

Archie raised his own glass with unwarranted energy, and the liquid in it sloshed alarmingly. "We've not heard anything about the noble experiment in a great while," he said with a smack of his lips. "What's happened to all the electricity around here? Have we lost it?"

Cravenly, I kept my eyes on my plate, wondering how Oskar would respond. Archie Johnston was rude, and I didn't like to see my husband embarrassed, but I, too, wished for answers to questions somewhat like these.

"Lost it?" Oskar said. "No, it's just . . ." He shrugged in the defeated way that had become familiar. "Just that I can't find it, I guess. But it's here. Electricity can never be lost. It remains even after we die."

Mr. Crawley nodded as he picked a bit of orange pulp from between his teeth. Euphemia looked as if she were waiting for something mildly unpleasant to cease. But Archie seemed sincerely interested. "Are you talking about the spirit world, then?"

"Not in the sense of table-turning or any of that nonsense," Oskar said. "That's been thoroughly debunked. But certainly, electromagnetism is the life force that never dies."

"So electromagnetism is God?" Euphemia said dryly.

"You mock, Effie, because you don't understand a man's need to do something more than trudge around and around like a donkey in harness. It's all right for you and old Henry here, tending that light like a couple of nursemaids. But some of us want more. Isn't that right, Oskar?"

"The light saves lives," Euphemia said calmly. "It's important work."

"For women, maybe. Women like that sort of thing, keeping things tidy and on schedule."

"Well, now!" Mr. Crawley clapped his hands. "Don't you have a little surprise in the kitchen, Euphemia?"

Euphemia gave her brother a long look, clearly reluctant to give up the argument without having the last word, but she placed both palms on the table and pushed herself dramatically to her feet.

The surprise was a honeycomb she'd been squirreling away, and the children were as excited by the sweet as she'd anticipated. They reached with their butter knives as soon as she'd set it on the table, and Jane, in her excitement, brought her little arm too close to one of the candles. She dropped her knife and howled as if her hand had been sliced clean away.

Instantly, Archie snatched the girl from her chair and pulled her into his lap. The roughness with which he handled her made her wail all the harder, and she reached for her mother. He let her go reluctantly.

"For heaven's sake," Euphemia said, disentangling the child's arm from her neck to study the skin, "it's only a little burn. Look, it's hardly pink."

In fact, it was impossible to tell any color in that dim light.

Euphemia touched her lips to Jane's inner arm, and the child stopped crying. "Bedtime," Euphemia said.

"Yes, children," Archie said, "if your mother says it doesn't hurt, then there's no pain, and if she tells you to go to bed, you must drop off immediately. So go to bed. Go to bed!" he roared.

"Now, Archie," Mr. Crawley began, his voice like thin milk. He put one hand on his brother-in-law's arm. "Exercise some self-control."

Euphemia had shooed the children out. We could hear them running up the stairs of their house. She came to stand beside her brother. He looked puny and weak in his chair beneath her great height and beside her wide skirt.

"You'd best see to the light, Archie," Euphemia said. Her voice was like iron. I, for one, could not have stood up to it.

"She thinks she can boss me," he said, keeping his eyes on Oskar. "She's got me stuck up here, keeps my woman in the rocks, rations my liquor."

I may have emitted an audible sound of surprise when he mentioned the woman. Archie and Euphemia so thoroughly commanded everyone's attention that no one noticed.

Archie, pretending that he controlled the scene, raised his glass and drained it ostentatiously. He turned his head to look up at Euphemia. "Always in the right, aren't you?"

She stood silent, unwavering, holding his gaze, a pillar of rectitude.

At last he looked away, almost sheepish. "Oh, yes, the damned light. You'd think it was the star of Bethlehem." But obediently, he went out.

CHAPTER 23

EUPHEMIA BEGAN NOISILY to clear the dishes. I was afraid she'd snap at me, but I had to ask the question that beat furiously inside me like a fly against a window.

"The woman in the rocks—"

"That he blames me!" She crashed one lighthouse plate down upon another. "It's . . . "

She banged a few more plates together, mere words apparently being inadequate to express her feelings. Desperate with curiosity as I was, I was also uncomfortably conscious of possible chipping and was relieved when she ceased her crashing and sat down with a sigh.

"Perhaps a little more cheer," Oskar said, tipping the bottle over each of our glasses in turn. Euphemia didn't object.

"Archie's always depended on Euphemia, you see," Mr. Crawley began. "That's why we got him the place here along with us."

"He's no good on his own!"

"No, you're right, my dear," Mr. Crawley said soothingly. "He gets funny, you know," he explained. "Desperate-like and mean. Well, you saw him."

He reached to pat the back of his wife's hand. She was pressing salt to a purple wine stain beside Archie's plate and took no notice of his comfort. Finally, seeing that her ministrations were doing no good, she sank back into her chair, like a pillow that had lost its stuffing, and put

181

her hands over her face in an attitude I would not have believed her capable of.

"Archie was so delicate once," she said, speaking through her fingers at first, "like a sweet baby bird. He could practically fit in my mama's shoe when he was born; he was that little! Mama'd had quite a few that went wrong between him and me, so when he was born so small and fragile, Mama and I smothered him up with cooing and coddling. Maybe it was our fault that he turned out the way he did."

"Now, Euphemia," Mr. Crawley said, "I wouldn't say you did wrong."

"We had to build him up, you see, with special foods. Always honey on his oatmeal and sugar in his tea, extra butter for his bread. When my mother cooked a chicken, he got the livers fried in oil. And he loved buttermilk! He would bang his little cup on the table and shout, 'Mo! Mo!'" She sighed. "We were so pleased when he was greedy."

"Euphemia was like a mother to him, really," Mr. Crawley said. He'd lit a pipe and puffed at it with great concentration to get it burning. "Their mother ran off when he was just a little thing, and Euphemia was so much older. She took on the care of him, you see."

"He didn't thank me for it, though," Euphemia said. " 'You're not my mama,' he would scream, and then he would kick and bite like I aimed to torture him."

"Gave her a good poke once with a fork. Show 'em, Euphemia."

She shook her head; nevertheless, she pulled the collar of her dress a little way from her neck and tilted her head so that we could see in the dim candlelight the four pale dots on her skin.

"He had the most terrible cry," she said. "A wail as if he'd lost everything dear to him in the world and even the birds must bear witness. It drove my father mad."

I thought of Janie's cries. Yes, I could well imagine little Archie's sounds of pain and alarm and outrage. I didn't understand how a mother could run off. But there was a more pressing question.

"The woman in the rocks," I broke in.

"What I'm trying to say," Euphemia went on, "is that I did my best."

I couldn't tell whether she was answering or ignoring me.

"A lighthouse keeper can choose his own assistant," Mr. Crawley said, circling back. "That's how we got him this place."

"Henry and I were at Pigeon Point," Euphemia said, "but then Archie—he'd been working on one of the steamers—pulled a knife on his captain."

"He only let him see a bit of the blade," Mr. Crawley said. "He didn't hurt him."

Euphemia took a drink of her wine, neatly swallowing what I could well imagine might have been a retort.

"Henry got the judge to turn Archie over to us," she said, "but we had to agree to take him with us to this post and swear to keep him out of trouble. What trouble could a person get into here?" She made a sound like a laugh, tight and bitter.

"So this was an exile?" I suggested.

"Not for us!" Mr. Crawley said. "It was an honor, an appointment. It was a new station. They needed someone trustworthy and capable to get it going."

Euphemia nodded proudly. "It was quite a bit different around here then." She spoke more easily now that the talk had turned from her brother. "The lumber companies had just built a landing a little ways down the coast—had to dig a tunnel to get to it, but that didn't stop them when there was money to be made. They started bringing in men by the dozen, and they worked their way into the mountains, chopping and sawing and generally stirring up country that hadn't felt a man's boot for, oh, more than a century, I'd say, since the padres had come through. You'd be surprised at what we could hear all the way out on this morro. The axes thunking and thunking, the saws rasping. Did you know that trees scream when they fall?"

"It's the wood tearing apart," Mr. Crawley explained. "It's not really screaming."

Euphemia hardly paused. "After months of that, it got quiet all of a sudden. It was the strangest thing."

"Somebody found gold," Mr. Crawley said, nodding. "That's why. Gold beats trees."

"He'd been washing up in the creek, that's the story we heard, this fellow—who knows his name—and he hadn't sense enough to keep it quiet; he ran yelping high and low that the stuff was there for the taking," Euphemia said. "We couldn't hear that, but Henry went down to see why the trees had stopped falling, and that's what they told him. They'd followed the flecks upstream and discovered nuggets big enough to pay."

"The men were trying to use their ax heads as shovels. They wanted to know did we have shovels and picks up here!" Mr. Crawley clucked his tongue indignantly at the idea of using Lighthouse Service tools for such a task.

"Archie wanted to try his luck," Euphemia went on disdainfully. "That didn't surprise us. It was no use arguing that he had a duty here when it looked like easy riches just over the ridge. He took a hammer and a screwdriver and the kitchen sieve, and he was gone within an hour after Henry got back. Didn't bother to pack himself a blanket or a knapsack of food, just rode the steam donkey down the mountain and was gone."

"Did he find gold?" Oskar asked.

"Not an ounce!" Mr. Crawley said.

"He didn't find gold." Euphemia paused with dramatic flair. "What he found was a woman." She said it straightforwardly, but her look was rueful.

"Where did she come from?" I asked. "Was she a gold rusher?" I'd never imagined a woman panning for gold, but why not? "I mean, a prospector?"

"I doubt she cared about the gold," Euphemia said. "She showed up one morning in his camp, deranged with fever, weak from disease that was no doubt dysentery, among other things, caught from those dirty men using the creek as a toilet."

"She was lucky it was Archie who found her," Oskar said. "Who knows what some men might do in those circumstances?"

"Yes," Euphemia said dryly. "It's always surprising what some men will do."

No one said anything for a long time, thinking, I supposed, of the horrors that might have been.

"Archie traded the lighthouse tools for the use of a wagon," Euphemia said. "And he brought her up here."

"She was a sight!" Mr. Crawley said. "Hardly a woman at all, really, when she first come. Her hair was like black seaweed matted up, and she didn't have a stitch of clothes on! Not proper clothes, anyway."

"She was wearing a skirt made of soft bark—it was quite clever, really," Euphemia explained, "and a little apronlike shirt sewn from rabbit pelts. They were perfectly good clothes, considering. Of course, I had to dispose of them. If they weren't full of disease, they were filthy beyond cleaning."

"Where had she come from?"

Euphemia shrugged. "From somewhere in the mountains. She was obviously an Indian."

"An Indian!" Oskar's eyes were wide. "A wild Indian? No one has seen Indians here for decades."

"Yes, we read that in the Lighthouse Service pamphlet," I said, ever the earnest schoolgirl.

"That may be true," Mr. Crawley said. "Before the loggers, who was here to do the seeing? Anyone might have been living there."

"Obviously, she was," Euphemia finished.

"Do you think there are others?" Oskar asked eagerly.

"We don't believe so," Mr. Crawley said.

"I thought she might have people to go to. But she didn't," Euphemia added sadly.

"That's terrible!" I burst out.

"The last of her tribe," Oskar breathed.

"What's her name?" I asked.

"Oh, her words were impossible!" Euphemia said. "I can't even repeat them. She sounded lots of them low in her throat, like growling."

"You mean her language was guttural? Like German?" I asked.

"I don't know German." Euphemia dismissed my suggestion with a wave of her hand. "There was some sound like an 'h' and something like an 'n.'"

"So we called her Helen," Mr. Crawley finished.

"This house, your house, was empty," Euphemia went on. "So we made up a bed for her here, and we treated her ailments as well as we could."

"Euphemia did it," Mr. Crawley said. "She's the one fixed her up."

Euphemia brushed off his pride. "There's no cure for dysentery. You either get better or you don't, so I don't credit myself with her recovery except that I gave her fresh water to drink. Obviously, she did get better after a time. One day she came sniffing her way out, real cautious, like an animal creeping out of a den, and there she stood, blinking in that doorway." She pointed at our door.

"That's right! I remember she smelled the air. Like a dog," Mr. Crawley said.

I wanted to say that of course she did. These people had grown so used to the smells of the sea and the beach that they no longer registered them. I was no longer assailed by their sharpness, but to one who'd just arrived, the very air was strange.

"Her tribe had probably used the resources of the coast," Oskar said. "I suppose she was remembering other journeys here."

After all, she and I were not the same.

"She did like to sit and look out at the water," Euphemia said. "Well, I oughtn't to say she liked it—how could I know what she liked? All I can say is that's what she did, and she looked very strange doing it. I'd given her my red calico, but she wouldn't put it on. Just kept wearing my old nightdress. And her head was nearly bald. I'd tried to comb her hair out for her, but she wouldn't let me, kept pushing my hands away."

"She burned it," Mr. Crawley said with satisfaction. "Burned it all off. Now, that was a stink. And her ears stuck straight out!"

"It wasn't a bad idea, though," Mrs. Crawley said. "Who knows what disease was caught in all that hair? I appreciated her getting rid of it."

"Probably some sort of ritual," Oskar said. "I've read that some western tribes burn off their hair as a sign of mourning."

The excitement in his voice caught my attention, and I looked at him. His face was animated; he was beginning to resemble the old Oskar.

Euphemia nodded. "Maybe so."

"Remember how she liked the water, Phemia?" Mr. Crawley said. "Remember how we'd look down and see her rolling around in the waves, just like an otter?"

I thought of the dark head that had scared the seals off their rock.

"She was a great deal of trouble," Euphemia said, but her tone was fond, as if she were speaking of an exasperating child. "She was afraid of the light and especially of the foghorn. She wouldn't touch any of the canned food, only the pilot bread and the cornmeal."

"She caught fish, though," Mr. Crawley said. "And brought up abalones as big as this plate. Bigger. And she was good with the children. She's the one started them picking up all that junk, shells and whatnot."

We didn't seem to be getting at the heart of the matter.

"Why isn't she here now?" I asked. "Why does she live—"

"Like an Indian?" Oskar broke in. "I imagine this life was uncomfortable to her. Indians can commune with nature, you know, in a way that we've lost. I would think she would have longed to return to her traditional way of life. Isn't that right?"

Henry, absorbed in his pipe, made no effort to reply. Euphemia, too, said nothing for some time. She kept her eyes on a stretch of tablecloth in front of one of the children's empty places. I assumed she was considering Oskar's suggestion.

"She just didn't take," she offered grudgingly. "She is, after all, a wild Indian, like Oskar said. One morning she was gone." She sighed. "It's true that she prefers her ways, and I believe it's best to leave her to herself. That's what she wishes. We can't force her to live here."

I thought of that first day on the beach with the children, when Euphemia had appeared, striding out of what I'd understood to be nowhere. "You visit her!"

Euphemia frowned. "I leave her a few things from time to time, yes."

The children visit her, too, I thought, but I kept quiet about this.

"We were docked for that blanket," Mr. Crawley grumbled.

Euphemia shrugged.

"Did Archie love her?" I asked recklessly. The idea of him rescuing her struck me as very romantic.

"If he did, it was a twisted sort of love," Euphemia said. She rose from the table, reverting to the stony and practical Mrs. Crawley who'd met us when we first arrived. "I did my best, but he ruined everything." She hoisted the large stack of plates she'd accumulated and went into the kitchen.

I stood to collect the glasses. Euphemia was already scraping slops into a bucket for the chickens when I stepped into the kitchen. The slump of her shoulders told me that it was she who had loved the Indian.

CHAPTER 24

As SOON AS we'd closed the door behind the Crawleys, Oskar turned to me. "You have to show me that cave."

"I told you she was interesting." I couldn't keep some irritation from my voice; he'd hardly paid attention when I first told him about her.

"You didn't say she was an Indian. A wild Indian. An Indian unsullied by contact with whites."

"She had contact!" I protested. "She was living here!" Exactly here, I thought, looking around the room with new understanding.

He waved one hand vaguely in the air, as if this fact were a fly he could brush away. "Before that."

"Before that, we have no idea how she lived." I began to gather the flotsam we'd scattered over the floor, separating the remains of the shipwrecks from the stuff of the sea.

"Exactly! Exactly! We have no idea. Don't you want to know? She may show us things about her people that no white man has ever seen. Can you find that cave again, do you think?"

I, too, wanted to go back to the cave, though the idea of bringing Oskar with me made me nervous. While his renewed energy pleased me, I knew that it was a beam to be focused with care, and the Indian woman seemed a fragile subject.

"I think I can find it," I said. "We'll have to wait for drier weather."

"Why? What's a little wet? Are you afraid you'll melt?" he teased.

"Oskar, please be careful!" He'd begun to help me tidy the room, but his hands on the delicate objects were far too eager and rough. Gently, I took from him a dried crab with all eight of its legs attached. "I just don't believe it's safe, that's all. Anyway, she's been there for years. I'm sure she'll be there when the rain stops."

Would she? It was difficult to see how she survived. I realized that until tonight I'd considered her almost a natural curiosity, more akin to the mussels and sea stars and octopi than a real human being who would feel the cold and grow hungry. Had she huddled in her cave for all these soaking days, much as we'd huddled in our houses? The logs I'd seen, tangled and bleached among the rocks, must have come sweeping down from the mountains like battering rams in churning rivers of rainwater, and I pictured them piling up at the entrance to the cave, trapping her. I could envision the water washing inside, the sealskin floor wet through, the acorns floating away, the pyramid of cans tumbled down, and a body, with the small black head that I'd glimpsed in the ocean, lying among abalone shells and fish bones in one corner, nearly dead, as the baby otter had been.

I started when Oskar touched my shoulder. He let his hand slip down my arm until his fingers interlaced with mine. "We have a little time," he said, "before my shift."

In our bed—had this been her bed, too?—I could tell it was not contemplation of me that had brought this on but the thought of the Indian woman.

CHAPTER 25

O SKAR DIDN'T COME home for breakfast after his shift the next morning. I took little notice, though his habits had been extremely regular since he'd given up electricity. Often repairs or maintenance required two keepers, and he would stay on at the tower. When he didn't appear at lunch, I wondered, but I wasn't alarmed, nor was I eager to go searching for him among the rain-lashed outbuildings. Our meal was cold duck. His portion could wait.

At three or four in the afternoon, the waning of what light had shimmied through the heavy clouds made me restless at last to know his whereabouts. Annoyed, I put on my Lighthouse Service oilskin and plunged into the rain. I splashed to the workshop and then to the barn, climbed to the top of the lighthouse, looked into the storeroom, and knocked on the Crawleys' and Archie Johnston's doors. I walked around the residence, checked to see whether the steam donkey had gone down the mountain, searched the upstairs of our house—in case he'd come back while I was out—and went back to the lighthouse. No one had seen him since the Crawleys had left us the night before. Anxiety began to press at me. It occurred to me that he might have tried to find the cave, and I was as uncomfortable with the idea of his drinking in its wonders without my supervision as I was with the worry that he'd gotten lost among the rocks.

Archie heard him finally from the catwalk, his call a thin bleat that the wind by some freakish turn happened to carry up from the beach. That morning, before his shift had officially ended, Oskar had started down the children's way, lost his footing on the rain-slick rocks and mud halfway down, and tumbled the rest of the way. He'd been lying in the rain for hours, water streaming down the morro around and over him, one leg twisted away from his body at an impossible angle.

"This is a merry Christmas," Euphemia said.

He gasped when I touched him.

"I'm no doctor," Euphemia said, "but I can assure you this will hurt." She turned to her brother. "Find me a bit of wood. About this big." She held up one hand, showing the spread between her index finger and thumb.

The storms had thrown up a good deal of driftwood; Archie didn't have to scrounge for long before he returned with a piece. "What's it for?" He handed it to Euphemia. "You can't make a splint out of that."

"To keep him from biting his tongue in two."

She pushed the stick into Oskar's mouth, which stopped his teeth from chattering, although it seemed to make the rest of his body shake more violently, despite the sodden blankets I'd tried to wrap him in. I squeezed his hand, which meant I couldn't press my palms to my ears to dull his screams.

I was frightened when he fell into a faint as Euphemia struggled to straighten his leg, but she said it was a mercy. She tied the leg to a pole with rags, and Oskar came to consciousness as Mr. Crawley and Archie, using a ladder to stand in for a stretcher, carried him around the bottom of the mountain to the steam donkey.

When we'd gotten him into our bed, Euphemia gave me from her stores a large bottle of laudanum with which to dose him.

"Keep it up regular," she warned. "Don't let the pain sneak up on him, or you'll have a dickens of a time rooting it out." She turned to Oskar indignantly. "Where did you think you were going?"

"To the beach," he said between gritted teeth.

"You've caused a lot of trouble. And it's only just begun. You'll be in this bed for over a month, at least. Was it the electricity you were after?"

He shut his eyes so that she might believe he'd fainted again.

Later, when I was certain he was safe, I took my turn. "For heaven's sake! Why couldn't you for once in your life wait?"

"I must see her!"

"'I must! I must!'" I mocked. "You help yourself to whatever you please and never mind what I say or feel. I told you not to go!"

He bit his lip and turned away. He was badly hurt and helpless, and I felt ashamed of my anger. Nevertheless, although I had no clear idea of his intentions and neither, I believed, did he, I wasn't sorry that he'd have no chance of finding the Indian for a very long time.

For the next few weeks, my days were made of running: up the stairs with food and drink and down again with the chamber pot and soiled dishes. Every few hours, the laudanum had to be spooned and the pillows pounded, pencil shavings brushed from the bed, fallen books retrieved from the floor. In between, I kept up the children's lessons as well as I could, setting them tasks that I could oversee in spurts between the kitchen and the bedroom and the outhouse. We would start a chapter of history or some long division or a bit of Latin vocabulary, and inevitably, his voice would come through the door. Could he have more water? He'd finished his book. His back was uncomfortable; what could be done about it? He had some questions for Archie; would I find him?

Archie? I would have felt shy around Archie Johnston after the anger he'd revealed on Christmas Eve and the story that had come of it, but the confusion and worry and bustle over Oskar's accident had wiped that slate clean. He came, his gaze straying everywhere as he passed through the parlor and climbed the stairs. He shut the bedroom door behind him, but his voice and Oskar's rumbled loudly enough to cause me to close the schoolroom door as well, so we could concentrate on the task of adding three-digit numbers. After that, Archie began to show up regularly around ten o'clock, his boots clumping up the narrow wooden steps.

I complained to Oskar as I rubbed his back with liniment to keep bedsores from forming. "I don't like it that he just lets himself in."

"That way he doesn't interrupt your lessons. Don't you have enough trips up and down as it is?"

"What do you talk about so long?" What difference did it make? I scolded myself. I ought to be relieved that someone else was seeing to Oskar for an hour or two.

"The Indian. I'm writing down everything he can remember. The circumstances under which he found her. Her clothing and habits. Her words and gestures." He touched the logbook beside him on the bed. "I'm not sure what'll turn out to be anthropologically significant, so I want to be thorough."

"Anthropologically significant?" I riffled through the pages with my thumb. To me, they were impenetrable, densely covered with his frenzied shorthand.

"You remember what Philip was saying? About California Indians being nearly extinct and the importance of gathering information about their culture and language, their whole way of life?"

"You think the people at the university would be interested in her?"

"Of course they would! I'm going to be the one to study her, though. She's my find."

"She's not a find, exactly, is she? I mean, she's a woman they all knew here. She's not, you know, a phenomenon of nature, like electromagnetism. You're not planning to do experiments on her, are you?"

He laughed. "I'm only learning what I can about her. I do think she must be approached scientifically. The way Franz Boas studied the Eskimos. She's a fantastic opportunity for science."

"And for you, I suppose."

"Well." He shrugged. "I'm not afraid to have greatness thrust upon me. Come, you can't say you aren't curious, too."

I could not, so I said nothing.

He yawned. "I'm awfully tired. It's more work than you'd imagine, trying to keep Archie focused on useful information. He keeps wanting to talk about how Euphemia made her go."

"Made her go? Why would she do that?"

He'd already closed his eyes. "I don't know. Maybe to spite her brother. That's what he seems to think. Anyway, I'm grateful to her. If that Indian had been living here all this time, she'd be pretty much spoiled."

I grabbed my own sleep here and there, because I had to cover Oskar's shift at the light, as well as care for him during the day. On stormy nights, Euphemia joined me, claiming that she wanted to be sure I didn't blow away. That did seem a real possibility. When we walked to the light, we had to bend nearly double against the wind that threatened to turn our skirts to sails, and pull ourselves forward hand over hand on the rail to cross the little bridge. Twice a shift, wearing the black spectacles, we edged our way around the outside of the glass cage that housed the light, one hand clutching a brass handhold, the other wiping salt streaks from the panes as strenuously as the tearing wind allowed. To release the handhold while on that narrow catwalk, with only the thin ribbon of an iron rail to interrupt a fall, would be flirting with suicide, but I was more invigorated than afraid. My hands were strong; I wouldn't let go. Most frightening was the walk home in the morning, when the wind pushed us along, shoving violently at our backs, as if it meant to sweep us right off the rock into the lashing water and black rocks below.

Euphemia was ecstatic. "This is why we're needed," she said more than once, gazing up at the light that seemed as much a beacon to us as to those at sea. "This is when the light does its real work."

I was grateful for her company not only when we were struggling through the wind and rain but also at the other extreme, when I was trying to stay awake in the warm boiler room.

"What was she like?" I asked tentatively one night, when we were seated with mending in our laps from the basket we kept handy to fill these odd hours. I'd come close to this question several times but backed away, afraid of Euphemia's annoyance. Clearly, the woman in the rocks was an uncomfortable topic.

"Who?"

"The Indian woman. Helen." Our conversation proceeded in fits and starts between blasts of the foghorn.

Euphemia's needle moved quickly, forming serviceable but sloppy stitches. Neither my mother nor my domestic sciences teacher would have approved. "She wasn't much use," she said, repeating the assessment she'd given at Christmas.

"Did you like her company?" I insisted. "Was she a friend to you?"

She stopped sewing and tugged firmly on the patch, making certain it was secure. "Not a friend, exactly, no," she said slowly. The newly mended garment, a threadbare pinafore, covered her lap. It had a pink flower on the bib, obviously appliquéd in her own loose style, and she began to pick those stitches out. "Pink is Mary's color," she explained. "Janie likes blue."

She was quiet through two blasts of the horn, and I feared I would have to prompt her, but she went on, holding her work close to her face in the dim light. "She was afraid at first, of Archie and Henry especially. Who knows what had happened to her on that mountain, among all those screaming trees? No wonder she was afraid! Even from a distance, she would look at the men only out of the corner of her eye, and when they were close, she would look away and freeze, like a fawn hoping not to be noticed, waiting for them to pass.

"Archie had an idea, I think, that he was like some prince in a fairy tale. Because he'd found her, I suppose. He picked wildflowers for her once—you'd be surprised how many blooms come out of this rock in the spring. When she wouldn't take them from his hands, he laid them in her lap." She squeezed her eyes tightly shut for a moment, perhaps to refresh them for her sewing, although it seemed to me that she was trying to pinch off the painful scene she was remembering. "She kept her face turned away from him, willing herself elsewhere, it looked like. I should have called him away. But I hoped . . . well . . ." She stopped speaking and then started fresh. "When he'd gone, she stood and let the flowers fall from her lap. They shriveled in an hour. Blew away. Wildflowers aren't meant to be picked," she added with a touch of her old imperiousness.

"She was happiest with the children," she continued, speaking more lightly as she squinted to thread her needle with blue. "They were so much littler then, of course! Just babies. She was always rocking Nicholas, singing her peculiar songs. Such a harsh sound to my ears. I was a little alarmed when I saw her brown fingers on his soft skin. I wanted to take him away from her. But she was gentle with him, and he seemed to welcome her touch, so I let them alone. I considered that we must frighten her, our language and ways being as strange to her as hers were to us, and the baby, being much like any other baby, must have been a comfort. She played with Mary and little Edward, too, some game having to do with throwing stones and feathers into the air and another with pebbles. She would laugh as if she enjoyed it as much as they did. Or she would spin Mary—you know how you do, with your hands locked around each other's wrists. The children don't remember any of it.

"They brought her things—bits of ribbon, colored rocks, cans with pictures that they liked. What else did they have to give? She didn't much like the food, but she stacked the cans on the table like a centerpiece. As Henry said, she brought the children things from the beach, little shells and suchlike. Well, you know their mess."

Yes, I knew it. While Euphemia had been speaking, I'd been darning, repairing a hole in one of Oskar's socks. I stroked the newly woven patch with my thumb, thinking that their mess was my mess now, and Helen had begun it. The idea made me feel close to her.

"No." Euphemia shook her head as if she'd been reading my mind. "She wasn't like you. When she was well and no longer haggard, I realized that she was very young, more of a girl than a woman. You are a friend to me, but she was more like a daughter, needing to be taught, oh, everything! How to set a table and how to brush her teeth. Even how to sit in a chair!"

"How could you make her go, then?" I didn't mean to say it aloud and accusingly, but the notion that Euphemia could push away someone she regarded as nearly a daughter shocked me.

"Make her go?" she repeated with disgust. She stabbed at the pinafore with such force that I feared she would draw blood. "That's what he says, does he? I'll tell you something!" She threw down the mending and stared at me fiercely. "I wish I *had* made her go! I wish I'd pushed her right back down the morro the day he brought her up here. It would have been unthinkably cruel, but it would have been far better than what I did do. What I let him do." She'd risen and began to pace the room, obviously tormented.

"Yes, I helped her go. After I caught him sneaking out of her house. I knew what he'd been up to while Henry and I were occupied at the light. I understood why she was so afraid of him. Yes, after that, I helped her go. Escape, I call it. I thought—and maybe she thought, too—that she'd find more like herself. Her own people."

"Why didn't you send *him* away?" It was a wail of futility. It was too late, far too late, for any course except the one she'd chosen. "How can you stand to see him? To live here with him?" How could I?

"Oh, we tried to make him go. I thought it would be easy. After all, he hated it here. But he reminded us of the judge's order; we'd promised to keep him; that was the reason we had this post. And then he threatened to tell the inspector we'd been harboring a savage, feeding her our rations, allowing her to cause all manner of damage." Here, Euphemia imitated her brother's drawl. "'An uncivilized creature like that might even destroy your precious Fresnel lens.'" She laughed unpleasantly. "He thought we were helpless. That he had us all trapped and he could have his way. I'm not saying what I did was right. Probably it would have been better to push him off the edge. But you must be prepared to go far to thwart a person like my brother, and I'm ashamed to say that I wasn't. He is my brother, after all. Anyway," she went on with a little shake of her head, deliberately changing her mood, "no point crying over spilled milk. Helen was here for a short and unhappy time, and now she's returned to a life that's not much different, I would guess, from the one she had before he found her. It was the best I could do." At this, she shouldered the shovel and began to march up the stairs. It was dawn, time to dispose of the birds that had flown into our false sun.

I was relieved that Oskar had finished his talks with Archie. I didn't want Archie Johnston coming into our house again.

CHAPTER 26

Eventually, the rain and wind faltered, and for stretches of days the sky was a clear, washed blue and the sun burned steadily. It was foreign weather to me, the air being cold but the sun fierce, so that both extremes of temperature made themselves felt at once. The gold-tinged landscape I'd grown accustomed to in the fall had become vivid with greens and blues. Shoots pushed up between cracks in the rock and seemed to spread by the hour until the morro had bejeweled itself in orange paintbrush and yellow lupine. I thought of Archie piling flowers in Helen's lap.

I'd begun to look askance at Archie Johnston. I couldn't decide whether he'd hoped she might love him or whether he was simply a monster, so I kept well clear of him.

The pain in Oskar's leg lessened, and he became restless. He complained that he'd read through all of the library and that he was tired of pilot bread and bully beef. Indeed, we were all sick of the sailors' rations to which we'd been reduced. Though we joked about scurvy, constant expectation and repeated disappointment had made us all, even mild Mr. Crawley, irritable by the time a longboat landed on the beach on a gray and dripping day in February. I eagerly opened a bulky package addressed to me in a familiar slanted hand.

Dear Trudy—

I'm delighted to hear from you. What fascinating experiences you must be enjoying. It was most kind of you to send these specimens. Some are well known to me from pictures, but some I've never seen before. I wonder if you might be willing to ship more of these creatures to Milwaukee so that I could use them in my class. We could study the external features of dried specimens—in that case, variety is wanted—but I would also like at least thirty of a single type preserved in a flexible state. Since I don't know in what quantity these items present themselves, I must leave the choice as to which in your hands.

I've enclosed some issues of a magazine that prints, among its last pages, advertisements from companies that sell preserving alcohol and appropriate containers. I've also taken the liberty of enclosing a check for ten dollars from my college account to act as a down payment. If this proposition is of no interest to you, simply tear it up.

Your drawings are very fine, and I do encourage you to continue with them, with an eye toward eventual publication as a catalog of Pacific tidal life. I can find no record of several of the organisms you've represented, so you would be doing biology a great service, indeed, were you to commit all of your discoveries to paper.

Yours very truly,

Cecelia Dodson

I read the letter twice. Admittedly, the flatness of the first few lines was a disappointment. I'd hoped, I saw now, for a livelier interest in my life and a more intimate correspondence. Still, I experienced a frisson at the signature. I'd been aware of Miss Dodson's first name but had never presumed to think of her as anything other than "Miss." And her proposal—the idea that things I collected could become a part of Miss Dodson's class, that girls in Milwaukee, even Miss Dodson (Cecelia Dodson!) herself, would examine them, marking down what they observed in their laboratory books—delighted me. Even more exciting was the thought that a catalog I could devise would interest my teacher, not in the condescending way she would note the efforts of a student but as work that would truly expand her knowledge.

Since Euphemia and I had grown closer, I'd realized that she'd been starving for friendship. Now I saw that whether she'd been aware of it or not, she'd also been in need of a means by which to reach into the world beyond our mountain, for she was as animated as I by Miss Dodson's plan. In the lighthouse at night, I paged through the scientific journals Miss Dodson had sent and read out choice bits. One of our favorite articles involved experiments performed on my old friend the sea urchin. It seemed that a fellow in Switzerland had divided an urchin egg in two, and from each half egg, he'd grown half an urchin.

"What was the point," Euphemia said, laughing, "of growing half an urchin?"

I explained that if only half a creature grew from a divided egg, it would mean that every cell, even in the tiniest of eggs, had been assigned from the moment of its existence—maybe before—to be a crumb of the heart or the stomach and, in the case of more complex creatures, the fingers, toes, ears, or tongue. Each cell had its role, and that role was preordained, maybe not by God, exactly, but by its nature. It would be impossible to change that nature, no matter how hard one might try.

Then a second scientist said the first was dead wrong. When he repeated the experiment, the half-eggs grew into whole urchins. I found this notion pleasing, believing it meant that if something were damaged—even cut entirely in two—it might adapt and, given time enough to grow, become whole again. In a leap of the kind Oskar might make between the physical and philosophical realms, I conceived of myself as a being that had been severed in two when I'd left the place that had formed me and come to this world where so little was familiar. I was beginning to feel filaments start to grow from the half that remained, and I sensed I was adapting and becoming whole again.

We also studied the advertisements. Before I could collect any specimens to preserve "in a flexible state," I'd have to procure containers that would neither corrode nor easily break—heavy glass, probably—and enough ethanol or some such chemical to act as a preservative. I liked the serious sound of the Chicago Scientific Company, "supplier of reliable apparatus and chemical glassware," along with "a complete line of reagents, stains, lacquers, and cements." I could make over Miss Dodson's check to them and ask them to send thirty jars.

"Better make it thirty-five," Euphemia said. "Some are bound to break." She then did the figures in the margin of our logbook and determined that I had enough money for seventy jars and the alcohol to fill them. "If we're going to have a business," she said, "we'd best be prepared for future orders."

The avidity with which she tackled what had almost immediately become *our* endeavor surprised me. She'd always been energetic, but in a grim, dutiful way. Now she brightened and bubbled; it was as if the idea of organizing a business had opened some long-dammed passage inside her, and her enthusiasm and ideas rushed forth. Through night after stormy night in the lighthouse, collecting and selling biological specimens became our electromagnetism. The long, dark stretches of time between the trimming and the filling, together with our awareness of the long, dark stretches of space that surrounded us, encouraged us to lose perspective as we bandied our plans about. "How many colleges would you say this country has?" Euphemia asked one night. "Wouldn't all of 'em need specimens?"

We decided that the children could help gather. It was what they did, anyway. I must handle the chemicals, because they could be flammable and, Euphemia suspected, dangerous in other ways as well. She wouldn't want to see any of her children pickled!

We would pack the jars of preserved specimens and the boxes of dry ones in grass and sawdust, as I'd done with my samples. Henry Crawley could be doing plenty more sawing, Euphemia said. The animal pens needed repair; the steam donkey could use a new platform. Oskar could make those shelves he'd promised. That would generate packing material for a good while.

"And we always have plenty of empty barrels," I added.

Even figuring shipping into our costs, we determined that in two or three years, we likely would have built up a profitable business, supplying schools and laboratories all over the continent with crates of specimens preserved and dried.

When our empire began to spread to Europe—"Think," Euphemia said, "what the Swiss could do with *our* urchins!"—I reminded her that we must first compose an order to the Chicago Scientific Company.

Without hesitation, she opened a fresh logbook, ripped a page from it, and handed it to me. "Write it on this."

CHAPTER 27

ALTHOUGH OUR ORDER was soon ready and the check enclosed, it had to await the tender, which would have to come twice before we could begin collecting specimens to preserve. In the meantime, I determined to work on the catalog. I surveyed the basic sketches I'd done of the creatures in our tubs. They were competent and detailed, reasonably good as far as they went, though I understood little about what I'd drawn and each picture stood alone, unrelated to the others. Bestowing some meaningful organization on a comprehensive volume would be difficult. I was irritated with myself for my lack of attention in my biology classes and wished for a more complete taxonomy than *Some Species* provided.

What I was sure I could produce, and probably render better than nearly anyone else Miss Dodson knew, were studies that would show an entire tide pool and the arrangement of the creatures within it, perhaps indicate how they coexisted. I began to send the children to Oskar, so he could conduct morning lessons from his bed, while I went to the beach with one of the purloined logbooks under my arm.

My custom was to wear shoes (my kid leather pair, because my work shoes were in the Indian's care) until I'd slithered down the side of the morro, since its stones were sharp, but abandon them along with my stockings as soon as I reached the sand. I acquired the knack of walking on the packed stuff at the water's edge, where my feet seemed to skim the surface, leaving a trail that vanished in the space of a wave. When I reached the rocks, I tucked the skirt of my duster into my bloomers—no one would see me, after all—and plunged into the froth, working my way around the spit of rock that marked the end of our beach and the beginning of what I thought of as "her" territory.

The pool lined with urchins was my favorite. I could spend two hours there easily, perched on a certain comfortable rock, drawing and turning in my mind the problems Nature set for me. I asked myself what business these creatures had being bright and beautiful—the dark red and the brilliant blue starfish, the violet sea urchins, the aqua anemones. It seemed dangerous for them to call attention to themselves; it must make them easy prey for those that might want to pluck them out and eat them. Surely it would be safer to meld with the gray and black of the rocks or the green of the weeds. I tried to observe what frightened these creatures and what tempted them forward, the means by which they moved and the ways in which they protected themselves. I thought about their small scope, whole lives passed in a basin, neither knowing nor caring what lay beyond the rock wall beside them. While they stayed still, their surroundings changed; with every tide, old water seeped away and a fresh supply replaced it. Whatever the waves carried in was invisible to me, but it was obviously essential to these creatures.

Inevitably, while I was in this place, my mind would stray to thoughts of that other being who made her home here. As a child, I'd read that Indians could become nearly invisible, so completely could they blend with their surroundings. I often studied the shadows between the rocks, trying to determine whether a dark curve might be a hank of black hair or whether a flutter of light was the movement of the hem of a bark skirt.

More than once, pretending even to myself that I was merely searching for new pools, I made my way down the narrow passage to her cave and stood again in the doorway, examining the silky floor and the shell bowls and the tightly woven baskets. As far as I could tell, the place hadn't changed since the children had shown it to me. I worried that, wary of our smell, she'd abandoned it, like a bird its nest. I felt inexplicably desolate at the thought.

One afternoon I saw that she had come to my tide pool before me. Arranged in a perfect circle on my rock was a single abalone shell on a leather thong. I knew it was a gift for me.

That day I did no drawing but wandered in widening rings, peering half hopefully, half fearfully into hidey-holes between the rocks and among the piles of logs. I longed to see her; at the same time, I shrank from an encounter. I was terrified that she might be like the Indian I'd seen from the train, shuffling and gaping, dirty and debased. Perhaps she would beg, as that woman had. I wondered if I would appear marvelous and strange to her, and whether she would want to touch my fine hair and the refined fabric of my dress, the way Indians did in books. I searched as long as I dared, knowing that the tide would come in relentlessly and the sun would inevitably dart below the horizon. I found no other sign of her.

I arrived home much later than usual, and I let more time ebb away while I built up the fire in the stove and absently stirred some sort of meat and vegetable in a pan for our supper. When I came into our bedroom with the tray at last, Oskar was standing beside the bed. He'd begun recently to test his leg, hobbling between the two rooms upstairs. He feared it had lost a little of its length in the healing, but since it wouldn't bear his full weight, he couldn't tell.

He lowered himself onto the mattress, closing his eyes briefly with the pain of that movement. "Where've you been?"

I'd used those same words and peevish tone months before, when he'd not shown up for dinner at the time I'd expected. How changed I was as I stood here wearing my duster, my hair as carelessly pinned as Euphemia's, barefoot, with an Indian's amulet hanging from my neck. The only evidence of the Milwaukee girl that my family and friends might have recognized was the coral necklace that had been my Christmas present over a year before. The necklace he'd taken so as to feel close to me.

I'd tucked the abalone shell into my dress while I'd heated our dinner, unsure whether I wished to share it. But the sight of Little O, hurt and helpless, moved me. I remembered following his fingers down the pages of his books as he opened the world for me. I remembered how his eager eyes had appreciated me as no one else's had. I remembered the rapture of his hand on mine.

"I went to the rocks. Look." With the care that seemed to befit its import, I lifted the thong over my head and held it out to him.

"What's this? Something the children made?"

"No. It's from her. She left it for me."

His eyes brightened, as I'd known they would. He turned the abalone over several times and ran his fingers along the leather.

It was nothing, really. The children could have made it. Abalone shells come equipped with breathing holes, so she'd needed to do nothing more than thread the leather through one of them and tie a knot. What had impressed me was that she'd given it to me.

But Oskar was curious about the object itself. "What is it used for, I wonder. Is it spiritual or practical?"

"Isn't it just a necklace?" I reached to take it back. He ignored my hand.

"I doubt it. It may not be meant to be worn around the neck." He frowned. "Give me your notebook."

I passed him my catalog-in-progress. He flipped haphazardly through the pages until he found a clean one.

"I'll need a pencil as well." He was impatient to begin. "Get me a ruler from the workshop, would you?"

I obliged him in this, too, wondering what information he might glean. What I saw as a token from one woman to another, he perceived as an artifact that might reveal a sliver of humankind's very nature.

While I looked on, Oskar measured, weighed, described, and traced; he noted that one edge had some dirt clinging to it and another appeared worn. In the end, however, his rendition of the thing on paper didn't much resemble the actual object.

"Here," I said. "Let me draw it." I couldn't capture the iridescence of the abalone, but my sketch recorded the correct shape and size and the relative roughness and smoothness of the surfaces. In other words, I drew a convincing picture of a shell on a string.

"Do we know anything more?" I asked, returning to the bedroom sometime later with the dinner I'd reheated. He'd apparently finished his examination, and the pendant hung from one of the knobs at the head of the bed.

"I suppose not." He shrugged. "It's just one piece, completely out of context. We need a much fuller picture if we're going to make anything of it."

CHAPTER 28

Between the time I'd spent among the rocks and the hours I'd devoted to examining the pendant with Oskar, I'd lost all opportunity for sleep. When I reported to the lighthouse for my shift, I'd been awake for over twenty-four hours. I finished my first round of chores—refilling the oil reservoirs, clipping the wicks, changing the mantles, and setting the chain at the top of the tower—and then pulled the table underneath the spot where the chain of the foghorn came inching down, climbed onto it, and folded a rag under my head. I counted on the chain's cold, heavy touch to awaken me, knowing that then I would have the time it would take for the chain to travel the distance from the tabletop to the floor in which to run up the stairs and pull it to the top so as to keep the horn sounding its proper rhythm. The table was a hard bed, but I was asleep the moment I closed my eyes. In what seemed like minutes later, I was awakened not by the chain but by a hand on my arm.

"Dangerous," Archie Johnston said, "sleeping by a burning lantern." His breath was sharp with liquor, and he smelled unwashed. "I saw you today on the beach. Far down the beach. What were you doing there?"

"Drawing. I'm making a catalog of—"

He shook his head violently. "Not that. I don't care about that." He clutched my arm again. "What you had around your neck. It's hers, isn't it? Did she give it to you?"

"Yes. Well, I don't know for certain," I said, pulling my arm away and pushing myself into a sitting position on the table. "I found it."

"So you haven't seen her?"

I shook my head.

"It's for scaring snakes," he said. "She showed Euphemia once. The women wear them when they're harvesting. The shell flashes in the sun—zing, zing!" He made a quick motion with his hands near my eyes, and I drew back, startled. "That keeps the snakes away." He pushed his face as close to mine as he could. "Do you need protection from snakes?"

"She was mine, you know!" he said suddenly, pulling back and beginning to pace, propelled by anger. "'Stay away from her,' my sister says to me, as if she's my keeper. But when she wanted something, she took it. She makes out like she's so superior, but she's no better than anyone else, my sister."

He stopped speaking and looked into the distance, or perhaps toward the house where Euphemia presumably lay asleep, there being no reason on this calm night that I should need her help. Then he leaned toward me, his breath heavy on my face. I could see the black dots where his beard grew.

"Listen," he hissed, "whatever you do with her, you and Swann, I get a share. She's mine, after all. I found her."

"What are you talking about? We're not *doing* anything with her!"

The first link of the foghorn's iron chain fell against my shoulder. "The horn!" I exclaimed, alarmed.

To my relief, he made no attempt to stop me as I slipped off the far side of the table and rushed upstairs. I stayed there a good while, calming myself by deliberately performing the tasks the light required. When I could find no more to do, I crept as quietly as I could halfway down and bent low to peek into the boiler room. Archie had gone.

*　*　*

Oskar was sitting on the side of the bed when I came in the next morning, doing what he called his "strengthening exercises." He'd put a can of green corn into our valise, hooked the handles over the ankle of his bad leg, and was lifting it, sweating with the effort. He counted quietly as I told him what Archie had said.

"And he was drunk! It was disgusting!" Archie's smell lingered in my nostrils. I inhaled it with every breath.

"I wouldn't take him too seriously . . . two, three, four . . . He's obviously angry . . . two, three . . . frustrated . . . four . . . under the Dragon's thumb."

"I would have thought you'd be more concerned for my safety!" Weeks ago, I'd told him the gist of Euphemia's story, and he'd been suitably appalled.

"If you'd screamed, I would have come," he promised. "Broken leg or no. Obviously, he didn't do anything terrible enough to make you scream."

I shook my head, though it was true that Archie hadn't hurt me, and I was far too tired to argue. I pulled the covers back and began to climb into the bed without bothering to change into my nightdress or let down my hair.

"What are you doing?"

"I told Euphemia there'd be no lessons today. I haven't slept in so long!"

"No, no." His hand was on my arm, as Archie's had been. "You have to go back to where you found this." He fingered the pendant hanging from the bedpost.

Later, I would tell him Archie's story about its purpose, I thought, closing my eyes. Oskar had been right that it was more than a necklace.

"Trudy, I'm serious. If I could go, I would. I'd be there already."

I was nearly asleep.

He shook me. "What if she left something else? She'll be expecting you."

He kept at it until his conviction that she might be waiting for me or have left some other object fully entered my mind and began to nag at me. I sat up and pushed my bare feet into my shoes.

"All right," I said, stumbling around the room. "I should bring her something. A gift in exchange for the pendant. What do you think she'd like?" I thought of some of the loose items on the table in the parlor. A steel crochet hook? A thimble? A pen? What did I have that she might desire? I pulled a clean lace-trimmed handkerchief from my pocket. It was pretty, and she would have none like it.

Oskar snatched it from my hand. "No! Trudy! You mustn't corrupt her! If she uses our things, how will she be different from us?"

It was remarkable that I didn't fall down the mountain, as Oskar had done, so unsteady was I on my feet. At the bottom, I kicked off my shoes and splashed into the freezing water, which, together with the stiff wind, braced me for a time. Soon I was barely plodding, nearly unconscious, hypnotized by the regular wash of the surf, too tired to turn back. More than once, I nearly lay down on the sand.

At last I reached my tide pool and saw that the stone where the pendant had been was bare. I circled the pool gamely, grabbing up a crooked stick of driftwood and a shattered shell. The first had obviously been tossed up by the sea or washed down by the rains; the second, dropped by a passing gull. There was nothing human in them. Disheartened, I lay on the sun-soaked rock to rest awhile before plodding back.

CHAPTER 29

I WAS AWAKENED THIS time by the slight sting of pebbles, like hail, striking my hand, my foot, my cheek. Abruptly, I sat up.

She was standing beside a large rock, and she was wearing a corset, my corset (although she hadn't tied the laces), over a dress of gray and green rags. She held a slingshot before her face, cocked in my direction.

A pebble hit my neck.

"Ow!" I covered my throat with my hand.

I was afraid. Having heard her story—at least as much of it as Euphemia and the children could tell—and having seen her home, with its strange but obvious domesticity, and having received her gift, I'd had no thought that she might harm me. But I realized now that I was entirely at her mercy.

She lowered the slingshot. She was smiling, her face, with its sharp nose and cheekbones, an echo of the jagged copper-brown mountains to the east. She bent to lift something off the ground, then held whatever it was behind her back as she began to move slowly toward me. I sat motionless, almost without breathing, as though she weren't a woman but a wild animal approaching. It occurred to me that the object she was hiding might be the spear the children had told me about.

When she'd come within a few feet, I perceived that the gray-green rags were seaweed, dried and somehow woven or knitted together. Around her neck was a whole loop of abalone shells, or pieces of shells, at any rate, like the string Mrs. Crawley had taken from Jane on our first night at the lighthouse. Around her waist on a cord was a kitchen knife precisely like the one in the drawer beside my sink.

I was startled to discover that it was I who wished to reach out my fingers. I wanted to feel the blackness that was her hair, hanging in long shanks over her shoulders, so that it looked like a hooded cape. I wanted to feel the lacy tangle that was her dress. I refrained, of course.

She brought her hand forward, revealing her surprise: my shoes. She held them out to me, and I took them. The leather was stiff, twisted, and rimed with salt from its tumble in the sea.

She moved her lips, and a voice emerged, rough and oddly inflected. Her expectant look, more than the syllables themselves, made me realize in a second or two that she'd said, "How do?"

"Very well," I answered at last, aware that this mundane dialogue was strange, almost ludicrous, in this context. But how else should we proceed? "And how do you do?"

"Good."

Or at least that's what I assumed she said.

She sat down beside me, the woven weed dress bending to accommodate her movements. I was struck by what was obviously an offer of friendship and wished to offer something in return. Thanks to Oskar, I'd brought nothing.

I held out the boots that lay heavy in my lap. "Would you like to keep these?"

She took one from me and frowned with concentration as she set herself what must have been the unfamiliar task of opening the top and pulling forward the tongue. She bent to push her toes into it, as far as they would go, which was hardly any distance at all. The skin on her feet was rough, thick, and grayed, like the bark of a tree. The feet themselves were remarkably wide at the toes, nearly as wide as they were long, and so resembled . . . well . . . flippers. She waggled the shoe on the end of those toes and laughed, a rusty but mirthful sound that caused me to laugh, too, and then she took off the shoe and handed it back to me with a little toss of her raven head. My gift was useless to her.

She reached one hand toward me, her expression serious. Her face was weathered and her teeth yellow and worn to stubs. Her fingernails were sharp and ragged. A few nails were long, those on the littlest fingers especially, like the nails of the opium eaters I'd seen in Chinatown. Like claws. They scratched my neck. I began to lift my own hand, ready to push hers away with all the strength I could muster.

Gently, she lifted the coral necklace a few inches off my throat and bent, squinting, toward it. I saw grains of sand in the part of her hair. She smelled of smoke and grease and the green odor of the sea.

I believed she wanted the necklace, but I had so little left of the old life that I couldn't give it up. I stayed still and waited, allowing her to examine it with her eyes and fingers, until she sat back on her heels.

She folded her forearms together under her breasts and moved them gently from side to side, as if rocking a baby. Was she rocking a baby? Was this a universal sign?

I shook my head. "No," I said. "I don't have a baby."

She held her hand palm down at about her waist and then moved it up, marking three more imaginary spots. Then she raked her fingers through the air toward her, like Jane imitating an eagle.

The children. She wanted me to bring the children. A burst of alarm traveled from my crown to my toes.

I scrambled to my feet, and she jumped at my quick movement, a wild animal again. Now that I was standing, I could see the water had already come up very far; I'd stayed too long. I pointed at the ocean. "I have to go."

"Go," she repeated. Or perhaps commanded. It was impossible to say which.

She disappeared more quickly than I, somehow absorbed by the landscape. I was reduced to sliding and scrabbling as before, my misshapen shoes clutched awkwardly to my chest. I'd grown more agile with practice. My toes understood how to grip the stone, and I knew which routes would be free of treacherous slime and dead ends. Still, by the time I reached the final stretch through the water that would take me back to the safety of the beach, the waves were swelling as high as my chest. I assumed I would have to abandon my ruined shoes again, so I could use my hands to keep my balance or perhaps to swim. In the end, I held them easily over my head as I pushed through the water. My elation at having at last encountered the woman in the rocks seemed to be all I needed to carry me through.

As I strode toward our mountain far in the distance, I congratulated myself on drawing the elusive mermaid from her hiding place. I had discovered the ultimate treasure of this natural world, a human being who was as comfortable living among the stones as a crab. Still more exciting, I had enticed for myself a friend, someone who was in at least one essential way like me; she'd been separated from her people and was having to make her life as best she could at the edge of the earth. It was not until I had walked the whole of the beach and begun to climb the morro that I was struck by another thought: had I lured her or she me?

Oskar took copious notes on all that I reported about the woman's appearance and gestures. He'd not been happy when I'd produced my shoes.

"It's no good her giving you your own things back. What can we learn from that?"

"She knows who I am. She's been watching me. That must be important."

"That's just personal," he said. "Don't you realize how much bigger she is than that? This woman is the remnant of a lost culture. You saw how it was from the train; people like us have spread all over this country like dandelions, choking out those who've lived here for tens of centuries. She may be all that's left. The only evidence of a former, more primitive phase of humanity that can never be experienced again."

He asked me to sketch her from memory. After his reaction to the shoes, I decided to omit the corset.

"I think she wants me to bring the children to her." I said this tentatively, keeping my eyes on my sketch. I hoped his reaction might help me decide how to respond to this notion.

"I'm not sure if that's a good idea. We don't want them influencing her, teaching her to behave like little Crawleys. On the other hand, it might be enlightening to see what she does with them."

"What she does with them!" This sounded alarmingly like Archie.

He shook his head, impatient with my fright. "I'm not suggesting she's going to cook and eat them. I mean observing her with them will help us discover aspects of her. Is she childlike—does she want to play with them? Or does she mean to teach them some skill? Does she plan to give something to them, some token of herself, or is there something they have that she wants? Those are just some possibilities."

I thought of the way her fingers had worked through the air in the gesture of beckoning. Although I knew she possessed no real powers, there was something of the sorceress in her wild costume and her cape of hair, in her very existence. I imagined that somehow the children could feel the tug of her. I certainly could.

CHAPTER 30

THE FOLLOWING WEEK, Oskar resumed his shift at the light. Now that he could walk more than a few feet at a time, he began pestering me to take him into the rocks. I was to guide him first to the tide pool where I'd found the amulet (the place I considered "our" tide pool, meaning Helen's and mine) and then to her cave. I was to bring a logbook as well, so I could make a complete record in words and pictures of everything we observed. This would be important work, he explained, that we could do together.

"And we have to go early. I can't move fast, so we must have plenty of time. Tell Euphemia you're canceling school because you need to get on with your catalog."

I remained uncertain about exposing the cave to Oskar. I did want to share this wonder with him. I could imagine no one appreciating it more. After all, he'd been eager to share with me all the wonders he'd observed. But my connection to Helen relied on stillness and waiting; I didn't think Oskar was capable of that.

Nevertheless, he *would* go. I couldn't hope that he would break another leg. If he were to go crashing around the rocks, better that I be with him.

*   *   *

We used the steam donkey to get down the morro; that was simple enough. As usual, I removed my shoes and stockings at the bottom. Oskar stood beside me, waiting, repeatedly plunging a walking stick he'd made from a piece of driftwood into the sand to mark his impatience.

"It's easier to walk here with bare feet," I explained.

"Maybe for you, who've been doing it for months, but my feet aren't accustomed to it."

The going was tedious. The uneven, dry sand was a labor to cross even for a person with two good legs, so Oskar had to plant his stick deep with every step. By the time we reached the packed sand, his face was twisted with the effort of coaxing his injured limb to rise and fall through the soft stuff and to bear his weight, and his forehead was slick with sweat. Even on the harder surface, his leg was obviously paining him.

"Maybe we should wait another week or so," I suggested.

He shook his head without taking his eyes off the distant rocks that were our goal, and kept doggedly on.

It was difficult to slow my pace to match his. I couldn't skim along as I usually did but frequently had to catch myself and wait, dragging rainbows in the sand with my toes to relieve my taut muscles. Physically trying as the experience was, I welcomed the delay, hoping that our window of tide might close before we reached it. Helen would be safe from his fierce scrutiny, at least for some time longer.

But the water was shallow, and once we'd stumbled through it and reached the rough and uneven rocks beyond, Oskar became surprisingly agile, using his hands to climb like a monkey. In some areas, he could move faster than I. To save the soles of my feet, I had to skirt the clusters of mussels and colonies of periwinkles with their sharp little peaks, but he walked right over them in his heavy shoes.

"Be careful!" I called as he started over a rock packed with the pursed mouths of closed anemones. "You'll crush the animals." He was far enough ahead to pretend he hadn't heard me.

At the purple pool, I searched the surrounding shadows diligently, but Helen was nowhere near, or she was keeping herself well hidden, wary of Oskar. He couldn't stay ahead of me for long, because he had no idea where he was going, at least until we entered the narrow channel that led directly to the cave. There, we started out together; as the passage between the rocks steadily narrowed, we brushed against each other, knocking first shoulders, then hips. At last the passage became so tight that we couldn't walk abreast. Though I ought to have been the one to step into the lead, he pushed forward, not roughly but with an insistence that I couldn't challenge without becoming ridiculous. He went ahead into the funnel while I fell back farther and farther, as every few steps I stopped to scan the rocks. There was no sign of her.

When I caught up with him, he was standing at the entrance to the cave, peering into that dim space. I could see he was overwhelmed at the scene that was now familiar to me. The tools she'd fashioned of stone and bone and the shell bowls filled with acorns and seaweeds were arranged in their places along the base of the walls. Strings of abalone and mussel shells were looped, as always, over bits of protruding rock. The sealskins stretched, impossibly rich, over the floor.

"This is marvelous," Oskar breathed. "She *is* a real Indian."

"Of course she is."

"I wasn't sure. What do you and the Crawleys know of Indians?"

I wanted to retort that I doubted he knew any more than I, but I couldn't bring myself to speak as arrogantly as he. "We had Indians in Wisconsin."

"Not wild ones."

"Helen's not exactly wild, either." I used her name, reminding him that I knew her better.

"That's not really her name," he said.

Standing there with Oskar, staring at the accoutrements of her life, felt all at once like an intrusion, and I stepped back. "I'm not sure—" I began. "Oskar! Stop!"

He'd walked into the cave.

I was sincerely shocked. Although the place had no real door, even the children had known to hang back. How dare he breach her walls? Instinctively, I looked over my shoulders, right and then left. Was she watching him? Us?

"Oskar, come out!"

"Just a moment." His boots trampled the sealskin.

"You shouldn't be in there."

"Why not?"

"It's her home. You're trespassing."

"I'm not hurting anything."

But he was fingering everything. Not only fingering but palming. I saw him slip something into his pocket.

"You can't take that!" I plunged into the cave myself, the sealskin on the soles of my bare feet as soft as my mother's blue velvet drapes. Already he'd lifted another item, a string of rocks, green like Chinese jade. I grabbed his wrist, and he turned on me.

"These are important artifacts," he said.

"No! These are hers!"

He didn't answer, but he must have heard the shrill horror in my voice, because he looked startled, as if I'd woken him from a dream. "You're right. Of course you're right. We shouldn't disturb her things." He let me take his arm and lead him back through the entrance until we were standing outside again. He looked about uncertainly, chastened by what he'd done but unwilling to leave the spot. "I tell you what we'll do. We'll just sit here outside the door, and you draw everything you can see. A sketch of the whole and then studies of some of the more detailed items. That would be all right, wouldn't it? Look at those baskets, for instance. See how fine the weave is?" He pointed to a large round one near the entrance. "This jagged pattern—I bet it's unique to her tribe. I wonder if it's meant to symbolize water."

Although I was still angry with Oskar, I felt more comfortable now that we were outside the cave, and I didn't see how sketching was any different from staring, which I'd indulged in often enough. I began the project grudgingly, grumbling at the hardness of my rocky seat, the inadequacy of the light, and the difficulty of the angle, but once I began to sketch, the hours became among the best I had ever spent with Oskar. We reveled in the spectacle before us and felt transported by it, as if we were again viewing the panorama of Athens. As my drawing grew, Oskar studied it in relation to the scene, praising my use of perspective and pointing out details he thought should be emphasized—the texture of the baskets, the arrangement of what appeared to be fishhooks in a length of leather on the wall. He guided me to look so closely and methodically that I noticed details I'd overlooked on my own. While most of the baskets, for instance, had a dark design worked on a light background, on a few this pattern was reversed, as if she'd been trying an experiment or, as Oskar suggested, sometimes had access to different materials. He encouraged me to include every facet of every object, but he stopped me when I began to pencil in the pyramid of canned goods.

"Leave those out," he said. "They shouldn't be there."

"But they are there," I insisted stubbornly.

I could tell she treasured the cans and had arranged them with care. I had a notion that they, along with the neatly folded Lighthouse Service blanket, might be as important to her as the blue velvet drapes were to my mother and the wooden teeth were to Euphemia. It felt wrong to eliminate them.

"They're imposed on her," Oskar said. "They're not authentic."

I obeyed his wishes—after all, the drawing had been his idea—though I marked the placement of these objects in my mind, planning to do another copy for myself.

From time to time, Oskar moved around, studying the evidence of Helen's life outside the cave. He pressed his fingertips against the fish scales that dusted the rocks, and when he held up his hand, his skin glittered as if covered in sequins.

"Are these from fish she eats?" he asked. "Or are they here for some other purpose? How does she catch them? Does she use those hooks, or does she have nets?"

"She spears them," I said, experiencing a little flush of pleasure at being the one who knew.

We went on in this way for some hours, until I began to worry that the tide would be closing our route home, and I shut the logbook.

"Now, Oskar." I'd decided to try wheedling, as if he were a little boy. "Before we go, I must be sure you've put everything back. She'll miss her things if we take them."

"I'm not going to *take* anything. I'm only borrowing. And it's only this." He held up a small piece of bone the color of oatmeal, one end sharply pointed, the other with a small hole drilled through. A needle. "I just want something to study at my leisure, so I can take measurements and make some notes when I have time to think. And you'll draw it. This"—he swept his hand grandly across the entrance to the cave— "should be the subject of your catalog. When we're finished, we'll bring it back. Of course."

I thought of the way she'd laughed with her toes in my shoe, and of the pendant she'd left for me. I convinced myself that she wouldn't object to our borrowing such a small item. Probably she wouldn't even notice it was missing.

We returned in the same tedious manner in which we'd come, although Oskar planted his stick with energy, exhilarated despite his pain, whereas I dragged my feet, drained by the tension of the day.

There was no time for a proper sleep before his shift, and he didn't attempt it. Instead, he sat at the kitchen table and began to study the needle with such thoroughness that it might have been a relic of Christ.

Later, when he'd gone to tend the light, I looked at the pages he'd covered with coded notes. What could he have found to say about that bit of bone to fill a page with such a turmoil of symbols?

I was meticulous with my drawings. I did one close view to show texture and one with a ruler beside it to indicate size. I passed a thread through the eye and pushed the point into some material and drew the whole to indicate how the thing might be used. I tried to show the needle's slightness and the spots where it had been worn down by fingers. In the morning, I set the children some compositions so I could complete my work.

"I've done every possible rendering," I said, handing Oskar the book at dinner that evening. "So we can take it back."

"Yes," he said absently, turning the pages. "These are very good."

"I'll cancel school for tomorrow morning, then, and we can take it back," I repeated.

We were eating oxtail stew again, and he paused to work a bone from his mouth before answering. "I'm going tonight."

"Tonight? It'll be dark soon. And what about your shift?"

"I thought you'd cover that. You don't mind, do you?"

I didn't want him to go alone. "Why risk your neck in the dark? This is as foolish as going in the middle of a rainstorm. Why not wait until tomorrow?"

"Because I think night is the best time to catch her there, and I want to see her. She obviously keeps away from the place during the day." He cracked a square of pilot bread over the remains of his stew and stirred it vigorously in the gravy. "Don't worry; I'm not going to go in the dark. I'm going to start immediately after I eat, give myself plenty of time to find a good place to hide. I'll wait. Sooner or later, I bet she shows."

I could tell that it was a good plan by the degree to which it dismayed me. "She obviously doesn't want you to see her. Maybe she's afraid of you. As she was of Archie. You don't want to frighten her."

"That's silly. She has nothing to fear from me. I'm not going to hurt her."

I tried a different tack. "I'm very tired. I don't think I can manage your shift tonight."

He shrugged. "We'll have to hope for the best, then. What are the chances that a ship will need our signal on this particular night?"

I stared at him. "You wouldn't leave the light without a keeper!"

"I think the important point," he said, spooning up the last of his stew with gusto, "is that you wouldn't."

CHAPTER 31

I WENT TO THE lighthouse at the proper time and did Oskar's duty with the oil and the scissors. If anyone had seen him go, I was to say he was exercising his leg by walking on the sand. It was an unbelievable story, but as he said, it was his business what he did as long as the light was tended.

When I'd finished my tasks, I was too anxious to sit down to the usual mending. I'd brought a book; that couldn't hold me to the chair, either. Soon enough, I allowed myself to go up the stairs and then onto the catwalk, careful to avoid exposing my unprotected eyes to the beam as it swung over me. I stood for a long while staring north, trying to bore through the blackness to discover what Oskar was doing. Of course, I could see nothing. By now he would be squeezed into some hole in the rocks.

The night was extremely still, without wind or bird cry. Far below, the water rocked gently in its bed. If it had not been for the steady hiccup of the light, I might have imagined myself in the womb.

And then I heard a small stone roll across the face of the rock, just below where I stood. It gathered speed and knocked against other rocks until, with a crack, it fell silent. At first I didn't grope for explanation. After all, rocks must often spontaneously dislodge from their seats. Indeed, such phenomena must have been happening for millennia, as evidenced by the jagged black teeth at the foot of the morro. Then another stone began to roll some yards farther to the south, and I heard a sort of scrabbling. Something large was moving below me. My heart beat with a sudden, painful force, and I let out a small, distinct gasp. The scrabbling stopped.

I'd clearly frightened whatever animal had come to this place. I recalled Jane telling me there were no predators on the rock except eagles. Could it be an eagle? Or was it Archie Johnston going to visit his child's grave? Would he move so surreptitiously? Bravely, I hung over the rail as far as I dared, my loose hair streaming around my face like a waterfall.

"Trudy?" Euphemia's voice came not from beneath me but from the bridge that connected the top of the light to the level where our houses stood. "What's the matter?" She came on, her footsteps louder when they left the wooden bridge and landed on the metal catwalk. "Why're you here? Leg paining him?"

I held my finger to my lips, but she couldn't see that in the dark. "Shhh," I said. "I hear something." I pointed over the rail.

"It's probably a possum. Or a fox." She pulled open the door to the tower. "Come in."

The beam passed over me in a brilliant bath of light, and I had to close my eyes quickly to avoid burning them. "Jane said there were no foxes."

"Trudy, come in now!"

I disobeyed. I turned back to the rail and jackknifed my body over it again. When the light swept past, I spotted the cairn and possibly something else, though I couldn't make it out behind the flash of brightness that clung to my eyes like a caul, a ghost of light blocking what was real.

"I think it's Helen!"

I said this, but my words were overwhelmed by an enormous crash, as the window behind me shattered. I recoiled, stumbled, and fell onto the catwalk along with the glass. Instantly, Euphemia's large hands gripped my arms. She pulled me to my feet. Pieces of glass that had stuck to my clothes and skin fell a second time to the floor and broke into smaller bits.

"Come away from here." This time I followed helplessly.

"Why did she do that?" I held my arm close against my body, trying to keep the blood from dripping onto the stairs.

"I believe she's unhappy sometimes," Euphemia clanked down the steps ahead of me. "Maybe because of her baby."

"'Baby Johnston born and buried,'" I said, finally realizing what I should have understood for months. I couldn't remember whose hand had written that line, although it rang of Euphemia's efficient way with words.

"She hardly knew the child. Still, it's a terrible loss for a mother." She gathered a handful of what was left of my sleeve at the shoulder seam. With a sharp pull, she ripped the fabric, revealing the gashed flesh beneath.

"When did she have a baby? You said she'd gone back to the mountains. You said nothing about a baby!"

"Stand here." She positioned me beside the pitcher and basin we kept for washing up. She wet a clean rag and began dabbing at my arm with a sureness that calmed me. "When she left, there was no baby," she said simply, rinsing her rag and dabbing some more. "But she came back. It was a different season by then. It was June, when we get the fog. I'd had another baby by that time myself. I used to make a little nest of blankets on the floor right there." She pointed, the bloodstained rag dangling from her hand.

The thought of a tiny Janie, snuggled in like a kitten, made me remember that my own child would have been in such a nest by now.

Euphemia bent to lift a worn shirt of Archie's from the mending basket and pressed it against my arm. "Sit down and hold this awhile.

"All of a sudden, here she was one night, right here in the boiler room," she went on, selecting a thin needle from her keeper. "I like to believe that she hoped to find me here, but it may have been Archie she meant to give it to, even Henry. Or maybe she didn't care who had it just so long as it wasn't her. Some mothers are like that." She paused.

"I don't understand—" I began.

"I'm telling you," she said impatiently. "It isn't an easy thing, you know. One, two, three." She snapped her fingers. "This, that, and the other. There are circumstances. There are things we can only conjecture." She turned up the flame of the lamp and passed the needle back and forth through it several times.

"I'm sorry," I said.

"She was standing at the bottom of the staircase when I came down from feeding the light, and I was so amazed that I was lucky not to drop the oil I was carrying." Euphemia unspooled a length of black thread and bit it off. "You know, I believed for an instant that she might be a ghost or a trick of my mind. I'd thought of her so often, you see, but I'd never expected to see her again in the flesh. Her hair had grown in; her face was rounder. She didn't appear to have suffered since she'd left. I remember feeling a good deal of relief at that.

"I was glad to see her." She squinted, lining up the eye of her needle with her thread. "I was nervous, too. Where would I hide her? How could I spirit her away again before Archie found her? That's what I was thinking. She had her own plans. She didn't need me. Not to take care of *her*, anyway.

"Here, now," she said. "Put your elbow there." She nodded at the table between us.

She pulled the lamp close and then, holding the edges of my skin together with her left hand, passed the needle through with her right. I sucked in my breath and gritted my teeth at the pinch of it. I could feel the thread running through my skin. Deftly, she tied a knot and bent to bite off the thread again, her lips grazing my skin.

"She knelt right there," she said, indicating the spot with her needle, "and she slipped her arms from the straps around her shoulders."

I hardly felt the needle puncturing my skin, so intent was I on her story.

"I'd assumed it was bedding she carried on her back, but when she got that pack around to her knees, I saw what her burden was. Laced right into the basket was a newborn, a tiny nut of a baby.

"It cried a little when she lifted it from its cocoon." She poked the needle in yet again. "It was a smart little thing; it knew that release from the basket meant it would soon be fed. But she didn't nurse it. Instead, she held it out to me. I thought she wanted me to admire it. As I said, she'd been a sort of daughter to me; it seemed the natural thing, despite unnatural circumstances. She'd wrapped it in a bit of my old red calico. Can you imagine?

"It cried more when I took it. I smelled wrong, I suppose. But by the time you've had four, a crying baby isn't agitating. I tried to soothe it, jostling it on my shoulder, wrapping my arms tight around it, because I'd seen that it was used to confinement. Babies like what they know.

"I remember smiling at it—thinking what a funny-looking little moppet it was. It had a thick mat of dark hair laying at all angles, and ears poking out like the little round handles of a jug."

She'd finished her stitches and was gazing at nothing in particular, some spot in the air, recalling, as people do, the scene in her mind's eye. Now she looked at me, studying my face.

"And then?" I asked. It seemed to me somehow that she wasn't telling the story in the right order. I glanced at my arm. Although I knew the stitches were necessary, the wound hurt more than before she'd applied her needle.

Euphemia wrapped her arms around herself, as if she were the babe who needed swaddling. "I looked to her. I remember I was smiling and I thought she would be pleased to see my pleasure in her child." She shook her head. "She was gone."

"Gone where?"

"Gone away. She left that baby. With me."

The image of Euphemia raising a stone over the baby otter's head thrust itself unbidden into my mind.

"I didn't know that she meant for me to keep it. I thought she'd reappear in minutes, then by morning, then in a week or two weeks' time. Even months and months later, I expected her at every moment, especially those times when I was alone here in the light tower."

"Was it Archie's child?"

"Oh, yes. That was clear straight off. She looked just like him. But he pretended that he had nothing to do with her. No matter. I had no intention of giving an infant to the likes of him. It was me that child needed, and I made sure she got everything she required, the way babies do. Even in that first hour, her crying made my milk leak into my dress. She was much more demanding than my own." She sighed. "I had plenty for both. Nature does provide.

"I admit there were times I was almost frantic, wishing Helen would come for her. Two babies at once was not an easy thing, I can tell you! But she didn't come and she didn't come, and at last I let myself love that baby, love her as I loved my own."

"Oh!" The bleakness in her voice overwhelmed me, erasing entirely the sting of my arm. I knew what had happened to the child.

"Both of them sickened," she said. "One and then the other. It was just after the inspector came. I remember him saying that he had been a twin himself, and he very much admired mine. I did my best for them both. I promise you, I did." She looked at me almost beseechingly, as if I might harbor a doubt. "I managed to save only one." She was rubbing her forehead with her fingertips, as if she could erase the memory of it. "When Helen finally did come back, I had to show her the stones."

CHAPTER 32

COLD, STIFF, AND spent, his leg paining him almost beyond endurance, Oskar limped into the house the next morning. I had not waited breakfast for him but was already eating a soft-boiled egg with a slice of real bread and plum jelly.

"Did you see her?" I rose to boil another egg. I was afraid that if I looked at him, my face would reveal what I knew—that although he had gone to the Indian, the Indian had come to me. Well, almost to me.

I need not have worried. Oskar took no notice of me, though I must have looked peculiar with my mismatched sleeve, sewn from what remained of Archie's shirt.

He collapsed into a chair. "I suppose she spotted me. Or smelled me. It's clear she doesn't trust me." His jacket bulged at his sides; the seams strained at his shoulders. The pockets were stuffed full.

"You took more!"

He began to pull items out and lay them on the table. "Damned heavy."

They were stones, mostly. The jade-like necklace that I'd stopped him from taking the first time; a red rock, big as his palm, with an edge chipped away to make a blade; a white stone, smooth as kneaded dough, with a depression in its center, together with one that fitted comfortably into his hand—they seemed to work together like a mortar and pestle. There were more, some flat, some sharp, some worn smooth.

"Did you leave her anything?"

"Of course I did," he said calmly. As if I were the one behaving outrageously. "I only borrowed a few representative pieces. I did take this, though." He unbuttoned his shirt. Against his torso was a wad of blue silk. "It's as bad to give her things as to take them away, you know. Worse. You make a mockery of her with this frippery."

"Oskar," I answered indignantly, snatching the silk from him, "I have no idea how she got this. I had nothing to do with giving it to her, although I wish I had!" I held my dress by its shoulders and tried to shake the wrinkles out. "You've smashed the bustle!" I was crying, although I cared nothing for the state of the dress. I was thinking of the girl I'd been only a year before, when I'd worn it to the panorama and believed that my life was about to flower. I looked at my husband in his unbuttoned shirt and sagging jacket, caressing the loot he'd spread before him on the table.

"Mrs. Swann, why do you have the mermaid's dress?"

It was Jane's piping voice. Oskar, in his exhaustion, had neglected to shut the door behind him, and the children had come straight in, expecting to start their lessons.

I wiped my eyes quickly on the silk sleeve. "The mermaid's dress? This is my dress. Remember, I gave it to Mary to wear in our play?"

"I thought you said I could keep it." Mary's voice was slightly tremulous.

"I did. And you may. It's only that somehow it ended up with . . . well, the mermaid."

Oskar leaned toward them as if sharing a secret. I saw that his hair and beard had begun to grow into one another. "Do you know how this came to be in the cave?" he asked shrewdly.

"We gave it to her," Nicholas said.

"It didn't fit Mary very well, you know," Edward added.

"We didn't think you'd mind," Mary said. "We thought you'd given it to me for keeps."

"It was Jane's idea," Edward said.

"It seemed like the kind of dress a mermaid would wear," Jane explained in a quiet voice. "All watery-like."

"She was grateful to have it," Nicholas said, defending his sisters. "She let it fly up over her head in the wind, like a flag. It's much better as a flag than as a silly dress."

"You saw her with it?" Oskar looked from face to face. "You gave it to her with your own hands?"

"We put it on the stones for her, but when she'd got it, she came to find us," Jane said. "Like she always does."

CHAPTER 33

T HERE HAD BEEN fog on and off since we'd arrived, but it had never
been like what sat on us now, an opacity, clammy and cold, so thick
that I tried more than once to sweep it aside with my arms. It was
impervious to the sun, which was at best an exhausted glow behind the
gray. The foghorn bellowed day and night, an insistent mourner.

Oskar cut pieces of fabric of various sizes from the articles in the
mending basket and sewed them onto his jacket, inside and out, as
pockets. "This way," he explained, "my hands are free. And it's better
than a bag or a rucksack, because items don't jumble together and break.
Also, better balanced for the body. You ought to use something like this
when you gather your specimens."

He made several more trips to the cave with the modified jacket and
came home with the pockets loaded with booty, which he arranged on
a sheet spread on the floor of our bedroom. He painstakingly labeled
each of Helen's implements and baskets, her strings of nut- and sea-
shells, even the bones that presumably were the remnants of her meals.
He used English for this instead of code, because he planned eventually
to show his display to Philip and other members of the university community.

When I tried to return some items, he was angry with me and fetched
them back the following day.

"These are scientific evidence!" he snapped, matching labels to stones. "You might have destroyed a week's work with your sentimentality."

"You're stealing her things!"

"I'm not stealing them. I'm studying them."

"That distinction can mean nothing to Helen. You have the things; she does not."

He shook his head impatiently. "You don't seem to appreciate that these artifacts are evidence of her tribe, maybe the only evidence. She can sacrifice a few tools and ornaments to keep her people from disappearing into obscurity, entirely unmarked and unknown. Don't you care whether people know that these Indians existed on this earth? These things are far too important for one woman to keep to herself."

"What if she needs them?"

He went on about his work, as if my arguments were not worth answering. I suspected that he hoped she would come looking for her things, which might provide him an opportunity to observe her. She must have known where they were, since no one could have taken them but one of us from the light station. I was dismayed by the idea that she might think it was I who was betraying her by dismantling her home, and I was sharply aware that I'd introduced Oskar to her cave and that, though I had not carried them off, all of her treasures were spread at the foot of my bed.

It wasn't long before Lighthouse Service tools began to go missing from the workshop. A hammer, a saw, a drill, and a clamp, implements made of iron and steel paid for those of stone. One morning a hen was missing. The windows kept breaking night after night, so many that we ran out of glass to replace them, and the precious lens was exposed to the sky. Luckily, the horn was most important in this weather, for every errant breeze blew the light out. The keeper had to sit in the lamproom, wrapped in a blanket and wearing the black spectacles, ready to relight the wicks.

* * *

"She'll only break this one, too," Mr. Crawley said. "I don't know what's come over her."

We were attempting to cut the windows that remained at the back of the tower, so as to move them to the front to block the wind off the ocean. It was risky, because the glass was likely to shatter either in the cutting or in the moving, and then we'd be worse off than ever, but Oskar had had to relight the wick two dozen times in the course of his shift the night before. At this rate, we would run out of matches.

The Crawleys and Archie Johnston were fatalistic about Helen's behavior, as if it were a force of nature, like a bout of bad weather. But they worried about the damage to the lighthouse, especially because the inspector was likely to arrive on the next tender. In anticipation, every knob and ball bearing, every hinge and windowpane, every gear, wheel, pulley, lever, and handle, each and every screw, had to be made to shine; and the quantity of wicks and the frequency of trimming, the quality of the wood and the appetite of the boiler, the duration of each barrel of oil, the number of ships and steamers observed and their approximate distance from the land, the gallons of paint used and the number of brushes worn to a nub, all had to be accurately accounted for in the logbook. Both appearances and records were severely wanting, thanks to Helen's recent activities.

"He'll say we're not managing properly," Mr. Crawley fretted.

"We're not," Euphemia said.

We struggled for an hour, Mr. Crawley and Oskar delicately slicing the caulking away; Euphemia, Archie, and I supporting the glass with our palms and easing the pane from its frame. We managed to move two panes, but we broke two others. Mr. Crawley closed his knife, shaking his head.

"I've been thinking," Oskar said in his old casually confident tone that seemed to brook no argument, "that the Indian ought to be in a place where others will take an interest in her, help her. Humans aren't meant to live alone."

"That's impossible," Euphemia said quickly. "She can't live here."

"No, I don't mean here," Oskar said.

"You mean find another tribe for her?" I suggested.

He shook his head. "No, that's impossible, naive. Even if we could find an intact tribe somewhere, it would be as foreign to her as we are. I've been thinking that a scientific community would be best. Anthropologists would revere her culture and preserve it. I—well, Trudy and I—could take her to someone we know at the University of California in Berkeley."

"Take her?" My voice came out choked, I was so shocked.

"Yes, I've been thinking," he repeated coolly, "and it seems the reasonable course." Oskar described Philip's work with Mrs. Hearst's collection and his interest in studying local Indians. "He's associated with the university. He could introduce us to the right people, those who would understand her importance."

The Crawleys were baffled. "It's nothing to do with electricity, is it?" Mr. Crawley asked suspiciously. "We wouldn't want her electrocuted."

Oskar assured them that anthropology wasn't dangerous. She would be a boon to humanity, he said. Instead of a nuisance to the light station.

And she would bring him the recognition he craved, I thought. I pictured him explaining the possible functions of various stones to a roomful of bearded scientists, and I knew he was imagining something much the same. With Helen, Oskar would dazzle them. I wondered how long he'd been planning it.

Archie Johnston nodded. "I'm going, too. I found her. I have a right."

"You'll not get within twenty paces of her," Euphemia said.

"It's only money he wants," I said, remembering what he'd told me at the light. It occurred to me that Oskar might have given Archie an inkling of this scheme as long ago as those bedridden days after Christmas.

"There won't be any money," Oskar said. "What do you think? People are going to put down their pennies to get a glimpse of the wild woman?

We're not going to stick her in a cage and dress her in furs. She'll help us to deepen our understanding of humanity. There's no money in that."

"It's your fault she's destroying the light station," I said, not for the first time, when we were alone.

He shrugged. "Maybe. But it can't be helped."

"You could return her things." I was beginning to sound tedious even to myself. "Then she might stop."

"She might not. I admit that I've angered her, but I don't know that putting things back the way they were will assuage her."

"We could try. After all, you already have so many notes and pictures." Despite my objections to keeping the objects, I'd gone on drawing them. I'd believed that having such a record would make him more willing to return the things, as I was now suggesting, but if I were honest, I had to admit that I'd felt as excited as he by the project of compiling a catalog of the artifacts.

"Don't you see that pictures and words aren't enough? We must have the real things."

He meant he had to have the real woman; I could see that clearly enough. Gradually, Oskar wore me down, just as he did the Crawleys.

"I'm sure she doesn't want to live alone," he repeated more than once. "It isn't natural." He told us that if the university couldn't supply rooms immediately, Philip would know of a suitable place.

"She can't pay for a room," Mr. Crawley objected.

Oskar said he would pay for it himself out of banked wages. He said he knew the way universities worked. Within a month, the gears would be grinding and a cottage would be supplied. A lady scientist would live with Helen as a companion and friend; the Crawleys shouldn't worry, Oskar said, the university wouldn't try to turn the Indian into a white woman. There would be no dressing in muslin or eating of tarts, was how he put it.

"I think she'd like tarts," Euphemia said.

"She did like sweets," Mr. Crawley added.

I liked to think of Helen in the university's cottage, even if it meant she would have to sit in a chair and eat with a knife and fork. I imagined a flower garden at the front, and I wondered if peonies grew in San Francisco.

"She would have stayed with the Crawleys if not for Archie," Oskar said, pressing his case. "Obviously, she doesn't want to live like a hermit."

It was true that none of us knew that she wished to live by herself in the rocks, only that she didn't leave. I believed her life would be better in many ways if she were in a safer, cleaner place. If she had a home and people who cared for her, as I was sure the lady scientist would.

"Do you think she'll be happy in Berkeley?" I asked.

The question annoyed Oskar. "I can't guarantee that. Do you think she's happy here? Anyway, you'll be there to get her settled. You can see to her happiness."

"You mean that I would be the lady scientist?"

"No one could be more suited to the job."

"I don't know anything about anthropology."

"That doesn't matter! I know very little of anthropology specifically, but I observe and think as well as anyone trained in the discipline, so there's no reason I can't make an important contribution. That's what all of science depends on, Trudy, close, thorough, and honest observation. And who observes with more care and honesty than you? Remember how you spotted the schooner?

"Besides," he went on before I could respond that the discovery of the schooner had been no more than luck, "she trusts you. I doubt that anyone else could make her more comfortable than you could."

So I would be the lady scientist, at least for a few months. I would make her at home, introducing her to her rooms and perhaps to the city, while Oskar arranged her role at the university. This idea soothed my fears, for I could protect Helen from anything that might make her unhappy. I admit that it intrigued me as well. I would be in a position to observe Helen more closely than anyone, then. Maybe I, too, would make a contribution to anthropology.

Euphemia refused to take Oskar seriously, as if this plan were as far-fetched as his wireless telegraph. "It's all well and good to say you're going to take her to Berkeley," she said with a laugh, "but I doubt you can get her to the boat."

Oskar had a scheme, and I was its key. "She trusts you," he repeated. "I think you can persuade her."

"She doesn't speak English, and I don't speak her language," I protested. "How will I explain something so complex? It's impossible."

"You'll take the children with you," he said. "If they show her that they want her to come along with them to the lighthouse, don't you think she might?"

"Deceive her? And use the children to do it? Oskar, think what you're proposing! It's horrible."

"You've said yourself that there's no way to explain things to her. This is clearly a case in which the ends justify the means. She's like a child, Trudy. We're doing this for her own good. Besides, all you'd be doing is bringing her to the longboat and presenting her with the option. You could get in first to reassure her, and she could follow if she chooses. If we can't persuade her to come here, how can we give her the choice?"

"What about the children? Won't they be upset to see her go?"

He shrugged. "She isn't their pet. We can't compromise her life so that they can go on exchanging their little gifts."

"We'll return her things to her? When she gets into the longboat?"

"Of course. We'll be taking all of her things with us. She'll see that we're not making her abandon her home; we're moving her home to a new place, a place that'll be better for her."

"And you think she'll want to go?"

"For pity's sake, I've already told you that I can't know what she wants. I'm convinced that it's best for her not to live like an animal, Trudy. You must agree with that. Anyway, a university's not a jail. If she doesn't like it, she can always come back. She can book her passage on the tender."

He had an answer for every worry and objection. Childishly, I let him convince me, wanting the man I loved to be admirable, the husband to whom I'd yoked myself to know what was right and act accordingly.

"Roberts always inspects in the fog," Euphemia complained, as if the man himself had ordered the weather.

"Isn't it exciting," I asked, "to see someone new for a change?"

"Not him," Mr. Crawley said. "Some inspectors try to help you do right, but Roberts is happy to find us in the wrong so he can write us up in his little book. He doesn't miss a thing, and he won't like them windows or all the missing tools."

"Nor should he," Euphemia said. "You can't blame him for that."

Euphemia and I planned a special lunch for Inspector Roberts. She'd kept a few choice cans aside for the occasion, as she had at Christmas; more, because there'd be no time for hunting or fishing. New barrels would arrive with the inspector, but we'd not have a chance to empty them before the meal. Anyway, they'd be saved for a barrel-opening ceremony after he'd gone; Roberts disapproved of bonfires. Lessons were put on hold in these days of preparation. We paid little attention to the children other than to order them to do small jobs and keep everything they touched tidy. Mostly, they careened in and out of the fog, consumed by their own inscrutable affairs.

The fog was so thick that the earth seemed to have vanished except for the few buildings where we lived and worked. Claustrophobia squeezed me into a panic, and I had to beat down an impulse to try to claw a hole in the sky with my fingernails. I often inadvertently strayed off the paths. More than once, I found myself at the edge of the morro when I'd thought I was yards away. I began to hobble my steps and keep my feet close to the ground when I walked, praying I would feel the brink with my toes in time to keep from stepping over it.

So we had no warning at all.

CHAPTER 34

"YOO-HOO! HELLO, UP there! Yoo-hoo!" The voice came one morning from the base of the rock and rose thin and muffled through the clouds.

Footsteps thumped heavily across the bridge from the light. Mr. Crawley, who'd been repairing a bit of the railing, was running. "It's Roberts!" he hissed. "Roberts is here!" He ran behind the house to the steam donkey. "Half an hour till I get this winch running!" he shouted into the gray. Silence from below.

Calling over his shoulder for Archie to stay at his post in the lamproom and for Euphemia to start the lunch, Mr. Crawley fed the fire in the steam donkey's boiler. There could be no bad luck; no part could break or come loose or appear worn today. Mr. Crawley took on a different personality in this moment of crisis, shedding his easygoing ways and replacing them with those of a commander. Euphemia looked proud as she set off for the barn.

Our valise, heavy with artifacts, was waiting at the front door when I went in to change from my duster into a dress in which I wouldn't be embarrassed to step off the tender in San Francisco. My frequent treks across the sand had caused me to lose flesh, and I could fit into all of my garments even without a corset. Oskar was in the bedroom, sewing closed the pockets he'd stuffed tightly with the implements he believed to be of most scientific value and didn't dare risk losing.

251

"The inspection should give you plenty of time," he said. "If she shows up."

His role would be to delay the tender, if necessary. He was confident the captain and the inspector would be willing to wait, if they could be made to understand the importance of their cargo. If they weren't agreeable, there were other, less cordial ways to postpone the boat's departure.

I'd planned to take all of the children with me; between the fog and the distraction the inspector was causing, I thought it would be easy enough to slip away unnoticed. But Euphemia had sent the boys to set up the plank table and had pulled Mary into the kitchen with her. Clearly, they would be expected to do their part to make the inspection go well.

However, I found Jane moping behind the house. "She says I'm not much use."

"Do you want to come with me?"

I held out my hand, and she took it willingly. She didn't even ask where we were going until we'd reached the bottom of the morro. The surf was large and loud. The wet air amplified the water's threatening boom as it toppled over itself and its frustrated hiss as it was sucked back into the sea. On the beach, two sailors were unloading barrels from the longboat. They took no notice of us.

I'd expected, and maybe half hoped, to wait fruitlessly by our tide pool, but when we arrived, Helen was sitting on my rock wearing her seaweed dress and corset. Obviously, Jane was the charm. Helen would have heard us coming—Janie was full of observations, and her voice carried like a gull's. The Indian smiled and nodded shyly at me, though it was Jane who commanded her attention. Euphemia had been right; she did like the children best. She took the girl's hand so greedily that I was startled. Jane didn't seem to mind, and I remembered that she'd visited "the mermaid" before, perhaps often.

Helen drew the little girl to the pool, pointing out a type of crab that in all my looking, I'd not yet spotted. I wondered if she'd introduced it there. While Jane studied the water, the Indian studied Jane, tracing the circle of the girl's ear with a fingertip, stroking and lifting her hair. She clearly craved human touch. From time to time, the girl absently brushed the woman's hands away with a casualness that brought tears to my eyes but did not discourage Helen. I wished that I had brought all the children with me for the woman to dote on.

For all that Oskar had persuaded me that Berkeley would be best for Helen, I felt uncertain. Watching her, I was aware that her life, while unusual, was not without its compensations. True, she had no one to take care of her, but she lived well enough without caretaking. I envied her independence; she was subject to neither the demands of a husband nor of a light. I admired her resourcefulness and her intimacy with nature. I could see she had a relationship with the children that was obviously loving, even maternal; clearly, they afforded her a sort of sustaining companionship. All of this would end if she chose to go with us, and maybe a cottage and a lady scientist wouldn't be worth the price.

We were charging ahead so quickly because of the damage she was inflicting on the lighthouse. If she could be convinced to stop that, we might have time to think things through. With more time, maybe we could learn to communicate with her well enough for her to think things through herself. While Jane was occupied with mounding sand, I touched Helen on the shoulder so she would pay attention to me.

"You must stop breaking the windows," I said, pretending to pick up a rock and hurl it high into the air. I made fists and then threw my hands open, splaying my fingers and widening my eyes and then clapping my hands over my ears in a mime I hoped conveyed the violent shattering of the glass. I furrowed my brow and shook my head in a stern "no." I repeated these actions several times, hoping she might eventually catch my meaning, but she only shook her head more and more vehemently in response. It seemed my playacting was communicating nothing to her but gibberish. Or maybe she understood and was refusing to comply.

Over half an hour had passed by this time. I would have to go ahead or give up the whole plan.

"Shall we bring the mermaid back to the lighthouse with us, Janie?" I made myself say these words although I could hardly look at either of them as I did so. I was deceiving them both. Jane would be heartbroken if we got into the longboat. I could almost hear her angry wail. I couldn't imagine what the mermaid would think; her view was so foreign to me. I reminded myself that all I was doing was leading her there; after that, she would be free to make her own choice.

Jane took Helen's hand and gave it a little tug, and that was all she needed to do. The woman followed her even after their hands unclasped, as if she were joined to the child by an invisible thread.

It felt strange to walk with Helen along the beach. I realized that despite the heft of her tools and ornaments, despite our merry exchange over my shoes, despite the barrel of broken glass she'd caused us to pitch into the ocean, I half believed she was a mythical being who would evaporate in the real world. But her footprints interlaced with ours in the sand; she was solid as any of us.

The fog on the beach had thickened, and we could see almost nothing through it; I judged our progress by the increasing intensity of the horn. I wondered how much time had passed since Jane and I had left the morro. Would the inspector have finished? Had Oskar been able to hold the tender? I almost wished it gone.

Eventually, the longboat emerged, a dark gray solid in the light gray air. It was waiting in shallow water, loaded with empty barrels, and the sailors squatted patiently nearby, spitting tobacco into the sand. At first I thought they were alone; then I saw that others were a little farther up the beach. They stood together in a clump, stiff and dark, like a colony of mussels. There was Oskar, his jacket so crammed with Helen's stones and shells that his arms couldn't hang freely at his sides, and Euphemia and Mr. Crawley, and a little man with a round head and belly like a chickadee whom I took to be Inspector Roberts.

I had imagined the three of us—Helen, Jane, and me—coming alone upon the boat and so being able to let Helen examine it as she wished. I had thought that I would step in first to demonstrate the vessel's safety. And then we might all three sit in it for a while. This was inconceivable with the others crowding around.

Jane ran to her mother. "We've brought the mermaid! Look, Mama! It's the mermaid!"

Euphemia pulled her daughter tightly against her body. "Yes, I see her, Janie." She looked steadily at Helen with a wary expression. She didn't step forward to embrace the woman or even to greet her, as I might have thought she would.

Oskar's mouth had opened slightly when he saw Helen. I suppose he, too, had believed she might not be real. "Mr. Roberts agrees it would be best to take her to San Francisco." He was speaking to me, but his eyes were on her.

"Can't have people destroying lighthouse property, stealing tools," Mr. Roberts said. He had a pipe in his hand, and he smacked it smartly to dislodge the old tobacco. "Criminal behavior, that's what that is."

"She's not a criminal," I said. I'd meant to speak firmly, but my voice carried a note of alarm, and Helen, who until now had stood beside me, watchful yet calm, began to shrink back.

"Oskar," I said, "give Helen her things. The jade necklace. Give her that so she understands we're her friends."

"When we get on the tender," he said, stepping forward. "Let's get into the boat first. Let's get going."

When he moved, I saw that our trunk—my trunk—had been behind him. "Why have you brought the trunk? We don't need all our things for a few months in San Francisco."

Oskar was focused on Helen and didn't answer. As he came nearer, she tensed; like a skittish horse, she was gauging his movements. Slowly, he reached for her arm. She stood taut but quiet. He wrapped his hand around her wrist. The motion was gentle, but he had her.

"Trudy," he said, still not looking at me, "why don't you get in first? Show her it's all right."

"You said it would be her choice," I reminded him.

"It's not a real choice if it's based on fear," he said. "Get in and show her it's all right."

The water around the boat was growing steadily deeper. The tide would help us launch. I remembered disembarking from this same boat nearly a year before. Oskar had given me his hand then so that I could step out like a lady, and I'd soaked my boots. Now, without ceremony, I clambered over the gunwale in bare feet and sat tensely on one of the benches.

"My shoes . . ." I began, thinking that someone would have to fetch them from the base of the morro. I would need them in the city.

Before I could finish, an anguished wail erupted from the beach. Jane was screaming as if she'd been stung by a jellyfish. She was pointing at me, and I understood her meaning. My going was wounding her. I started to climb out again, thinking to go and comfort her, to assure her that I would be back.

The child's panic seemed to awaken Helen. The arm Oskar held jumped and twisted like a fish leaping from the water. Unsteady on his feet, he lost his grip, and she darted away.

She was seized again almost immediately and this time with more force. Archie Johnston had emerged from the fog and somehow—perhaps when I was climbing into the boat, concerned only with keeping my skirt dry—made his way behind her.

"Here, now," he said in an unctuous voice I hadn't heard him use before, "you don't want to go running off again." Slowly, so that it wouldn't look as if he were pushing her, he eased her toward the boat and me. She stumbled slightly, her feet catching in his because he held her so close. "We're taking you to a nice place now. You and me, we're going together."

"Archie." Euphemia stepped forward. "I told you to stay at the light."

"I don't take orders from you," he said. "The light is your concern. She's mine."

I suspected that he'd drunk the wine we'd saved out for the inspector's lunch.

"You do take orders from me," Mr. Crawley said. "And my orders are that you go back up to the lighthouse. We don't need you here."

"It's me that don't need *you*, Henry. This is my business. She doesn't belong to you." Almost caressingly, he passed his hand over Helen's hip and closed his fingers around the handle of her knife. "Lighthouse Service–issue, I believe," he said, displaying the blade. "*You*"—he looked to Oskar disdainfully—"would have let her get away."

"It's the damn leg. I'm still off balance. I suppose we'll have to tie her," Oskar said. With some difficulty, he opened the heavy flaps of his jacket. Wrapped around his waist was a length of rope. Two lengths.

"What are you doing?" I'd gotten out of the boat and was splashing back through the cold water. "You can't take her prisoner!"

"Get back in the boat, Trudy," Oskar said sharply. He was wrapping one of the ropes around her wrists, binding them together. "She's not a prisoner. This is only until we get her onto the tender. She can't be thrashing around on the longboat. She might capsize it. If you can lift her," he said to Archie, "I'll get her feet."

"Oskar!"

Helen was twisting in Archie's arms, kicking so that Oskar couldn't hold her feet. I grabbed at Oskar's wrist, but with one violent jerk, he thrust me off, and my back hit the sand with a thud. I gasped, as shocked by my own puniness as by what he'd done.

Helen, too, was weaker than the men. The rope was around her ankles, and though she still bucked and plunged, Archie held her fast.

When I'd charged at Oskar, Mr. Crawley and the inspector had run, too. I expected them to pull Helen free, but they came to me. They helped me to my feet and held me there, lightly but firmly, while the sailors, who saw where authority lay, helped Oskar finish his tying. Helen hung from Archie's arms, helpless. He carried her to the boat, an unwilling bride.

"It's best if she goes, Trudy," Mr. Crawley said. "Oskar's right. She'll be better off at the university. With people to take care of her."

"Yes," the inspector agreed, brushing sand from his trousers. "The Lighthouse Service isn't equipped to deal with irregularities like this. If the university wants her, by all means, let them have her. She won't last long anyway. These people are weak, you know, when it comes to disease. They lack disciplined habits; that's their trouble."

"Come on, now, Trudy." Oskar held out his hand to me. "It'll be better once we're away."

Unsure, I looked to Euphemia. But she'd turned away from the scene long before. She had Jane by the hand and was helping the little girl trudge through the soft sand back toward the mountain. They were nearly to the path, their forms softening in the fog. I wished I were scrambling up with them, shut of all of this.

"Euphemia!"

At my call, Euphemia and Jane turned. For an instant, they stood frozen, staring, but then Jane, taking advantage of her mother's distraction, pulled her hand free with a tug. Without hesitation, she began running headlong, away from the security of her mother and her home, over the pitted sand and the dark tangles of kelp toward me, her body jolted by her own stiff, still babyish steps, her face lighting with the pleasure of her speed.

"Janie, stop!" Euphemia came after her with long strides, but Jane had a head start.

Archie turned from the boat, where he'd deposited Helen among the empty barrels that crowded the bow. He scooped the little girl up. "All right," he said. "I'll take her, too."

Oskar squeezed my hand. "Don't argue with him," he said quietly. "Once we get the Indian to the tender, we'll bring Jane back."

The inspector's head jerked birdlike as he looked at each of us in turn. "What's going on here?"

With relief, I saw that Euphemia had reached her brother. I knew that she would take Jane from him and put him in his place. She would demand that he untie Helen. She would put right again all that had somehow gone wrong. What happened next alarmed me more than any of the horrors that had come so far: Euphemia fell to her knees in the sand.

"Archie." Mr. Crawley had reverted to his skim-milk voice. "You don't want to take Jane. What will you do with a child?"

"Put that girl down," the inspector ordered. "What's going on here, Crawley?"

"What's going on," Archie said quickly, before Mr. Crawley could speak, "is that I'm taking my wife and my child away from this place. As I have every right to do."

"You can't take Jane!" Euphemia and I said the same words together. My tone was outraged; hers was plaintive, desperate, a tone that didn't sit right in the mouth of Euphemia Crawley.

"I can."

The girl, who at first had sat trustingly in her uncle's arms, an elbow hooked around his neck, bent away from him like a drooping flower and reached for her mother.

"I have a right," Archie said. "She's mine."

He'd been undone, I saw, by grief and unhappiness. I understood the power of these emotions now.

"She's not yours," I insisted calmly and firmly. "Your baby died."

Helen's voice came from the boat. She was speaking in her own tongue, a stream of urgent, incomprehensible syllables.

"She's right." Oskar let go of my hand and stepped toward Archie tentatively, as if approaching a madman. "I'm sorry, but your child died years ago. You know that."

Archie didn't look at us. He kept his eyes on Euphemia, sister and mother both to him, and she looked steadily back. She held her arms out. "Please, Archie, think of Janie. Give her to me."

I thought I saw his shoulders shift, as if he were readying his arms to do as she asked.

"That's right," Inspector Roberts broke in. "Your baby is dead, Johnston. Yes, it was recorded in the logbook. It was some time ago, but I have a memory for these details. 'Baby Johnston born and buried.'"

Jane had straightened herself. Anxiously, she rubbed the blue appliquéd flower on the bib of her pinafore with sandy fingers.

Archie gave her a little shake so that her head bobbed up and down. "Jane is Baby Johnston," he snapped. "She belongs to me."

Inspector Roberts looked from Archie to the Crawleys. "I suppose you expect me to order that the child be cut in half." He shook his head in disgust. "We've got to go before this fog gets any thicker, or we'll miss our chance. We'll sort this out in San Francisco and send her back, if need be." He wiped his palms together briskly, ridding himself of the last grains of sand, the dirt of this place, and climbed into the boat.

As the two sailors heaved at the hull with their shoulders, its flat bottom began to slide along the wet sand.

"Goddammit, Archie. Put Jane down!" Mr. Crawley lunged for his brother-in-law, but Archie was too quick. He dropped Jane onto one of the seats and jumped in after her.

"Trudy! Come on!" Oskar was sitting on the gunwale, one leg in and one leg out of the boat. He stretched out his hand to me.

Jane was howling piteously; Helen's face was hidden by her hands and her hair. The thought of being any part of this kidnapping revolted me, but I knew that I'd already caused enormous damage, and I wouldn't compound it by abandoning them. I grasped Oskar's fingers and let him pull me into the boat.

Immediately, Jane scrambled into my lap. "I don't want to go on the boat!" she cried. "I want my mama!"

I tried to soothe her as the sailors pushed us away from the shore. They held the boat steady until they were nearly shoulder-deep in the water, and then they hoisted themselves over the gunwales with practiced ease and each grabbed an oar. The surf was breaking directly before us. The trick, I saw, was to get the boat over the foaming curl without being forced back to shore or, worse, capsized. To me, the feat seemed impossible, and the inspector, who was struggling to control the tiller, looked as if he agreed.

"We're too heavy," he barked. "Too low in the water."

We yawed suddenly, caught by the force of the break, and our bow slipped north. I could feel the wave catching hold, lifting the starboard side high, tilting the port gunwale dangerously close to the water.

Jane shrieked, her mouth against my neck.

"For God's sake, can't you shut her up?" Archie said.

Oskar scrambled over the seats to the back of the boat and shouldered the inspector brusquely aside. He tucked the tiller under his arm and hugged it against his chest. Once I might have admired the skill with which he encouraged the boat to nose over the top of the wave and then steadied it as it collapsed into the trough, but now the way he controlled our course struck me as arrogant and his confidence unnatural.

The bow teetered upward as another wave, traveling just behind the first, caught us. I clutched Jane with one hand, grasping the edge of my seat as well as I could with the other to keep from tipping backward off the bench. As the wave passed beneath us, we tottered forward, and I braced my feet against the floor, buckling at the waist, trying to keep from spilling headfirst onto Helen and the empty barrels in the bow. Spray shot in all directions, pummeling our faces with cold, salty wet.

Beside me, our steamer trunk rocked on its end. The sailors had loaded it into the boat while I had been focused on Helen and Jane. I understood what its presence meant. Oskar was going back in triumph; we wouldn't come here again.

Helen's face was still buried in her hands. All I could see were her fingers and her hair, which hung heavy and tangled as kelp. I'd reduced her to this, a hopeless, faceless thing.

Over and over we plunged, I assumed toward the tender, which must have been anchored not too far from the shore, although I could see nothing but gray fog and darker gray water. The boat shuddered with every fall as the waves punished us for this journey and tried to drive us back. Sickness, my own internal waves, rose high in my throat, sickness at what we were doing, ripping this woman up by the roots. And what about Jane? Oskar had promised to take her back when we reached the tender, but I no longer believed he would do anything that didn't suit his purposes.

I turned and shouted over my shoulder. "Oskar! Go back! Turn back!"

"What?"

"I want to go back!"

A blast of water, cold as if there'd been no spring, hit me in the face.

"No!" he shouted. "Look! We're nearly there!"

Indeed, the fog had momentarily thinned, and I could differentiate the dark form of the tender from the thick air. We *were* nearly there. The hideous sickness rose in me again. I knew the inspector was right. Helen would die; she would be a subject, a specimen, delivered to other Oskars and other Archies to be examined under a microscope until she succumbed to tuberculosis or measles or one of the other ills our civilization harbored. I had delivered her. I may as well have popped her into a jar of embalming fluid.

And what would happen to Jane?

"I'm sorry." My voice was drowned out by the wind; my tears were indistinguishable from the ocean water that ran down my face. My sorrow was compounded by the futility of my apology. Neither of them would understand me anyway.

And then, as we lurched over the crest of yet another wave, a buffet of wind lifted a hank of Helen's hair, and I saw that she was not bent over herself in despair. She was biting, gnawing steadily, with her yellow, worn teeth on the rope that bound her wrists.

"Helen!"

I heaved myself to my feet, Jane wrapped tightly around me, and began to stagger awkwardly toward the bow.

"What are you doing? Sit down!" the inspector snapped.

The boat dipped and I with it, nearly losing my balance. Another dose of cold water flew over the gunwale, soaking the front of my dress and the back of Jane's.

"Sit down, Trudy!" Oskar yelled. "What are you doing? You'll tip the boat!"

What *was* I doing? I felt as if I were yanking myself free of a current in which I'd been caught. I had loved him, joined him, gone with him, followed him, but now I could think of nothing but stopping the destruction we two had set in motion.

"Sit down!" Archie made a lunge at me.

"No! We're going back! We're going back!"

Helen had freed her hands, and she bent over her feet, tugging at the ropes, trying to find the weak points. The tender stood out clearly, only about fifty yards away. The captain had seen us and was calling to the boilerman to stoke the engine.

Archie's arms closed around Jane and me together, as if we were one of the barrels. He dragged at us, trying to force me back onto the bench. Then Helen rose. I can't say there was understanding between us, but we were bent to a common cause. When the next swell began to lift the boat, we leaned together, Helen, Jane, and I, concentrating our combined weight against the gunwale that was already dipping dangerously low. We leaned together, and we overturned the boat.

It's one thing to have cold water splash your skin and another to be submerged in it. I remember the shock and the freezing rush around my ears as I plunged. Little Jane was like a stone around my neck, and my heavy skirt tangled around my legs like a mermaid's fingers.

I buried my fingers in the crossed straps of Jane's pinafore to hold her tight against my chest, and then I kicked and kicked, drawing my legs together, as I'd seen little octopi do in our tubs.

Jane and I surfaced as a two-headed creature, gulping the breathable air. For a moment I could see nothing but the gray-green slope of the next wave that bore down upon us, but rather than break over us, it lifted us to its crest along with a small, empty kerosene keg over which I easily threw my free arm. The tender had dropped its lifeboat, and within minutes I was twisting Jane's straps around a boat hook that the captain himself held out to us.

They'd come to our rescue first, but the rest were close by. While the captain wrapped Jane in a blanket, I looked anxiously for Helen's dark head among the men. She wasn't beside the two sailors who'd heaved themselves over the hull of the capsized longboat, nor near the inspector who'd grabbed one of the floating oars. Nor was she with Archie, who clung to a large barrel. I craned my neck, but in every direction I could see only waves, riding relentlessly toward the shore now shrouded in murk. I was hopeful; I didn't think a woman who could dive for abalones and spear fish while swimming was likely to drown when the shore was in reach.

I searched for Oskar, too, and when I didn't spot him at once, I assumed that he was beyond the next wave or on the far side of the capsized boat or hidden by one barrel or another. After all, he had no reason to swim away. But soon I was screaming his name, standing on the seat to extend my view and trying to scrape at the fog with my eyes. This time no one tried to make me sit down.

We rowed in widening circles for an hour while the foghorn moaned. Jane was shaking with cold and I with a fear that made me vomit over the side. We found the mail pouch and all of the barrels, but Oskar, along with our valise and our trunk, was gone.

"A drowned man ought to float," the captain insisted stubbornly.

It was then I remembered all he'd sewn into his pockets—the ax head; the pestle; the flat rock "possibly for grinding acorns"; the scraper "perhaps used to clean hides or peel bark"; the smaller version of the same "likely used for scaling fish"; the pieces of jade, bored through and strung on a twenty-six-inch length of braided hair, "ornamental, ceremonial, or spiritual"; among many others, more than enough to drag him to the bottom.

At last the captain would search no longer, and we rowed back to the beach. The captain and the inspector rode the platform with us to the top, and they waited while Archie packed his things. The inspector said he'd overlook the kidnapping, since the child had been returned, but he couldn't allow a man who'd been insubordinate to his superior to keep a post at a lighthouse. Archie muttered that he was done with the place anyway and couldn't wait to be quit of it.

Euphemia told me later that the captain had come to her and Henry. "I may know what happened to the young man," he'd said. "But it's a raw thing for the widow to hear." He told them that from the deck of the tender, before he'd stepped into the lifeboat, he'd seen Helen, or as he described her, "a strange beast with a human head and arms but a fish's tail"—she'd not, apparently, been able to untie her feet in time—cutting through the waves like a porpoise in the direction of the beach. Such a creature, he maintained, might easily have consumed a man.

EPILOGUE

FOR SOME MONTHS, I was in a dark state and unable to pick up my old routine of schoolteaching and housework. Nevertheless, the lighthouse had to be tended, and only the Crawleys and I remained to do it, so I took my turn there, insisting on covering Oskar's night shift. Sleep was impossible for me, anyway. Through the long stretches in the boiler room, I tried to read or develop new lessons for the children, but my mind wouldn't take hold of the words or figures. I couldn't even sew. An hour after I'd taken a garment into my lap, I would discover myself sitting idle, having added only two loose stitches to a seam or a patch.

Nightly, I was drawn to the catwalk, where I would stand with my waist pressed against the slender rail, leaning into the blackness, looking. Although I didn't dare articulate my yearning, I wished fiercely for both Oskar and Helen to materialize again. I imagined so vividly each lying on the sand or caught in the rocks, in need of me, that I often thought I heard a human cry below or sensed a human movement on the moonlit beach, and I strained my ears and eyes for more. Inevitably, I had to admit that these signs had been created by my own mind, not by them. In the light of day, I had no hopes or illusions.

Euphemia, kindly, left meals in my kitchen, from which I swallowed a little soup or chewed a bit of pilot bread while standing among the cans and sacks and bottles of provisions that had come with the inspector. Euphemia had stacked them as neatly as possible but, being strict

267

about the organization of her own kitchen, thoughtfully left the putting away for the time when I was ready to face it. Two of our three store cupboards had been entirely bare by the time the tender had arrived, and at last I began with these, thinking to wipe them out with warm water and vinegar before filling them. When I opened the first, I discovered my mother's linen tablecloth rolled into a bundle. I lifted it—it was surprisingly heavy—and unrolled it on the kitchen table. One by one appeared the tools from the workshop that we'd believed Helen had stolen. Her insistent "no," when I'd gestured to her about the wholesale breaking of the windows, I now saw had been a denial.

Philip sent a letter of condolence.

But what is this about a woman? he added in a postscript. *I understand that she drowned as well, but was she really an Indian, as Roberts seems to think? No one has reported a local native, you know, for at least a quarter century. Should I come and investigate?*

I replied that Oskar had indeed believed her to be an Indian, but who could say for sure? Oskar, I reminded him, had been imaginative and prone to enthusiasms. I implied that she might have been an eccentric, like the Yale man people talked about. Along with my letter, I sent a few primitive items that I'd asked the children to make—an awkward grass basket, a pinecone and mussel-shell "scraper," a tool made of driftwood and a sharp bit of tin can. I claimed that we'd found these in the woman's hut. Did he think they were, as Oskar had speculated, evidence of her Indianness? It hurt me to betray Oskar in this way, making him look a fool, but I'd learned to do what needed doing. Though Philip and I corresponded for many more years, he never mentioned the Indian again.

Euphemia had remembered to put my letter to the Chicago Scientific Company into the mail pouch. Although it must have been dampened by its time in the ocean, it was obviously legible, since the jars and chemicals arrived on the next tender. Our business slowly grew much in the way we'd envisioned it during those nights we'd kept the light together; we were careful to cull only a few specimens, the way my mother had taught me to cut flowers from her garden, so that there would always be more.

Within the first year, it was clear that we were observed at our work, because prettily woven baskets full of whatever we were hunting appeared on the cairn. I wondered what Helen imagined we were doing with these things, but I was grateful less for the specimens themselves than for the evidence that she was alive and considered herself a friend to us.

Euphemia drove us to expand, scouring the journals to which I was soon subscribing, picking out biologists who might be interested in our "authentic Pacific Coast specimens," as she put it in the letters she sent. Our lighthouse logo, a duplicate of the china print, was her idea, and she affixed it with great satisfaction to each crate.

After what seemed a very few years, Mary went to San Francisco to enroll in business college, and the boys, one after the other, joined the navy. They wanted to see some of the places we'd marked with pebbles on my trunk. I had hope that Jane would stay to work with me. She'd developed a keen interest in biology and had always taken pleasure in her drawing. I thought together we might produce a finer, more comprehensive edition of the catalog. But she was infected with the longing to make her own life or create her own destiny or some such youthful nonsense. One day she left on the tender that took her to the train in San Francisco that took her to a normal school in San Jose. I never saw her again.

Only a little time later, the Crawleys left me, too, following their youngest daughter to San Jose. Although we did not, in the end, provide urchins to Switzerland, we were by that time supplying enough colleges and universities in the United States and Canada with specimens "dried and preserved" that Euphemia and Henry could afford to retire from the Lighthouse Service and open a grocery store.

Oskar's ambitions had made me fear the consequences of anyone else discovering Helen, and so that I might keep the world away from Point Lucia, I fought for permission to tend the light without assistants when I became chief lighthouse keeper. The new inspector, Mr. Roberts's successor, understood that I couldn't easily be replaced, especially since he himself wasn't familiar with all the procedures at the light station, and when he saw that I was capable of making life unpleasant for whomever was sent to assist me, he agreed to give me a fair chance—a week's observation—to prove myself. In his later years as chief, Mr. Crawley had built an ingenious system of pulleys and platforms so that the oil could be transported to the light with little effort, and the mechanism that controlled the foghorn had been improved so that it could go hours longer without resetting. (That Oskar might have engineered such advancements, had he been less concerned with dazzling, wasn't lost on me.) In the end, the Lighthouse Service wasn't sorry to save itself a great deal of money in salaries and supplies. They set me up with a radiotelegraph— apparently, electricity *was* in the air—and told me to study the code so that I could communicate with a passing ship in case of emergency.

Since the Crawleys have gone, I've collected fewer specimens, having become uncomfortably aware that I'm doing to these helpless creatures precisely what Oskar wished to do to Helen. I concentrate on my own studies instead. My hours of gazing into the tide pools have made me think of these tiny bodies of water as simplified versions of the world at large, and so as convenient opportunities to examine the ways in which each species, and perhaps each individual organism affects the others with which it shares its limited world. It's a romantic notion, I admit, but I've written a handful of articles on the subject, and the scientific community has been for the most part gratifyingly receptive.

My parents did visit. I had not, after all, crossed an ocean in the nineteenth century, as they had done. They urged me to return "home" now that, as my mother said, nothing held me "to the edge of the earth." I declined, obviously, and by now my old world is mostly a shimmer of memory beyond the mountains, although Lucy and I correspond still. She can't imagine my life nor I hers, and her descriptions of concerts and cookery and her work at the Settlement House have the same fairy-tale quality that my mother's stories of the gilt-legged tables and ceramic shepherdesses of Hamburg had for me as a child. I once asked Philip to visit the shop in San Francisco where we had pawned our things. The silver toilet set and the pocketknife were gone. He sent me a pickle fork, but I don't think it was the right one.

I've recently begun a new project—although Euphemia would laugh—a sort of collage affixed to the tower. I pretend it's a monument, a way of melding the lighthouse with its surroundings, but it's a means of preserving the last of what I can't bear to lose, the detritus and wonders the children collected, the occupants of my nursery.

I have not been entirely alone. Not long after the baskets of specimens appeared on the cairn, the children began meeting Helen again among the rocks. The space between us began to dissolve. It may have been because Archie had gone, although I like to think that my coming, too, had a hand in it. First she met us openly on the beach. Eventually, she and I taught the children to swim, and then she took them farther out and taught them how to dive for abalone. At last she showed herself at the top of the morro, delivering her offerings in person, rather than leaving them on the cairn, and she stayed to eat with us at the plank table above the sea. She would never move into the empty house, although the Crawleys and I did our best to make clear she was welcome. At the end of an evening, she would always go back down the mountain.

So even after all the others had gone, I had a friend who helped me gather plants and animals from deep water where I feared to dive, who arranged my cans in pyramids when she came to visit me, for whom I named a crab in my catalog—*Pugettia Helena*—although, as Oskar would have pointed out, that wasn't her real name.

She lived for twenty-six more years, and I suspect she knew when her life was nearly over, for she spent many months carefully fashioning a dress of fully feathered bird skins. I have more than once displayed it to Oskar in my dreams. When I found her lying still and cold, she was wearing the dress along with the coral necklace that I'd given her at last some years before. If her body is ever disinterred, I wonder what theory will arise from the discovery of a California Indian in a necklace made of Florida coral. No one will guess that it came to her by way of Wisconsin.

I'm free to go now, I suppose, but I believe I'll stay. Here, I've experienced a world beyond my imagining; here, I've walked on my own feet. Here, at the edge of the earth, I am content.

Jane
1977

WE'VE SEEN ALL through the buildings, watched the filmstrip and drunk the cocoa, and been encouraged to buy a key chain or a mug or a postcard of the Fresnel lens. The teenagers are beginning to slouch back down the morro of their own accord, their faces hidden in the wings of their hair. The little boy is hanging off his mother's hand, suspending himself at a forty-five-degree angle to the ground. It's time to go.

As we're making the turn at the base of the light tower, I think of one last thing. I walk to the edge and lean out to take a look at the cairn. Although it had always been difficult to see from this angle, I know just where to stand. But there's nothing there except more brown rock.

Lydia gives a little gasp, hurries over, and begins to pluck at my arm. "Please. You're far too close to the edge."

I step back as I turn to her. I don't want to give her a heart attack. "I was looking for the stones." I hadn't known it was a grave before I'd read Trudy Swann's story. To me, it had been more like an altar.

"What's that, dear?" Lydia's raincoat is folded over her arm. She holds a hand against her brow to shield her eyes from the sun as she squints at me, puzzled and a little impatient.

"The pile of smooth stones. It used to be below the light tower here."

"Oh, you mean the baby. Yes, I don't like to mention it if there are, you know, children in the group. It might upset them."

She doesn't ask how I know. Some people have no sense of curiosity.

"Someone threw the stones away. Probably the same who shot the windows up. You know how people are. It's better, I think, that the little body is unmarked. Who knows what people might do in a place like this?"

"So there's still a body there?"

"Oh, yes. Lucius Crawley. The name was carved right into the tiny coffin. I like to think of him as a little angel now. The angel of the lighthouse."

We were walking down, and I had to take Danny's arm and concentrate on where I was placing my feet and on not thinking about the pain in my knees. Then, too, at my age it takes a long time for understanding to bubble up through years of sludgy assumptions. It wasn't until I'd packed myself into his Japanese box and we were bowling along what I still think of as the "new" highway, looking west at the brave stand of buildings and that breast of a mountain upon which I'd been raised, that I realized that the little Crawley grave confirmed the suspicion I'd formed when I'd read Mrs. Swann's story. I was the mermaid's daughter.

Trudy Swann had written that she wanted "someone to know how she lived." The mermaid, I believed she meant, the woman she had saved. But now I saw how I, too, had lived. Three times I'd been delivered into the world, first by the one who had birthed me, then by the one who had raised me, and then by the one who had restored me to them both.

"Let me tell you," I said to Danny as we rounded a bend and Point Lucia was no more, "about Trudy Swann. I want someone to know how she lived."

ACKNOWLEDGMENTS

I'M GRATEFUL TO the resolute Jennifer Rudolph Walsh for her toughness and kindness, as well as for her insightful and generous reading. Because of her, I can make a living writing books. I'm grateful to the warm Greer Hendricks for her acute perception, meticulous care, and bolstering enthusiasm. It seems that I can't write a novel without Caitlin Flanagan to prop me up. In this case, I was particularly demanding and she met the almost daily challenge with her characteristic big-heartedness and dazzling creative instincts. So many friends honored drafts of this manuscript with their time, attention, and honest and helpful reactions: I thank Jennifer Stuart Wong, Jenny Kowal, Abigail Deser, Gina Hahn, Barbara Faculjak, Sonja Alarr, Cindy Davis Stephenson, Linda Rudell-Betts, and Alan and Kathy Buster. For help with German translations and spellings, I thank Belinda Cooper and Nick Meyer, who also explained some facts about electromagnetism. The scene on the western train platform owes much to Helen Hunt Jackson's poetic and lively account of her trip across the United States, *Bits of Travel at Home,* published in 1878. I'm indebted to Ben and Nicky Schwarz for their willingness to survive on pizza for weeks at a time. Above all, I trust Ben to tell me when I've gone wrong and when I've got it right. I'm grateful for his inflexible expectations, his unstinting commitment, and his uncompromising editorial eye. He is the best reader I know.

The
EDGE
of the
EARTH

CHRISTINA SCHWARZ

A READERS CLUB GUIDE

Topics and Questions for Discussion

1. Consider the novel's title—besides serving as a description of Point Lucia, what other meanings could it have? What does being at "the edge of the earth" mean for these characters?

2. On p. 35, Oskar says, "For a curious person, the world is full of opportunities." As a group, discuss the difference between curiosity and ambition, particularly in the context of Oskar's character. Is Oskar ultimately curious, or is he ambitious?

3. How does Schwarz create tension and atmosphere within the narrative?

4. Early in the novel, Trudy reflects, "I was a goose plumped for others' consumption" (p. 40). What does she mean by this? What has changed for Trudy by p. 220, when she compares herself to Helen, "[L]ike me, she'd been separated from her people and was having to make her life as best she could at the edge of the earth." Is this a fair comparison? Take into account each woman's degree of agency as you discuss this.

5. Discuss the significance of material objects—especially personal effects—within the novel. What do the things that each character treasures reveal about them? What do you think the book is saying about ownership and identity, materiality and corporeality?

6. Turn to p. 117, where Trudy and the children are dissecting the sea urchin, and discuss the larger meaning behind this scene. How is this also a commentary on the many ways of seeing? Can you find another instance in which Trudy's perspective on something she's never questioned suddenly switches?

7. How are masculinity and femininity represented in the novel? How are the traditional roles of men and women either upheld or subverted as the story progresses?

8. In what ways is illumination—light and dark, sight and blindness—a theme within the novel?

9. As a group, read aloud the conversation between Trudy, Oskar, and Mr. and Mrs. Hatch, when they observe through the train window the woman carrying her child on her back (pp. 130–132). Whose point of view did you most identify with in this scene?

10. Examine the instances in the text where Oskar and Archie speak of Helen, and compare them to the moments when Euphemia and Trudy do the same. How do both the content and the tone of what they're saying differ?

11. On p. 242, Oskar says to Trudy, "Don't you care whether people know that these Indians existed on this earth?" In regard to Helen, do you think Oskar believes he is working for a greater purpose—and if so, does this justify his treatment of her?

12. Of which character did your opinion evolve most dramatically over the course of the novel? How and why did this occur?

13. In what ways could this novel be considered a love story?

Enhance Your Book Club

1. As a group, read Schwarz's first novel, *Drowning Ruth*. Consider how the setting of each novel shapes the events of the narrative. What role does a sense of isolation play in the main characters' psyches?

2. The fictional Point Lucia is based on Big Sur, California. As a group, research the history of this lighthouse. You might begin by visiting: bigsurcalifornia.org/pointsur.htm.

3. Oskar defends removing Helen's objects from her cave by saying, "I'm not stealing them. I'm studying them." Trudy responds, "That distinction can mean nothing to Helen." Whose point of view resonates more with you? Can Trudy's perspective have other applications? Consider zoos or museums that hold artifacts that are a very long way from where they were originally located/discovered (an Egyptian temple in the New York Metropolitan Museum of Art, or the Rosetta Stone in the British Museum). Have the objects or creatures in these spaces been stolen, or are they being studied? Consider the extent to which power dynamics or perceived cultural inferiority/superiority might play in your answer. (For example, when Helen takes objects from the lighthouse, did it occur to you that she might be "studying" them?)

4. The classic children's novel *Island of the Blue Dolphins* also features an enigmatic Native American woman and is based on the true story of Juana Maria (or "The Lone Woman of San Nicolas"), who lived alone on an island off the coast of California between 1835–1853. To learn more about her and the recent discovery of the cave that may have been her home, go to: latimes.com/news/local/la-me-lone-woman-cave-20121027,0,1564818.story.